PRAISE FOR LEE GOLDBERG

PRAISE FOR *BONE CANYON*

"Lee Goldberg puts the *pro* in *police procedural*. *Bone Canyon* is fresh, sharp, and absorbing. Give me more Eve Ronin, ASAP."

—Meg Gardiner, international bestselling author

"Wow—what a novel! It is wonderful in so many ways. I could not put it down. *Bone Canyon* is wrenching and harrowing, full of wicked twists. Lee Goldberg captures the magic and danger of the Santa Monica Mountains and the predators who prowl them. Detective Eve Ronin takes on forgotten victims, fights for them, and nearly loses everything in the process. She's a riveting character, and I can't wait for her next case."

—Luanne Rice, *New York Times* bestselling author

"*Bone Canyon* is a propulsive procedural that provides high thrills in difficult terrain, grappling thoughtfully with sexual violence and police corruption, as well as the minefield of politics and media in Hollywood and suburban Los Angeles. Eve Ronin is a fantastic series lead—stubborn and driven, working twice as hard as her colleagues both to prove her worth and to deliver justice for the dead."

—Steph Cha, author of *Your House Will Pay*

"I didn't think Lee Goldberg could improve on the first Eve Ronin book, *Lost Hills*, but *Bone Canyon* is even better. The writing is lean and mean; the dialogue is pitch perfect; and the characters jump off the page with intensity, emotion, and wit. My only complaint is that I'll have to wait a year to read the next one!"

—Nick Petrie, author of the bestselling Peter Ash series

PRAISE FOR *LOST HILLS*

"A cop novel so good it makes much of the old guard read like they're going through the motions until they can retire . . . The real appeal here is Goldberg's lean prose, which imbues just-the-facts procedure with remarkable tension and cranks up to a stunning description of a fire that was like 'Christmas in hell.'"

—*Booklist*

"[The] suspense and drama are guaranteed to keep a reader spellbound . . ."

—Authorlink

"An energetic, resourceful procedural starring a heroine who deserves a series of her own."

—*Kirkus Reviews*

"This nimble, sure-footed series launch from bestseller Goldberg . . . builds to a thrilling, visually striking climax. Readers will cheer Ronin every step of the way."

—*Publishers Weekly*

"The first book in what promises to be a superb series—it's also that rare novel in which the formulaic elements of mainstream police procedurals share narrative space with a unique female protagonist. All that, and it's also a love letter to the chaos and diversity of California. There are a lot of series out there, but Eve Ronin and Goldberg's fast-paced prose should put this one on the radar of every crime fiction fan."

—National Public Radio

"This sterling thriller is carved straight out of the world of Harlan Coben and Lisa Gardner . . . *Lost Hills* is a book to be found and savored."

—*BookTrib*

"*Lost Hills* is Lee Goldberg at his best. Inspired by the real-world grit and glitz of LA County crime, this book takes no prisoners. And neither does Eve Ronin. Take a ride with her and you'll find yourself with a heroine for the ages. And you'll be left hoping for more."

—Michael Connelly, #1 *New York Times* bestselling author

"*Lost Hills* is what you get when you polish the police procedural to a shine: a gripping premise, a great twist, fresh spins and knowing winks to the genre conventions, and all the smart, snappy ease of an expert at work."

—Tana French, *New York Times* bestselling author

"Thrills and chills! *Lost Hills* is the perfect combination of action and suspense, not to mention Eve Ronin is one of the best new female characters in ages. You will race through the pages!"

—Lisa Gardner, #1 *New York Times* bestselling author

"Twenty-four-karat Goldberg—a top-notch procedural that shines like a true gem."

—Craig Johnson, *New York Times* bestselling author of the Longmire series

"A winner. Packed with procedure, forensics, vivid descriptions, and the right amount of humor. Fervent fans of Connelly and Crais, this is your next read."

—Kendra Elliot, *Wall Street Journal* and Amazon Charts bestselling author

"Brilliant! Eve Ronin rocks! With a baffling and brutal case, tight plotting, and a fascinating look at police procedure, *Lost Hills* is a stunning start to a new detective series. A must-read for crime fiction fans."

—Melinda Leigh, *Wall Street Journal* and #1 Amazon Charts bestselling author

"A tense, pacy read from one of America's greatest crime and thriller writers."

—Garry Disher, international bestselling author and Ned Kelly Award winner

PRAISE FOR *FAKE TRUTH*

"A winner from first page to last. Lee Goldberg has single-handedly invented a new genre of thriller. At once nail-bitingly suspenseful and gut-bustingly hilarious . . . but never less than a pedal-to-the-metal, full-on page-turner. *Fake Truth* is clever, edge-of-your-seat entertainment that I read in one glorious sitting. And that's no lie!"

—Christopher Reich, *New York Times* bestselling author

"Timely, satirical, and funny. Lee Goldberg's *Fake Truth* is deftly ironic and painfully observant."

—Robert Dugoni, *New York Times* bestselling author

"Hilariously surprising. The author's juggling of truth and fiction is almost as dexterous as his hero's."

—*Kirkus Reviews*

PRAISE FOR *KILLER THRILLER*

"*Killer Thriller* grabs you from page one with brilliant wit, sharply honed suspense, and a huge helping of pure originality."
— Jeffery Deaver, *New York Times* bestselling author

"A delight from start to finish, a round-the-world, thrill-a-minute, laser-guided missile of a book."
— Joseph Finder, *New York Times* bestselling author

"*Killer Thriller* is an action-packed treasure filled with intrigue, engaging characters, and exciting, well-rendered locales. With Goldberg's hyper-clever plotting, dialogue, and wit on every page, readers are in for a blast with this one!"
— Mark Greaney, *New York Times* bestselling author

PRAISE FOR *TRUE FICTION*

"Thriller fiction at its absolute finest—and it could happen for real. But not to me, I hope."
— Lee Child, #1 *New York Times* bestselling author

"This may be the most fun you'll ever have reading a thriller. It's a breathtaking rush of suspense, intrigue, and laughter that only Lee Goldberg could pull off. I loved it."
— Janet Evanovich, #1 *New York Times* bestselling author

"This is my life . . . in a thriller! *True Fiction* is great fun."
— Brad Meltzer, #1 *New York Times* bestselling author

"Fans of parodic thrillers will enjoy the exhilarating ride . . . [in] this Elmore Leonard mashed with *Get Smart* romp."

—*Publishers Weekly*

"A conspiracy thriller of the first order, a magical blend of fact and it-could-happen scary fiction. Nail-biting, page-turning, and laced with Goldberg's wry humor, *True Fiction* is a true delight, reminiscent of *Six Days of the Condor* and the best of Hitchcock's innocent-man-in-peril films."

—Paul Levine, bestselling author of *Bum Rap*

"Ian Ludlow is one of the coolest heroes to emerge in post-9/11 thrillers. A wonderful, classic yet modern, breakneck suspense novel. Lee Goldberg delivers a great story with a literary metafiction wink that makes its thrills resonate."

—James Grady, *New York Times* bestselling author of *Six Days of the Condor*

"Great fun that moves as fast as a jet. Goldberg walks a tightrope between suspense and humor and never slips."

—Linwood Barclay, *New York Times* bestselling author of *Elevator Pitch*

"I haven't read anything this much fun since Donald E. Westlake's comic-caper novels. Immensely entertaining, clever, and timely."

—David Morrell, *New York Times* bestselling author of *First Blood*

BONE
CANYON

OTHER TITLES BY LEE GOLDBERG

King City
The Walk
Watch Me Die
McGrave
Three Ways to Die
Fast Track

The Ian Ludlow Thrillers

True Fiction
Killer Thriller
Fake Truth

The Eve Ronin Series

Lost Hills

The Fox & O'Hare Series (coauthored with Janet Evanovich)

Pros & Cons (novella)
The Shell Game (novella)
The Heist
The Chase
The Job
The Scam
The Pursuit

The Diagnosis Murder Series

The Silent Partner
The Death Merchant
The Shooting Script
The Waking Nightmare
The Past Tense
The Dead Letter
The Double Life
The Last Word

The Monk Series

Mr. Monk Goes to the Firehouse
Mr. Monk Goes to Hawaii
Mr. Monk and the Blue Flu
Mr. Monk and the Two Assistants
Mr. Monk in Outer Space
Mr. Monk Goes to Germany
Mr. Monk Is Miserable
Mr. Monk and the Dirty Cop
Mr. Monk in Trouble
Mr. Monk Is Cleaned Out
Mr. Monk on the Road
Mr. Monk on the Couch
Mr. Monk on Patrol
Mr. Monk Is a Mess
Mr. Monk Gets Even

The Charlie Willis Series

My Gun Has Bullets
Dead Space

The Dead Man Series (coauthored with William Rabkin)

Face of Evil
Ring of Knives (with James Daniels)
Hell in Heaven
The Dead Woman (with David McAfee)
The Blood Mesa (with James Reasoner)
Kill Them All (with Harry Shannon)
The Beast Within (with James Daniels)
Fire & Ice (with Jude Hardin)
Carnival of Death (with Bill Crider)
Freaks Must Die (with Joel Goldman)
Slaves to Evil (with Lisa Klink)
The Midnight Special (with Phoef Sutton)
The Death March (with Christa Faust)
The Black Death (with Aric Davis)
The Killing Floor (with David Tully)
Colder Than Hell (with Anthony Neil Smith)
Evil to Burn (with Lisa Klink)
Streets of Blood (with Barry Napier)
Crucible of Fire (with Mel Odom)
The Dark Need (with Stant Litore)
The Rising Dead (with Stella Green)
Reborn (with Kate Danley, Phoef Sutton, and Lisa Klink)

The Jury Series

Judgment
Adjourned
Payback
Guilty

Nonfiction

The Best TV Shows You Never Saw
Unsold Television Pilots 1955–1989
Television Fast Forward
Science Fiction Filmmaking in the 1980s (cowritten with
William Rabkin, Randy Lofficier, and Jean-Marc Lofficier)
*The Dreamweavers: Interviews with Fantasy Filmmakers of
the 1980s* (cowritten with William Rabkin, Randy Lofficier, and
Jean-Marc Lofficier)
Successful Television Writing (cowritten with William Rabkin)

BONE
CANYON

LEE
GOLDBERG

Text copyright © 2021 by Adventures in Television, Inc.
All rights reserved.

Published by Thomas & Mercer, Seattle

www.apub.com

Amazon, the Amazon logo, and Thomas & Mercer are trademarks of Amazon.com, Inc., or its affiliates.

ISBN-13: 9781542042710 (hardcover)
ISBN-10: 1542042712 (hardcover)
ISBN-13: 9781542042772 (paperback)
ISBN-10: 1542042771 (paperback)

Cover design by Shasti O'Leary Soudant

Printed in the United States of America

First edition

For Valerie and Maddie, who always have my back.

CHAPTER ONE

The dead were rising in the fire-blackened Santa Monica Mountains and Eve Ronin, the youngest homicide detective in the history of the Los Angeles County Sheriff's Department, was on her way to examine one of them.

"Are you sure you ought to be driving?" asked her partner, Duncan Pavone, who took a bite out of his morning donut and rested it on a napkin that was spread out on his considerable belly. He was more than twice her age, three times as heavy, and four months away from retirement. "You just got the cast off your wrist yesterday. What if you have to make a sudden move?"

She'd been stuck at a desk for weeks, pushing paper while waiting for her wrist to heal. It was broken during the course of her first murder investigation as a member of the Robbery-Homicide Division at the Lost Hills sheriff's station in Calabasas, a small city on the northwest edge of the San Fernando Valley. Eve was eager to get out and do some real detective work again. So she was excited when they were dispatched to investigate a call from a homeowner in the Santa Monica Mountains who'd found bones in his backyard.

"My wrist is fine," Eve said, "and even if it wasn't, it's still safer than you driving with one hand on the wheel and the other holding your donut."

"What if a frightened deer leaps out in front of us?"

"From *where*?" Eve gestured to the desolate mountains all around them as they headed south on Kanan Dume Road in their plain-wrap Ford Explorer on a hot, muggy Monday morning in mid-January. "There's no place for a deer to hide."

Six weeks earlier, a raging wildfire in Valencia, thirty-three miles north of Los Angeles, was pushed southwest by scorching Santa Ana winds. The flames converged in the Santa Monica Mountains with another blaze in Topanga Canyon to create a cataclysmic firestorm that roared through one hundred thousand acres of dry mustard weed and chaparral, devouring sixteen hundred structures before it was finally put down.

Five residents and one firefighter were killed in the inferno. But in the days and weeks that followed, the burned remains of four other people were found, corpses that had been hidden in the brush and ravines before the flames revealed them.

"What about a death-crazed raccoon?" Duncan said.

"A *what*?"

"A raccoon driven mad after the fire by pain, hunger, and thirst."

"I'll run it over," she said. "We probably won't even feel a bump."

"That's heartless. I can't believe you'd do that."

"I'll be putting him out of his misery and protecting others from the danger he poses. What if he attacks a puppy or a newborn baby?"

"Why would he do that?"

"Because he's death crazed."

"That's ridiculous. Why would a puppy or a newborn baby be out here?"

"It's as likely as a raccoon hurling himself at a speeding SUV."

"I feel like the last man on earth in one of those *Twilight Zone* episodes," Duncan said, ignoring her comment and looking out the window at the desolation. "Like the guy who finally has eternity to indulge his love of reading books and then sits on his last pair of glasses."

Eve also thought there was an eerie, postapocalyptic feel to the naked mountains. There was virtually no traffic on the road. The only people in sight were utility workers installing new poles for the downed power and telephone lines.

"Then you better be careful you don't sit on your last donut," she said.

Duncan took her advice, ate the remainder of his glazed old-fashioned, then balled up his napkin and tossed it in the back seat. His nickname at the station was "Dunkin' Donuts" and this was how he'd earned it.

She made a left onto Hueso Canyon Road. The narrow strip of cracked asphalt was bordered on three sides by steep blackened slopes and above by a winding, perilous stretch of Latigo Canyon Road that ran just below the ragged ridgeline.

They passed a small winery that had been spared by the flames, but the homes on either side of the vineyard hadn't been so lucky. All that remained of them were twisted pipes, freestanding brick chimneys, toppled water heaters, and the hulks of a few burned-out cars. As Eve drove farther along, the random nature of the destruction became more evident. Four houses in a row, on the south side of the road, backed up to the mountain. The first two homes and the fourth were gone, but the third was untouched. That house was their destination.

It was two stories with a four-car garage, a red-tiled roof, and lots of stone cladding. There was something unnatural about how pristine the home and landscaping were, as if the property had been under a protective dome when the blaze swept through. The lawn and flowers, contrasted against the black ash everywhere else, struck Eve as outrageously colorful, like something out of *The Wizard of Oz*. The only thing on the property that had burned was the fence. A few scorched posts remained, marking the property's boundary with a ghostly dotted line.

A man stood in the cobblestone driveway, waiting for them. He was in his fifties, with a goatee and long gray-flecked hair tied into a ponytail. He wore a faded Fleetwood Mac T-shirt, jeans with holes in the knees, and flip-flops.

Eve parked the Explorer at the curb and the two detectives got out. She wore a white blouse, a loose-fitting navy-blue blazer to hide her hip-holstered Glock, and slacks. Duncan was in one of his many off-the-rack gray suits and ties.

The man smiled with recognition when he saw Eve, as if they were old friends, and that made her uncomfortable.

"Are you Sherwood Mintner?" Eve asked.

"Yes I am," Mintner said. "Are you the Deathfist?"

"I'm Detective Eve Ronin and this is Detective Duncan Pavone," she said, tipping her head toward her partner, who was grinning, enjoying her discomfort.

Mintner nodded a few times, eager to get her back to his point. "Yes, but you're the deputy who beat up Blake Largo, right?"

She was. Eight months ago, she'd been off duty, riding her bike on Mulholland, not far from where they were standing right now, when she saw the movie star assaulting a woman in a restaurant parking lot. Eve stepped between the couple, Largo took a swing at her, and she swiftly planted him facedown on the pavement. The incident was filmed by several astonished onlookers with their phones.

A video of a lean, radiantly blue-eyed young woman in a body-hugging bike jersey and shorts easily overpowering the muscled, internationally famous actor who played Deathfist, the invincible mixed-martial-arts-fighter-turned-vigilante, was irresistible clickbait. It immediately went viral, getting eleven million hits in a week.

"I didn't *beat* him," Eve said. "I *subdued* him."

"It was awesome." Mintner grinned, flashing his capped, too-white teeth. "The sequel was even better."

He was referring to another viral video, this one shot six weeks ago by a firefighter as Eve ran toward his rescue helicopter with a child in her arms, all of Malibu Creek State Park ablaze behind her. The video looked like the trailer for a Deathfist movie and only solidified her unwanted nickname within the department and among the public.

"Could I get a selfie with you?" Mintner asked, taking his phone out of his back pocket.

"No, sir," she said. His smile disappeared. No selfie. "We're here because you reported finding human remains on your property. Can you please show us what you found?"

"Yeah, this way," he said, his shoulders slumped in disappointment as he led them single file around the side of his property. "It's in my backyard. It's a piece of a skull, but it wasn't here before."

"Before what?" Duncan asked, walking behind him.

"The fire."

"How do you know?" Eve asked, bringing up the rear.

"Because I've lived here for twenty years and we've relandscaped the backyard a few times. We definitely would have noticed it. The skull is right on top of the dirt."

The backyard had a pergola that jutted out from the house, a stone firepit, a swimming pool, and a gazebo. The property backed up to the canyon walls, which Eve figured had once provided some privacy. But all the thick vegetation on the slopes had burned away and anyone on Latigo Canyon Road could now look directly down into their yard. The upside was there was nobody on the road and probably wouldn't be for a long time. Most of the homes above had burned down and the road was open only to locals until the cleanup was complete.

Duncan took a notepad out of his back pocket. "How did you discover the skull?"

"I was out here with a contractor, getting an estimate on building a new fence, and there it was." Mintner pointed beyond the pool, to where his property abutted the hillside. "It was like something out of a horror movie. I should know."

"Why is that?" Eve asked.

"I'm *the* Sherwood Mintner," he said, waiting a beat for the recognition that didn't come from Eve or Duncan. "The screenwriter of *Bloodbath Day Camp for Girls*." He paused for a reaction again, but still got nothing. "It's a horror classic, for Christ's sake."

"Where's the contractor?" Eve said.

"Probably on his way to Oregon. Seeing that empty eye socket scared the shit out of him. He peeled out while I was calling you."

"Because he's superstitious?" Duncan said.

"Because he's an illegal immigrant and an unlicensed contractor."

"But you were willing to hire him anyway," Eve said.

"I want to build a fence, not a nuclear reactor." Mintner led them around the pool, past the gazebo, to one of the scorched fence posts. He stopped and pointed at the ground. "Here it is."

A jagged piece of a human skull peeked out of the dirt. It was part of a forehead, the left eye socket, part of the nasal cavity, and the cheekbone. The charred fragment reminded Eve of the mask worn by the Phantom of the Opera.

"Ironic, isn't it?" Mintner asked.

"What is?" Duncan asked.

"*Hueso* is Spanish for *bone*," Mintner said. "This is Bone Canyon. It's one of the reasons I built a house here. It fits my brand."

"Is this a stunt for your brand?" Duncan asked.

Mintner held up his hands. "I have nothing to do with this bone being here. It's divine providence."

Eve looked at Mintner. "Have you touched it?"

"Nope," he said.

She gestured to the phone in his hand. "Have you taken a picture of it to enhance 'your brand'?"

Mintner shifted his weight between his feet. "A few."

"Have you posted them on social media?"

"Not yet," he said.

"Please don't," Duncan said.

"Would it be a crime if I did?" Mintner asked.

"No," Duncan said, tipping his head toward the skull. "But that's somebody's spouse, son, or daughter. It wouldn't be very sensitive to the families who loved this person to have those pictures out there, especially after we ID the remains."

"Oh well," he said with a sigh. "There goes a couple of hundred likes."

"That's important to you?" Duncan asked.

"Of course it is. Likes are power," Mintner said, and looked at Eve. "You know what I'm saying. Isn't that how you became a homicide detective?"

Everybody knew that. The YouTube video of her taking down the Deathfist made her a hero with the public and the media, right in the midst of a sheriff's department scandal involving deputies beating up prisoners at the county jail. The embattled sheriff wanted to keep Eve, and the positive press she was generating, at the top of the news cycle for as long as possible. So Sheriff Lansing offered her a promotion. She asked for Homicide and got it, making history and more headlines. The public loved it. The rank and file within the department didn't.

"We have to treat this like a crime scene and seal the area," she said. "That means your backyard is off-limits until we can get a forensic unit out here to process the evidence. You'll have to go back inside your house."

"You're kidding me," Mintner said.

"No she's not," Duncan said. "Please go inside, sir, and we'll get a formal statement from you in a few minutes."

Mintner sighed and walked away.

Eve glanced up at the barren slope. "I'll bet the body was up there, hidden in the brush, and tumbled into the yard after the fire burned everything away."

"It's a safe bet," Duncan said. "It's what's happened with four of the bodies that have been discovered since the fire."

Three of the four were executed gang members whose bullet-riddled or multiply stabbed bodies were tossed into ravines by their killers. Those homicide cases were all being handled by the LASD gang unit. The fourth body belonged to an elderly man who'd wandered away from an Alzheimer's care facility in Calabasas several years ago. The ME had determined that he'd died from a fall.

"Don't even think about climbing up there to look around," Duncan said.

"It's not that steep."

"It's not worth the risk."

"What risk?"

"To your wrist, you idiot. What if you slip?"

"My wrist is healed," she said.

"Are you in a hurry to break it again? Besides, it's not your job to collect bones and your first physical therapy appointment is in an hour."

She'd forgotten about the appointment, which was back in Calabasas, eight miles northeast. "I'll cancel it. This is more important."

"Go," Duncan said. "I'll stay here, get Mintner's statement, and call in the forensic unit. I promise you won't miss anything."

"You could get attacked by a death-crazed raccoon."

"Don't say that. I'm 118 days from retirement," Duncan said as she walked away. "With my luck, it'll happen."

CHAPTER TWO

Old Town Calabasas was the eastern entrance to the city, a short stretch of road that looked like the set of a Hollywood western, abandoned after the cancellation of *Gunsmoke* or *Bonanza*, and left standing between the busy Ventura Freeway to the north, the forty-eight-acre Motion Picture and Television Country House and Hospital to the south, and Mulholland Road to the east. The authentic clapboard storefronts, and the historic Leonis Adobe ranch house, were undercut by the ornamental hitching posts and sidewalks made of synthetic material designed to resemble wooden slats. Eve's physical therapy appointment was on the west end of Old Town in a contemporary two-story office building that stood out with its blandness and total rejection of the frontier theme.

Her therapist, one of several working in the clinic, was Mitch Sawyer, an athletic-looking guy in his late twenties with sun-bleached hair who wore an Aloha shirt and board shorts that showed off his dark tan and strong build.

He sat across from Eve at a table in a room full of exercise equipment. Mitch asked her to bend and turn her wrist while he took some measurements of her range of motion with a plastic ruler device.

While Mitch did that, Eve's gaze wandered to a flyer tacked on the wall behind him. The flyer asked people to look for Kendra Leigh, a sixty-five-year-old local woman who'd been missing for three weeks.

Leigh was pictured standing on a mountain somewhere in hiking gear, smiling into the camera. Eve had seen the flyer all over Calabasas and Agoura, sharing lamppost, store window, and bulletin board space with posters seeking lost cats, dogs, and even a parakeet.

"How does your wrist feel?" Mitch asked.

"Fine," she said. "Can I go now?"

"Squeeze this," he said, giving her a device with a gauge above the handle. She gripped the handle as hard as she could and he wrote down the reading on his notepad. "Are you experiencing any stiffness, numbness, or pain?"

"Nope, it feels great, so I really don't need any therapy."

"You do if you want to regain the grip strength and range of motion you had before you broke your wrist."

"No problem," she said and stood up. "If you print out the exercises for me, I'll be sure to do them at home."

"Yes, you will, but you will also do them with me, right here, three times a week," he said. "Unless you want me to file a negative physical assessment today with the department that will immediately put you back on desk duty."

She narrowed her eyes at him, wondering if this beach boy was the hard-ass he wanted her to think he was. She decided he was too blond, too tan, and therefore too laid-back to follow through on his threat. Besides, she'd been referred to him by her younger sister, Lisa, who was a nurse at West Hills Hospital. He wouldn't want to piss off Lisa, too.

Eve shook her head. "You wouldn't do that."

"I should do it right now. Your measurements are lousy." Mitch gestured to her wrist. "That's no Deathfist."

"Very funny." She'd assumed that Lisa would send her to someone located close to Lost Hills station who'd do a perfunctory assessment, give her a passing grade, and let her go on her merry way. Now Eve suspected that her sister had intentionally done the opposite, picking someone who'd be tough with her. "Did my sister put you up to this?"

"Lisa warned me that you'd be a reluctant patient."

"So she told you to be hard on me."

"I know I look like I'd rather be outside surfing, or climbing a mountain, or running a marathon than sitting here with you, but don't be fooled. I'm as serious about my job as you are about yours," he said. "I'm only asking for another thirty minutes today. What's the big rush?"

"We found some human remains off Kanan Dume."

Mitch looked over his shoulder at the poster on the wall. "Is it her?"

It wasn't likely, she thought, since the skull fragment was charred and Kendra Leigh disappeared weeks after the fire. But Eve supposed it was possible that somebody had murdered her, burned the body, and tossed the remains in the ravine to cover up the crime.

"I can't discuss my cases," Eve said.

"Understood." Mitch held up his hands in mock surrender. "So, here's the deal. The sooner we do our exercises, the faster you can get back to your investigation. What's it going to be?"

Eve knew when she was beaten. She sat down.

Eve spent the next half hour doing what initially seemed to be absurdly simple activities. They included raising, lowering, flipping, and waving her right hand and lifting, rolling, and squeezing a rubber ball. But by the time it was all over, her wrist was limp and sore. It felt like she'd been doing curls with heavy barbells.

"Would you like some ice?" Mitch asked.

Yes, she would, but she didn't have time and she didn't want to show any weakness. "No thanks. It's not necessary and I really have to go."

"Okay," he said, clearly not buying a word of it. "I'll see you the day after tomorrow. Does the same time work for you?"

"We'll see." Eve stood up and fought the urge to rub her wrist.

"So we're on. I'll put it in the calendar."

"I don't think you heard me."

"I can come to you. Your office, your home, wherever. Same ten-dollar deductible, same friendly service, so you have no excuse for missing a session."

"Lucky me," Eve said.

He filled out an appointment card and stapled it to a printout of her exercises. "My cell phone number is on the card. I want you to do these exercises at least once a day. You can do them anytime and anywhere."

"So why do I need to see you?"

Mitch grinned. "Because I'm so lovable."

She took the printout and made a mental note to talk to her sister about getting this jerk off her back.

The Los Angeles County Sheriff's Department was responsible for law enforcement in a jurisdictional patchwork of unincorporated areas, state parks, and municipalities that couldn't afford their own police departments.

The jurisdiction of the Lost Hills sheriff's station was bordered by Ventura County to the west and northwest, the City of Los Angeles to the east and northeast, and Santa Monica Bay to the south. Within those borders, the sheriff was the law in the Santa Monica Mountains and the communities of Malibu, Westlake Village, Agoura Hills, Hidden Hills, and Calabasas, where the station was located.

Eve's drive back to Mintner's house took her west on the Ventura Freeway, straight across their jurisdiction, then south on Kanan Dume Road, toward the center of it. The first thing she noticed when she arrived was that Duncan had strung yellow crime scene tape along the fence post stubs around Sherwood Mintner's property. There were no patrol cars or CSU vehicles parked on the street yet, just somebody's dusty old Ford Fusion. Duncan was right. She hadn't missed anything.

She parked the Explorer, walked to Mintner's front door, and rang the bell. Duncan opened the door as if he lived there.

"How was the PT?" he asked.

"A waste of time." Eve walked past him into the house, which had the stylish, coordinated, and utterly impersonal decor of a model home. She didn't understand why anybody hired decorators. "Where's the CSU?"

"They're wrapping things up at a drive-by shooting in Lancaster. They'll be here in an hour or so."

She knew that bones that had already been exposed to the elements for a long time weren't a high priority compared to collecting fresh evidence at a shooting. Still, she found the wait frustrating.

Sherwood Mintner joined them from another room. She peeked inside the doorway he came from and saw it was a home theater, complete with a big screen, reclining seats, art deco sconces, and a popcorn machine.

"Want to watch *Bloodbath Day Camp for Girls* while you're waiting?" Mintner said. "I've got it all cued up."

"No thanks," Duncan said. "I see enough blood in my job as it is. I like a good western, though."

"I've got every cowboy movie Clint Eastwood ever did."

"Perfect," Duncan said.

Eve left the two men in the home theater and went out to the backyard to look around. She got as far as the pool when she caught some movement in her peripheral vision.

There was a man wearing an Australian bush hat, a khaki shirt, cargo pants, and hiking boots in the backyard of the burned-out property next door. He was crouched in the dirt near the hillside and taking pictures of something on the ground.

She ducked under the yellow tape and marched over to him, taking her badge off her belt and holding it up as she got closer. "Excuse me. I'm Detective Eve Ronin with the Los Angeles Sheriff's Department. May I ask what you're doing here?"

He stood up and faced her. "Looking for bones."

The muscles in her shoulders tightened the way they always did when she anticipated conflict. "Are you a reporter?"

"You say that like you might shoot me if I say yes."

"I'd be tempted."

"You can save a bullet. I'm a forensic anthropologist. Dr. Daniel Brooks. I'm working as a consultant for the crime scene unit. Nan Baker sent me out to get started while she finishes up in Lancaster."

Nan was the head of the CSU. Eve felt the tension easing in her shoulders and gave him a closer look. He was in his early thirties, had curly brown hair, wore rimless glasses, and hadn't shaved in a few days, not because he was trying to be stylish, she thought, but because he was too busy, forgetful, or just didn't care.

She clipped her badge back to her belt and gestured to the taped-off yard behind her. "The crime scene is over there."

"Actually, it's fifty yards that way." Daniel jerked his thumb behind him, like he was hitchhiking. "And fifty yards that way." He nodded toward Mintner's backyard. "And along that entire hillside." He looked up at Latigo Canyon Road. "At least for now. It could expand another fifty or a hundred yards in any direction."

"Why such a large area?"

"Because there are over two hundred bones in the human body and they have probably been broken and scattered by animals, firefighters, the water and fire-retardant drops from aircraft, and the runoff from the rains we've had since then," Daniel said. She didn't detect even the slightest bit of condescension in his voice, but rather a joyful eagerness to share his task with her. "Besides the bones, I'm also looking for loose teeth, surgical implants, jewelry, and any personal effects belonging to the decedent that might still be around."

It all seemed obvious to her now that she'd heard his explanation and she felt stupid for not already knowing it. Her inexperience was showing. *Again.*

"We're going to need a lot more crime scene tape."

"I'm all out of little wire marker flags," Daniel said. "Do you have any?"

"No I don't. I've never had any. Why would I?"

"You can never have too many flags. I buy 'em in packs of a hundred every time I step into a Walmart and I still always run out. Do you have a pen I could borrow?"

"Sure." Eve reached into the inside pocket of her blazer and handed him a disposable ballpoint.

"Thank you." He bent over and stuck the pen in the dirt beside his foot. It was a good thing she hadn't loaned him a Montblanc, she thought.

Eve looked down and saw something white and partially buried in the loose black soil. "What's that?"

"One distal phalange," Daniel said and then added, before she could ask: "The tip of the little toe of the left foot."

"Where's the rest of the foot?"

"It could be anywhere. Or, rather, everywhere. When the soft tissues burn away, the tiny bones that make up the hands and feet are freed like the beads of a necklace after the string has been cut," Daniel said.

Now she knew why she needed little marker flags.

"Can you please show me the skull fragment?"

She lifted the crime scene tape and led him over to the area where the skull was. Daniel moved slowly and gingerly beside her, his eyes on the ground.

"Watch where you step," he said. "You never know if there might be a bone fragment underfoot. Think of it as walking on the beach and trying not to crush any shells."

Eve moved like she was in a minefield. Now that she was looking at her feet, she noticed to her annoyance that her new flat-heeled Oxfords were covered with soot. She hoped the shoes could be cleaned—otherwise she was out eighty bucks. It was a dumb mistake. She should have put disposable Tyvek shoe covers over her Oxfords or changed into the pair of boots that she kept in the trunk for slogging through mud.

They reached the skull fragment. Daniel took a picture, then pulled a tiny brush from one of his cargo pockets, crouched beside the bone, and gently removed some of the dirt from the surface. He studied it for a second. "This was a white woman in her twenties and she was dead long before the fire."

Eve was astonished by his casual pronouncement. "How can you tell all of that from a charred skull fragment?"

"The size of the skull, the rounded shape of the eye orbit, and the smooth, flat brow ridge are all indicators of the sex," he said and used his brush as a pointer. "The narrow nasal aperture suggests that she was white. The fusion lines, which fade as we grow older, hint at her age. The coloration of the bone, and the type of charring at the edges, tells me she was a skeleton before the flames got to her."

"How long before?"

"Your guess is as good as mine," Daniel said as he stood up. "I'm an anthropologist, not a psychic."

"You could have fooled me."

"I'll know a lot more once we find more of her bones. The good news is if fire, runoff, and animals are the only things that came into contact with the remains, the bones and other evidence should be on the surface, not buried. Even so, it's going to be a slow, methodical search and recovery."

"Is there anything I can do to speed things up?"

"How quickly this goes depends on how much manpower and resources are devoted to it," Daniel said. "And a search for old bones isn't going to get much of either. It's only sexy and urgent to me."

"And me, too," she said. "What can I do to help?"

"You can tape off the wider scene and keep out anybody except crime scene techs and starving, underpaid forensic anthropologists who disappointed their parents by never having a bar mitzvah."

"In other words," she said. "Keep out lead-footed detectives like me."

"I didn't say that. I'm sure you have very nice feet," he said, and then his cheeks reddened. "What I mean is, we just need to control the scene so nothing gets trampled."

"I can do that." She thought his embarrassment was adorable. Was he flirting with her, she wondered, or was he just awkward around women?

"I'll bring the bones we recover back to the mobile lab at Lost Hills and reconstruct the skeleton there. That will save us both a schlep to Monterey Park."

That was where LASD headquarters and the crime lab were located, seven miles east of downtown Los Angeles and an hour away from Calabasas on a good day, which meant ninety minutes to two hours stuck in bumper-to-bumper traffic most of the time.

The mobile lab was a thirty-six-by-ten-foot portable office trailer that had been placed in the Lost Hills parking lot during the wildfire to identify the victims, a process that had unexpectedly dragged on in the aftermath as the long-lost casualties of gang warfare and unlocked Alzheimer's units were discovered in the blackened ravines. And now there was one more body.

"Thank you, Dr. Brooks," she said. "I appreciate it."

"Please, call me Daniel."

"If you'll call me Eve."

"Short for Evelyn?"

"Just Eve."

"Like Adam and Eve," he said.

"Just Eve, no Adam," she said, surprising herself. Why the hell did she say that? "I'll get things moving."

She went back to the house, pulled Duncan out of a screening of *A Fistful of Dollars*, and told him what she'd learned from Dr. Brooks.

"Do you think we need to get a search warrant for the other properties?" she asked.

"The fences are gone and so are most of the houses. The fire department and utility workers have been trooping through here for weeks. There's no legitimate expectation of privacy and the bones are in plain view," Duncan said. "It's a free-for-all of exigent circumstances. We don't need a warrant."

So Duncan called the station to get some uniformed deputies out to secure the expanded crime scene while Eve used up their roll of yellow tape defining the new boundaries outside. With that done, she had nothing to do but wait.

She hated waiting.

CHAPTER THREE

Three hours later, Daniel Brooks and more than a dozen CSU techs in white Tyvek suits were working the expanded crime scene. Four backyards and a hundred yards of hillside were cordoned off with yellow tape and, in some areas, were already sectioned off with string and tiny stakes into grids of ten-by-ten-foot quadrants. In each quadrant, techs were crouched on the ground, working with hand shovels, trowels, and sifters. Elsewhere, four techs were walking in a line, shoulder to shoulder, through the backyards along the hillside, looking for bones and personal effects, several of them scanning the ground with metal detectors.

Daniel was one of three people up on the hillside, working thirty yards apart from each other and tethered by ropes to vehicles parked above them on Latigo Canyon Road. They were searching for bones and personal effects that hadn't slid to the ground below.

Eve and Duncan stood in Mintner's gazebo, where the bones and other items that had been recovered so far were laid out on a white sheet on the floor. Nan Baker, the head of the unit, was suited up in Tyvek and gloves, and photographing everything on the sheet and making notations on a notepad. She was an African American woman in her forties who was built like a linebacker and, as Eve knew, was just as formidable.

Eve watched Daniel photograph something on the hillside, then carefully place the item in a bag clipped to his belt. "I've never seen a forensic anthropologist at a crime scene before."

"You haven't been to a lot of crime scenes," Nan said.

It wasn't a criticism as much as it was a statement of fact, but it stung Eve anyway. She tried not to sound defensive when she spoke again. "Why did you bring him in?"

Nan pointed to a bone fragment on the sheet in front of her. "Because he can say that's a human bone and not a squirrel's."

"Can't you?"

"I could," Nan said. "But I need an anthropologist to make the definitive determination."

Duncan spoke up. "She means one that will stand up in court against some asshole defense attorney trying to cast doubt on the evidence."

"Couldn't an anthropologist make that same determination in the lab rather than out here?" Eve asked.

"Yes," Nan said. "But human remains that are completely or partially destroyed by fire are particularly difficult to analyze . . . and that's assuming you can find them. Fire breaks bones apart and a shard can easily be missed by an untrained eye."

Nan explained that the odds of identifying the victim, and determining what happened to him, improved dramatically if the anthropologist recovered the bones in situ at the scene. That way, he could see all the variables at play, including the relationship of the remains to everything else that burned, to determine the path, duration, and intensity of the fire.

"The downside to having an anthropologist around is that he makes himself the center of everything," Nan said.

"You think Dr. Brooks is pushy?"

"No, but he's a showboat. Just look at him playing Indiana Jones up there." Nan gestured to the hillside, where Daniel was rappelling to another position. "He's having way too much fun."

He did look like he was enjoying himself, Eve thought, but she didn't see what was wrong with that.

Duncan crouched beside the sheet and glanced at the tiny screws, a zipper head, and two blackened, curved wires that had been collected. He pointed to one of the wires. "What's that?"

Nan looked over his shoulder. "The underwire from a bra."

Duncan stood, his knees cracking, and hiked up his pants. "How can you tell?"

"The shape, size, and rigid curvature of the wires," Nan said. "And the tiny bits of melted nylon that's stuck to them. I'd say she was a C-cup."

"Like this?" Duncan held his hands way out in front of his chest like he was holding two heavy basketballs.

"You'd need scaffolding, not a bra, to hold those up," Nan said. "Your partner is a C."

Duncan lowered his hands and glanced at Eve's chest. "Good to know."

"Why is that good to know?" Eve said.

"Because every fact is important when you're trying to ID a Jane Doe."

Fair enough, Eve thought, and turned to Nan again. "Have you found any other clothing or personal effects?"

Nan shook her head. "The fire probably burned any clothing. But we might find jewelry, belt buckles, maybe some keys."

Duncan waved Eve away from the sheet of bones. "Let's go eat. I'm hungry and we're about as useful here as eye shadow on a mule."

"You've been watching too many westerns," Eve said, but she agreed with him. She was starving. They started walking toward the house and that was when she noticed a TV news van and a couple of print reporters milling around in the street. "Before we go, one of us should have a word with them."

"You do it," Duncan said. "You're more photogenic."

"That's sexist," Eve said.

"It's a fact. Just look at me."

"Physical appearance is not a factor in this discussion."

"It is for me," Duncan said. "The camera adds ten pounds. I'll look like a beluga whale that shops at Men's Wearhouse. Besides, you're taking the lead on this investigation, whatever it turns out to be."

"I am? Why?"

"Because I'm retiring in a few weeks. My job until then is to sit on my ass, push paper, and offer you pearls of wisdom," he said. "And I don't want to get myself killed like all the soon-to-retire cops in the movies just to add some tragic depth to your character. I've done enough for you already."

"That's a cliché and this isn't a movie."

"It still scares the crap out of me. I feel like I have a target on my back."

She knew the truth was that he was trying to give her the experience she'd need to stand on her own after he retired. And she knew that he thought she liked the media attention, but he was wrong. Eve hated it.

"Fine. I'll meet you in the car." Eve took a deep breath and approached the reporters. They saw her coming and headed for her, Kate Darrow at the front, her cameraman in tow. Darrow was a local celebrity, a sharp crime reporter who also looked like a top fashion model. But she was no fool.

"Nice to see you back in action," Darrow said.

"There isn't any action here," Eve said, choosing her words carefully and keeping her gaze on the reporter, not the camera. "Just some old bones."

"How old?" asked Pete Sanchez, a *Los Angeles Times* reporter who got his best stories by hanging out in bars with off-duty cops. He always smelled like a stale beer. Eve was tempted to give him a Breathalyzer test every time she saw him.

"Too soon to tell," Eve said.

But Pete wasn't ready to let go. "Do you know if it's a man or a woman, an adult or a child? How about the cause of death? Is it an accident or murder?"

"I can't discuss any details at this point."

"Can't or won't?" Darrow asked.

Eve smiled. "Both."

"Is it another executed gang member?" Darrow prodded anyway.

"I don't know."

"Since the fire, it seems like burned bodies are being found every few days," Darrow said. "How many more do you think you'll find?"

"I hope this is the last."

"Unless the ravines of the Santa Monica Mountains are where the street gangs have been dumping their dead for decades," Darrow said, more for the camera than Eve. "Then this could just be the beginning."

"That's all I've got for now. Have a good day," Eve said and headed for her Ford Explorer.

Darrow was obviously struggling to create a story where there wasn't one yet. Eve didn't blame her for that. If Eve had her way, Darrow wouldn't have to wait long. Every corpse, even one that was just scattered bones for now, had a story. It was Eve's job to find it.

Duncan and Eve grabbed lunch at a spicy fried chicken place tucked between an Italian deli and a pet store in one of the vast, aging shopping centers on Kanan Dume north of the Ventura Freeway. He managed to dribble hot sauce on his tie despite tucking a napkin into his collar. Eve escaped spotless.

Afterward, they drove six miles east on the freeway to the Lost Hills exit, where the new six-lane, $37 million overpass did double duty as the official gateway to Calabasas. The city's logo, a red-tailed hawk flying over the hills, was sculpted onto white pillars in the center of the bridge and CITY OF CALABASAS was etched on the broad footing at the off-ramp. The words, however, were obstructed by a huge electronic traffic sign posted directly in front of the footing. Today the sign warned motorists to keep their eyes on the road.

She made a right onto Agoura Road, and then a left into the Lost Hills sheriff's station parking lot, driving past the handful of cars belonging to the paparazzi on constant stakeout to photograph a celebrity brought in for booking. Lost Hills deputies covered Malibu, Calabasas, and Hidden Hills, collectively known as the "New Beverly Hills," so she knew it was one of the best places in Los Angeles County to spot the drunks, shoplifters, wife beaters, drug addicts, rapists, and murderers with verified Twitter accounts.

The gates opened automatically to let her Explorer into the restricted lot, which was reserved for official LASD vehicles, the personal cars of employees, a helicopter, and, for the time being, the mobile crime lab. She pulled into a parking spot behind the one-story station and saw Detective Stan Garvey leading a heavily tattooed young black man, dressed head to toe in Gucci, to an idling Hyundai Sonata.

"Look who's getting the star treatment from Tubbs," Duncan said, referring to Garvey, a black man who enthusiastically embraced his *Miami Vice*–inspired nickname. His white partner, Wally Biddle, was known as Crockett and wasn't amused by it at all. "Isn't that Raisin Bran, the rapper?"

"Coco Crispy," Eve said, recognizing the painfully thin rapper now that she got a closer look at him. His clothes seemed too large for his frail body.

"That's who I meant," Duncan said. "Do you know him?"

"Just his face." She watched Garvey open the back door of the Sonata for the rapper, who leaned inside to get something.

"He's twenty-two years old, drives a chrome-plated Bentley, lives in a mansion in the Oaks, and probably makes $10 million a year," Duncan said. "And yet he's done stupid shit like shoplifting a six-pack of beer from Ralphs."

Eve and Duncan got out of the Explorer as Coco Crispy fist-bumped Garvey, handed him an eight-by-ten photo, and then lay down in the back seat of the car. Garvey closed the car door, said a few words to the Hispanic woman in the driver's seat, and watched the Sonata drive out the gate with Coco Crispy hidden from view.

Duncan joined Garvey and tapped the photo in his hand. "Are you gonna frame that?"

Garvey shook his head. "It's the third one he's given me."

"So he's been here a lot," Eve said.

"Never for anything serious," Garvey said. "He's basically a good kid."

She didn't like Garvey much. Working out of Lost Hills, Garvey encountered lots of Hollywood power players and treated them all as if he were their personal law enforcement concierge.

"What did Coco Puffs do this time?" Duncan asked.

"Coco Crispy," Garvey said. "He had a little too much to drink and took a shit in his neighbor's Jacuzzi."

Duncan nodded knowingly. "So that's why he's slipping out the back door and sneaking away on the floor of his maid's car."

Something didn't smell right to Eve. "Why isn't there a mob of paparazzi out there waiting for him?"

"Because nobody knows he's here," Garvey said. "I booked him under Rodney Turner, his real name."

"That was thoughtful of you," she said.

Garvey picked up on the snide tone in her voice and glared at her. "Our job is to protect and to serve. Sometimes we forget that last part.

Other kids make the same kind of mistakes as Coco and nobody ever knows. But because he's a celebrity, he—"

"—can't take a shit in a neighbor's pool without everybody knowing about it." Duncan interrupted him and finished his thought. "And who among us hasn't done that?"

"I'm just giving him the same privacy to mess up that anybody else would have," Garvey said.

That's a fair argument, Eve thought. Most people didn't have to worry about the whole world knowing about every embarrassing mistake they ever made. It was different with celebrities.

"The neighbor could talk," Eve said.

Garvey shook his head. "While Coco was sobering up in a cell, I brokered an understanding between the two parties. Coco agreed to pay her pool-cleaning bill for as long as she lives there and she dropped the charges. Everybody wins."

"You should be an agent, Tubbs," Duncan said.

"I'd rather be a producer," Garvey said.

At least he's honest about it, Eve thought, and went inside the station.

Eve and Duncan spent the next few hours in their squad room cubicles, doing the tedious but necessary paperwork to start the investigation on the remains found in Sherwood Mintner's backyard. They assigned the case a file number, filled out a detailed report on all the facts they'd gathered so far, wrote up Mintner's statement, and started a chronological record of every step they'd made.

Eve was nearly finished with her half of the work when she got a call from Kurt, the front desk duty officer, that there was someone in the lobby to see her.

"Who is it?" she asked. Eve wasn't expecting any guests.

"Says he's Linwood Taggert from Creative Artists Agency."

Eve swore to herself. She'd been dodging the agent's calls for weeks. She knew that he wanted to represent her and pitch her story to Hollywood. She wasn't interested.

How did he know she was in the station? She glanced over at Garvey, who was in his cubicle, pretending to be busy. Eve told the duty officer she'd be right out, hung up the phone, got up, and walked over to Garvey's cubicle.

The three partitions of his cubicle were adorned with autographed celebrity photos, like the ones on display in almost every dry cleaner, mechanic's garage, restaurant, hair salon, and bar in Los Angeles. Garvey was in some of the pictures, too, with a chummy arm around the star's shoulder.

Eve leaned against the cubicle and looked down at Garvey. "Linwood Taggert from CAA is out front. Did you tell him I was here?"

Garvey raised his eyebrows. "Linwood Taggert is here? Really? That's *huge*. He's a senior partner."

"You didn't answer my question. I've been avoiding his calls for a reason."

"Think it through. Linwood lives in Hidden Hills and you've been ducking him. He was probably on his way home and figured he'd take a shot, stop by, and see if you were here. What's it cost him? Five minutes?" he said. "Linwood is a giant in the industry. You should be honored that he came to you. He never does that."

"I'll be sure to bow when I see him."

Duncan leaned out of his cubicle, his chair squeaking under his weight. "I think you mean curtsy."

Eve ignored his comment, marched out of the squad room, down the hall, and through the door to the front lobby.

Linwood was the only person out there besides Kurt, the uniformed deputy behind the front counter. The agent was in his fifties and wore a perfectly tailored Italian suit and an outrageously thick, titanium Swiss watch that could probably be worn to measure ocean depth while diving the Mariana Trench or used as an altimeter while skydiving.

"Mr. Taggert," she said. "I'm Eve Ronin."

"It's a pleasure to finally meet you, Detective. You're a hard woman to reach," he said. "Can we go somewhere to talk?"

She didn't move. "I'm very busy and you're wasting your time. I don't need an agent."

"Of course you do. Your story is out there. Someone is going to tell it and make a lot of money doing it," Linwood said. "Shouldn't that person be you?"

"The only thing I'm interested in is solving crimes."

"Bullshit." He said it with a smile but it didn't make the response any less offensive to her.

"What did you say?"

"Bullshit. You got where you are by leveraging your media exposure from that YouTube video. Then you solved a triple murder and pulled off a daring rescue, adding a narrative spine to your story. It was a brilliant use of social media."

Yes, she'd used the first YouTube video to her advantage. But he made it sound like she'd scripted and staged everything that had happened to her since. Eve had no idea how her first homicide investigation, a gruesome triple murder, would play out or that a firefighter would be there to film her escaping the wildfire with a child in her arms. It was all pure luck.

"I was just doing my job," she said, rubbing her sore wrist.

"And if you have any aspirations to reach a higher level in the department, a TV series or movie about you will get you there."

Eve didn't know what her aspirations were but they certainly didn't include anything to do with Hollywood. She despised the business after living through what it had done to her mother, Jen, who'd dreamed of making it as an actress, but for the last thirty years had mostly worked as a background extra, one of the anonymous people filling out a restaurant, office, or sidewalk behind the actors who were actually in front of the camera. Jen ended up as a single parent with three children fathered by three different men who were in the entertainment industry, too. Eve spent her teenage years trying to bring order to the chaos at home, raising her two younger siblings while her mom was off chasing roles and men. Eve resented her mother, her absentee father, and Hollywood for stealing her childhood.

"I'll establish myself in the department by closing cases and putting criminals behind bars," Eve said, rubbing her sore wrist.

"How was that working for you before you put Blake Largo on the ground?" Linwood asked.

The answer, she knew, was that she'd probably still be investigating residential burglaries and purse thefts in Lancaster instead of working homicides in Calabasas. They both knew it. The run-in with Largo was a lucky break that she used to her advantage. But what Linwood Taggert was proposing was something else entirely.

"A movie or TV series about you is going to get made," he said. "With or without your involvement or consent."

"I don't care."

Linwood cocked his head, as if examining her from a new angle. "So you don't mind if Eve Ronin is a big-boobed blonde in a low-cut blouse and stiletto heels who rides her Harley to work and caps every arrest with a wink and her catchphrase, 'Kiss this, honey'?"

"That won't happen." At least she hoped it wouldn't.

"It could if you let someone else tell your story. You need to control the message, and how you are portrayed, to get the most out of it, professionally and financially. I can do that for you, leaving you free to do this." He waved his hand in the air to indicate the sheriff's station and everything it represented.

"I already am," Eve said. "I don't need your help to do my job."

Linwood reached into his jacket, took out his card, and offered it to her. She took the card. It was embossed and the paper stock was heavy. "Think about it."

He smiled at her and walked out. She watched him go and she felt a percolating rage. Everybody in Hollywood was under the misguided, arrogant belief that everyone dreams of becoming a celebrity, and that there was no higher calling or greater achievement than being the center of a TV show or movie, either as the star, or the director, or the executive producer of the series. So naturally people were certain that Eve thought of her job only as a means to achieve fame and fortune. It rankled her that nobody could accept that being a good homicide detective was really all that she wanted.

Of course, it didn't help her argument that she'd leveraged her YouTube fame to get her promotion. So perhaps she had only herself to blame for the unwanted attention from Hollywood. That realization didn't make her feel any better about everyone's wrongheaded assumptions about her motives.

Eve went back down the hall to the squad room and tossed Linwood Taggert's business card on Garvey's desk as she walked by. "For your collection."

Garvey picked up the card and admired it. "I don't think you appreciate how powerful he is."

Eve took a seat at her cubicle, her back to Garvey. "I don't think you appreciate how little I care."

Duncan leaned out of his cubicle and looked at her. "Does this mean you didn't curtsy?"

CHAPTER FOUR

It was 7:00 p.m. when Eve walked out of the station. She was about to get into her Subaru Outback for the short drive home when she spotted a dusty old Ford Fusion parked beside the mobile crime lab. It was the same car she saw outside of Sherwood Mintner's house before she met Daniel Brooks. It wasn't a big deduction to guess who the car belonged to. She walked over to the lab, climbed the two steps to the door, and pressed the speaker button beside the keypad.

"Yes?" Daniel's voice crackled through the cheap speaker.

"It's Eve. Can I come in?"

"Of course." There was a buzz, she heard the door lock unlatch, and she went in.

It felt like she'd walked into a meat locker. The temperature must have been only ten or fifteen degrees above freezing. The room was white, with a metal examination table in the center. In the back, there was a refrigeration unit similar to what she'd seen in the morgue, with several drawers for holding bodies.

Daniel stood over the exam table, which was covered with bones, some intact and others fragments, laid out like a person on her back.

"How did it go out there today?" she asked. Her wrist ached again. She wondered if her wrist was really sore, or if it was all in her head, if seeing all the shattered bones had reminded her about her recent fracture.

"It went well," he said. She noticed that his nose was sunburned. "Would you like me to tell you what I know?"

She smiled at him. "Unless you'd prefer to be interrogated."

"Her body was on the hillside prior to the fire. I know that from the dispersal pattern of the bones."

"What kind of dispersal pattern is that?"

"Starting out small on the hill and spreading out wide at the bottom. The pieces of the skull, for example, were found in eight different places. That, and the charring patterns on the bones, tells me they were scattered during the fire and by the elements. Wind, water, that kind of thing."

"So she fell or was dumped from Latigo Canyon Road." Eve shivered in the cold room. If she stayed much longer, her teeth would start to chatter.

"That's correct. The fusion of her clavicle confirms my initial conclusion that she was in her twenties. I know that not long before her death, she broke her elbow and needed surgery to put it back together. We found a partial radius bone with a plate screwed onto it." He pointed the bone out. There was a thin band of titanium, resembling the sprockets on a strip of movie film, screwed into it. He picked up something off the table that looked like a silver bottle stopper and held it out to her. "We also found the loose titanium radial head that had been embedded in the bone."

"What is a radial head?" Eve asked.

"The knobby end where the radial bone meets the elbow," Daniel said, demonstrating by placing the titanium radial head into a hole at the tip of the bone, giving it a rounded end. "Her radial head was shattered, so the surgeon replaced it with this. Take a closer look at the implant."

He handed her the titanium radial head and a magnifying glass. Eve examined the implant under the glass and could see a string of numbers and some kind of logo. She felt her pulse quicken with excitement.

"Can we use this serial number to trace the implant back to the surgeon and the patient?"

"Absolutely. That's why it's there."

"To identify corpses?"

"That's a side benefit. Implants are engraved with individual serial numbers so they can be traced if a design or manufacturing flaw is discovered later that poses a threat to patients and requires a recall."

"You mean so they can cut you open again and take it out."

Daniel nodded. "Just like replacing a faulty part in a car."

"Ouch," Eve said. She'd been so fascinated by the implant, and what it meant, that she'd momentarily forgotten how cold she was. Now she was shivering. Daniel didn't seem bothered by the cold at all. She figured he was used to it.

"The implant manufacturer is back east," he said. "Nan probably won't be able to get the information to you until tomorrow morning."

"I can wait," she said. But that was a lie. She really wanted it now and wondered if she'd get into trouble calling the company's CEO at home. She didn't care about upsetting him, but she'd definitely piss off Nan, and that would have repercussions. So she'd wait. Patiently. At least until 9:00 a.m.

"I can also tell you, by looking at the healing of her broken radius bone, that she died within a few weeks of getting out of her cast."

"Do you know how she died?"

"Not yet," he said. "There are still a lot of bones we haven't found, like her lower jaw and most of the spine. It's frustrating, because I know they're out there."

She felt the same way about clues in an investigation. "Did you find anything else, like jewelry, keys, or maybe a bullet?"

"Wouldn't that be nice," he said.

"Is that a no?"

"All we found was a zipper, some screws from her implants, and the underwire from a bra."

She glanced at the wire. "A C-cup."

"You know your bras."

"I've had some experience."

"That's outside my range of expertise. I'm going back out to the scene to poke around while there's still some light," he said. "I won't give up until I recover every bone there is to find."

She thanked him and rushed back outside, where it was warm.

Eve was home five minutes later. That was because she lived only two miles away, on the other side of the 101 freeway, in a two-story street-front condo on the north end of Las Virgenes Road. All her furniture was purely functional screw-together stuff from IKEA, and the walls were bare. She didn't spend enough time at home to care about decoration. Her racing bike was parked behind the couch in the living room, because that was the most convenient place for it.

She went into the kitchen, opened the freezer, and got an ice pack out for her wrist and a chicken potpie out for her dinner. While the potpie was cooking in the microwave, she iced her wrist at the table and stared at her bike. It had been six weeks since she'd gone on a ride. She missed it. The microwave dinged at the same time her cell phone rang. The caller ID warned her that it was her mom. Eve answered it anyway.

"Hi, Mom."

"I saw you on TV." Jen had a scratchy voice that men found sexy. She got it by smoking Marlboros for years. Eve wondered if men would still find her mom's voice so sexy when she was dragging around an oxygen tank. "It's smart of you to stay in the public eye."

"That's not what I'm doing."

"You should be. You don't want people forgetting you."

"That's exactly what I want." Eve put her phone on speaker, set it down on the table, and used a hot pad to take her potpie out of the microwave. She slammed the door to the microwave shut with her free hand.

"You have to stop eating potpies," Jen said, reacting to both the sound from the microwave and her knowledge of her daughter's habits.

Eve brought the potpie back to the table and placed it beside the phone to cool off. "It's the perfect meal. It has everything. Meat, vegetables, and bread."

She'd learned to love them when she was a teenager and her mom was off partying somewhere, leaving her responsible for feeding her sister, Lisa, who was three years younger than her, and her little brother, Kenny, who was five years younger. Lisa's father was a grip, one of the guys who moved lights and equipment around on a movie set, and Kenny's was a struggling actor who gave up years ago and moved back to Green Bay.

"You're getting chubby," Jen said. "Nobody needs more than one chin, honey. The way it's going, pretty soon you won't have any neck at all."

Eve's shoulder muscles tightened as they always did when her mother started irritating her, which was practically every time Jen spoke. It was worse when they were together, so it was a good thing her mother lived in Ventura, a beach community forty miles north, and they rarely saw each other.

"I'm going to get back into my exercise routine again now that my cast is off."

"Good," Jen said. "Because your fitness is important. There aren't any fat actresses in your age bracket who are popular enough to carry a series."

"That's not why I want to stay in shape."

"How many cop shows have there been starring a fat actor who wasn't William Conrad?" Jen said. "I'll tell you. None. Did you know he made a pass at me when I guest-starred on *Jake and the Fatman*?"

You weren't a guest star, Eve thought. *You were an uncredited background extra who didn't have a name or a line.* But what Eve said was: "You've told me a thousand times."

"It was like being charged by a horny hippo."

Eve's shoulder muscles were as tight as a crowbar. Now the stiffness was spreading to her neck. Five more minutes talking to her mother and she wouldn't be able to turn her head tomorrow without pain. "Did you call just to tell me I look fat?"

"Of course not," Jen said. "I wanted to remind you that your niece's fifth birthday party is at Kenny's house on Saturday."

Kenny's girlfriend, Rachel, became pregnant when they were students at Cal State, Northridge, together, so he married her, quit school, and started a pool-cleaning business. They rented a house in Encino, in the same neighborhood where Eve and her two siblings grew up.

"I know," Eve said. "I'll be there."

"Get Cassidy something girlie, not another toy badge, ticket book, and gun."

"I loved the junior police officer kit when I was her age." Eve wrote her mom tickets for everything. Coming home late at night. Leaving dirty dishes in the sink. Making too much noise in the bedroom with her boyfriends.

"One cop in the family is plenty," Jen said. "Get her a makeup kit, or stick-on nails, or a princess costume. Or buy her a book. Every kid loves *The Cat in the Hat.*"

Eve hated *The Cat in the Hat.* It made her anxious. The cat was way too much like her mother, a tornado that left nothing but damage in her wake. Junior Cop Eve would have put that cat in prison.

"Good night, Mom."

"One more thing. Show a little cleavage next time you're on TV," Jen said. "It will draw attention away from your chins."

Eve clicked off the phone and stared at her chicken potpie. It was like she was looking at her entire childhood in a bowl. Her appetite was gone. She tossed the potpie in the garbage and took a shower instead.

Eve woke up starving at 6:00 a.m. on Tuesday. She ate three granola bars, got dressed, and rode her bike to work. It was a straight shot down Las Virgenes over the freeway, and then a right on Agoura Road, and then up a slight grade past a shopping center, several office parks, and a fire-damaged motel that was nearly destroyed by a rogue ember from the wildfire. The swift journey to the station with the wind in her hair, and the pleasing sensation of natural balance, was an invigorating start to the day. She didn't even break a sweat.

Daniel stepped out of the mobile lab as she was parking her bike near the back door of the station. He walked over to her.

"You ride a bike to work?" Daniel said it as if she'd arrived on a camel. In Eve's experience, anybody in Southern California who didn't drive a car for every journey, even if it was just to pick up the newspaper at the end of their driveway, was regarded as some kind of freak.

"It's no big deal. I practically live across the street," she said. "You're here early."

"I never left," he said, stating the obvious. He was still in the clothes he wore yesterday and it looked to Eve like he hadn't slept, either. "Let me show you something in the lab."

Eve was tempted to dash inside the station first and get a coat out of her locker, but that wouldn't look good. Instead, she followed him into the cold trailer. There were a lot more bones on the table now.

"I found this last night." Daniel picked up a lower jawbone lined with teeth.

Eve knew that if the dead woman had been reported missing, her dental X-rays were likely to be in the National Missing and Unidentified Persons System, a database containing DNA, dental charts, skeletal X-rays, and other distinguishable details about lost or unidentified people provided by families, law enforcement agencies, and other concerned parties. It was an important discovery.

"The teeth could tell us who the dead woman is or corroborate the ID we'll get off the radial head implant," Eve said. It was always good to have more than one piece of evidence to support the victim's ID when dealing with nothing but bones. She still hoped they'd find some jewelry or keys belonging to the victim that might have survived the inferno.

"Delighted to be of service," he said. "In the meantime, the incompletely erupted wisdom teeth indicate I was right about her age."

"Erupted?"

"The third set of molars haven't fully emerged. That happens when you're about twenty-five, assuming you don't have the teeth removed because they are impacted or there's no room for them in your mouth."

"I see you found some other bones. Do any of them give you a clue about how she died?" She could tell from the expression on Daniel's face that they did.

"It would just be a guess," he said.

"So guess," she said.

"That's not my job."

"You're afraid Nan will kill you if you speculate."

"That's one reason," Daniel said. "The other is that there are still a few more bones I'd like to find. But I need a shower and a nap first."

"Are you alert enough to drive home?"

"I'm not going anywhere," he said. "You have showers and cots here, don't you?"

Eve walked him into the station, showed him the men's locker room, then led him to a small, windowless room with two cots inside. It was essentially a repurposed supply closet.

"Welcome to the Four Seasons Lost Hills."

The cots were mostly used by deputies who lived far from Calabasas and ended up working an unexpected swing shift, or by deputies on morning watch who had to testify in court the following day. It didn't make sense in either case for the deputies to drive all the way home only to come right back again for their next shift. A sign above the door read PLOWDEN MANOR.

Daniel gestured to the sign. "What's that mean?"

"The story I heard is that Plowden was a deputy going through his third divorce with big debts and no money. He lost his apartment and his car was repossessed. So he lived here for a few months."

"Anybody living here now?"

"Not that I know of," she said, but the air was stale and smelled like dirty socks. She had no idea when or if the sheets were cleaned. "Are you sure you don't want to call an Uber?"

"Absolutely. This is a presidential suite compared to some of the places I've had to stay on the job."

Eve was intrigued and wanted to know more about those jobs, but he was clearly exhausted and she had work to do. It would have to wait until another time.

"Sweet dreams," she said and headed for the squad room.

Duncan was at his desk when she came in. He was drinking a cup of coffee and eating a Ding Dong that he'd bought from the vending machine.

"You're in early," she said.

"I got a text from Nan. I hate texts."

"You hate anything that's written on a screen. What did she want?"

"She says they found some implants belonging to our Jane Doe and traced them to an orthopedic surgeon in West Hills. His office was able to ID the patient," Duncan said. "Her name is Sabrina Morton, age twenty-four, and she lived in a guesthouse on Latigo Canyon Road."

That was the road that ran along the ridge above Sherwood Mintner's home in Hueso Canyon. "How long ago was the surgery?"

"Six years," Duncan said.

That was probably how long her body had been in the ravine, Eve thought, considering that Daniel was sure she'd died within a few weeks of getting out of her cast. All the facts were fitting together smoothly. "Did you run her name through the system?"

"I was waiting for you," Duncan said. "Because I know how worried you are about missing any excitement."

"You mean because you hate using the computer," she said.

"That too," he said.

Eve went to her desk, logged in to her computer, and entered Sabrina's name into CLETS, the California Law Enforcement Telecommunications System, a title that was coined in 1970 and that hadn't changed with evolution in the underpinning technology. CLETS combined several databases, including the FBI's National Crime Information Center and Department of Motor Vehicles records from multiple states. Sabrina's California DMV photo came up, along with her vital stats and most recent addresses. Sabrina was white, as Daniel said she'd be, with long brown hair and a doe-eyed innocence that was reflected by her lack of a criminal record or outstanding warrants.

Next she typed Sabrina's name into the in-house database to see if she'd ever had contact with the sheriff's department, anything from calling to complaining about a noisy neighbor to being interviewed as a witness to a crime. The first item that came up in the search results was a missing person report.

"Got something," Eve said, getting Duncan's attention. "Six years ago, Sabrina was reported missing by her parents, Albert and Claire Morton of Woodland Hills."

Another fact snapped into place with the others.

Eve went on, summarizing the report for Duncan as she browsed through it. "Sabrina worked at the winery in Hueso Canyon but had the day off. Her roommate says Sabrina was there when she left for work at eight a.m., but when she came back that night, Sabrina was gone. Which was odd, because Sabrina's car was still in the driveway and her purse, keys, and cell phone were on her dresser."

"That explains why all we found were her bones," Duncan said.

"But not why we haven't found any jewelry."

"Maybe she didn't wear any," Duncan said. "You don't."

"Only at work—otherwise I have a few necklaces that I like to wear. Seems to me we ought to turn up an earring or something." Eve went back to summarizing the report. "The roommate assumed Sabrina went out for a walk. When Sabrina didn't come back that night, the roommate became concerned and called her parents. They called us."

There were some related reports in the case file from the detective who interviewed her neighbors and the deputies who searched the area for Sabrina. The investigation had lurched on for a few more weeks without getting anywhere and there hadn't been any new notations in the file in six years.

Eve closed the file and returned to the search results. There was another case involving Sabrina, opened just two weeks before her disappearance.

Early on a Saturday morning in Malibu, Sabrina staggered into a gas station on Pacific Coast Highway wearing only bikini bottoms and a T-shirt, and asked the clerk if she could use the restroom. The clerk gave her the key. When she came out a few minutes later, she told the clerk to call the police.

Tell them, she said, that I've been raped.

CHAPTER FIVE

Duncan stayed in his chair and used his feet to wheel himself over to Eve's cubicle. "Who was the detective assigned to the case?"

Eve checked the screen. "Ted Nakamura. The same detective who handled her missing persons case. Did you know him?"

Duncan nodded. "He's Assistant Sheriff Nakamura now. Teddy was even more ambitious than you are."

"I'm not ambitious."

"If that were true, you wouldn't be sitting in his old chair."

Eve went back to reading through the file and giving Duncan the broad strokes as she went along.

Sabrina told Nakamura that she was partying on the beach with three male surfers she'd met on Friday night. They had a few drinks, she got dizzy, blacked out, and the next thing she knew, she woke up on the sand at dawn. The guys were gone, her bikini bottoms were off, and she hurt deep inside. She suspected that she'd had intercourse but couldn't remember a thing.

Sabrina put on her bottoms, went up to the gas station, and asked to use the restroom, and she bled when she peed. Now she was certain that she'd been raped. So she told the clerk to call the police.

The deputies took her to West Hills Hospital, where her bathing suit and T-shirt were bagged as evidence and a nurse swabbed her for pubic hairs and sperm. Blood and urine samples were also taken. All the evidence was placed in a rape kit and sent to the crime lab in Monterey Park. She was interviewed by Detective Ted Nakamura at the ER. She repeatedly refused any counseling and was given a ride home.

"Her blood and urine tests didn't reveal any traces of a roofie," Eve said.

"No surprise there," Duncan said. "It would have passed out of her with her first piss."

"But they did find traces of cocaine and marijuana."

"That's bad. It raises the possibility that she was so blitzed that she might've consented to the sex and forgot about it," he said. "A defense attorney would tear her apart."

It was a shit case, Eve thought. No doubt about that.

She scanned through more reports. "The rape kit was sent to the lab, but it was never processed."

That was no surprise to either of them. It was common knowledge that the backlog of untested rape kits at the crime lab numbered in the thousands and went back a decade. There wasn't enough money or the manpower to process them all. The situation was even worse in some other states.

"The investigation went nowhere," she said.

"Because she disappeared," Duncan said. "No victim, no case. We could be dealing with a suicide."

"The thought occurred to me, too."

"I'll give Teddy a call, ask him if he remembers anything about the investigations that might not be in his reports. I'll also see what else I can learn about Sabrina through public records and LexisNexis."

"In other words," Eve said, "you want me to go break the news to Sabrina's parents that she's dead."

"I've done that enough for one lifetime," Duncan said and wheeled himself back to his cubicle.

Eve called Claire Morton, introduced herself, and told her that she had some news about her daughter, but that she preferred to deliver it in person. Claire told her to come right over and that she'd call her husband at his office in Tarzana to meet them at the house.

On her way out, Eve passed by the sleep room. The door was ajar. She peeked inside. Daniel was asleep on a cot, in a UCLA T-shirt and shorts, his wet hair leaving a damp spot on the pillow. Eve wondered what drove him so hard. Was it scientific curiosity or was it the same need to put things in order, erase uncertainty, and get justice for the dead that drove her?

The Mortons lived in a rambling ranch-style house in a Woodland Hills cul-de-sac east of Valmar Road, their back fence an inch from the Calabasas border. Eve arrived at the same moment that Albert Morton pulled into the driveway in his Cadillac. He wore a suit and an expression so stony on his jowly face that he could have been a sculpture. Eve introduced herself and got a nod in response.

Albert led Eve into the house, where Claire waited in the living room, sitting up straight on a floral-patterned couch in her floral-patterned dress, her delicate, pale hands in her lap. The room smelled of lilacs, but the only flowers Eve could see were illustrations on fabric. Perhaps she was only imagining the scent.

"Have you found her body?" Albert asked as he sat beside his wife on the couch. Eve guessed they were both in their early sixties.

"Albert—" Claire began.

"It's obvious, Claire. You don't need to be a shrink to read this woman's body language."

Eve sat down in an armchair that faced them. "I'm afraid your husband is right."

"Where did you find her?" Albert asked.

"Hueso Canyon," she said. "The fire cleared away the brush, exposing her remains."

"That's practically outside her front door," Albert said. "And you didn't find her until now? That's unacceptable."

"What were the circumstances of her death?" Claire asked, her voice barely above a whisper.

"I don't know yet," Eve said. "But I promise you I won't rest until we know everything."

Albert bolted to his feet, startling Eve, and towered over her. "Now you care, after she's dead, when you didn't do a Goddamn thing to help her when she asked you for it."

"Albert," Claire said softly. "Detective Ronin didn't ignore Sabrina, the other detective did."

He turned to his wife. "What makes you think she's going to be any different?"

"Because she's a woman, not much older than Sabrina was when she was raped."

Albert sat back down on the couch and Claire placed a hand on his knee. Eve waited a moment before she spoke. She could only imagine the depth of this couple's pain or how they'd managed to deal with it over the years. It disturbed Eve, though, that Claire believed that a young female detective would be more motivated than a man to investigate the sexual assault of a woman. Was there any merit to that belief? Eve wondered how Claire would feel if it had been an older female detective who'd failed to find Sabrina's attackers . . . or if Claire's assumption about the impact of the gender and age of the detective on the investigation would change if Eve failed, too.

"What can you tell me about the sexual assault?" She knew the details from Nakamura's report, but she wanted to hear what Sabrina's parents said. There could be details Sabrina shared with them that she didn't mention to Nakamura.

Claire cleared her throat before speaking. "Sabrina always loved the water. She broke her elbow surfing, but as soon as she got her cast off, she returned to the beach. She wasn't ready to get back in the water yet, so she watched other surfers. One Saturday, she stayed until dark, socializing with some men on the beach. She drank a few beers and passed out . . ."

She couldn't go on, overcome with emotion, so her husband continued, an edge in his voice.

"They drugged her, gang-raped her, and just left her on the sand. She went straight to you and you did nothing about it."

Claire didn't correct her husband this time. Eve wasn't offended. She accepted that she represented the entire Los Angeles County Sheriff's Department—past, present, and future—to the Mortons.

"Whatever drug they gave her messed up her memory," Albert said. "Sabrina couldn't remember their names or their faces."

"She remembered their tattoos," Claire said so softly that Eve almost didn't hear it.

There was no mention of any tattoos in Nakamura's report. Her pulse quickened but she tried to keep her expression neutral.

"What tattoos?" Eve asked.

Albert answered. "On their calves. Sabrina said they all had the same one, but you never sent an artist. So she found one herself."

"A few days later, she was gone," Claire said.

"The rape was horrible, but being ignored by you was like being violated again," Albert said, his anger building once more. "It tore her apart."

Eve took a deep breath. Her next question was a tricky one. "How distraught was she?"

"What do you mean?" Claire asked.

"She left her place without her keys, her purse, or her phone . . ." Eve let her voice trail off.

Albert's face was getting red. "You're asking us if we think she walked out the door and threw herself off a cliff. The answer is hell no."

Claire gripped her husband's knee. "I've asked myself that question every day since she disappeared. I'd like to say the answer is no, but I can't be sure, not after what she went through."

Albert shook his head vehemently. "My daughter was a fighter. She wasn't suicidal, she was furious. That's why she had a drawing made of the tattoos." He glared at Eve. "She wasn't going to wait for you to do something. She was going to find the bastards herself."

Maybe she did, Eve thought, *or they found her.* This changed everything. "Do you have a copy of the drawing?"

"No," Claire said. "But we know who drew it."

"How did it go?" Duncan asked Eve as she came into the squad room. He was sitting in his cubicle, looking at a picture of the golf course view from the back of his Palm Springs condo. Only 117 days until that was home. He'd mentioned his running count so often that now Eve found herself keeping track of the days, too, though she wasn't looking forward to him leaving. She'd come to rely on him not only as her partner, but as a teacher, too. She'd miss him terribly when he was gone.

"The parents don't think we did enough to help their daughter before she disappeared." She stood next to his cubicle. "Did you talk to Nakamura?"

"I left a message. He's a busy guy."

"According to the parents, Sabrina said the three men who raped her all had the same tattoo, but there's no mention of a tattoo in any of Nakamura's reports."

"Maybe she didn't remember the tattoo when Teddy interviewed her the first time," Duncan said. "That happens, especially in cases like this. Memories come back in bits and pieces over a long period of time."

Eve knew that was true, but it still bothered her. "Do you know anybody at the crime lab who can get her rape kit tested?"

"No, I don't, but even if I did, the sexual assault happened six years ago and the victim is dead," he said. "What's my leverage to make her kit a priority over the six thousand others waiting to be tested?"

"Justice has been delayed long enough," she said. "And whoever attacked her could still be out there and still raping women."

"I get that, but we aren't sex crime detectives and there's no legitimate, pressing reason to move her kit to the top of the heap."

Not yet, she thought. "What did you learn about her?"

Duncan checked his notes, written in an illegible scrawl all over a legal pad, going in all directions, avoiding the lines altogether. She didn't get why he didn't use a blank sheet of printer paper instead.

"Those are definitely her bones. Her dental records match the teeth that were found. I've also got the names and current addresses of her former roommate and her employer," he said. "But there's no reason to talk to them now. We don't know yet if a crime has been committed."

"Yes we do," Eve said. "She was raped."

"Allegedly," he said.

"Sabrina got a friend to draw the tattoo for her," she said. "I've got his name. I'm going to track him down and see if he still has it."

Duncan sighed, expressing several lifetimes of weariness, the eternity of Sisyphus pushing his boulder up a mountain in Hades. "What is the point of that?"

"The tattoo might be the missing piece that connects her rape to another one out there and give us the leverage we need to finally get her kit tested."

"I remember when I was as noble, idealistic, and headstrong as you," he said.

"When was that?"

"The week in kindergarten when I was a junior crossing guard."

Eve knew that wasn't true. Duncan hadn't lost any of his dedication or his drive. He was just a lot more cynical and tired than he was when he'd started out. Or at least he pretended to be. She wondered if that was the inevitable result of experience and age, or if it came from years of repeated disappointment and failure, of living with the cases that he'd never solved, and if there was any way to stop it from happening to her.

She didn't know. But for now, she believed the key was to keep pushing forward, to keep fighting against the obstacles until either they fell . . . or she did.

Eve went to her cubicle and was about to fire up her computer to track down the artist when Detective Wally Biddle, Garvey's partner, approached her. His hair was parted in the middle, like Don Johnson, which was one reason why the Crockett nickname stuck.

"Hey, I've got something for you." Biddle handed her a manila envelope. "My next-door neighbor is an actress. She thinks she'd be perfect to play you in the movie."

"There is no movie," she said, handing the envelope back.

"Take a look," he insisted.

Eve opened the envelope and took out an eight by ten of a blonde in her twenties with pouty lips and huge boobs, wearing a low-cut shirt and pointing an enormous gun at the camera. Her name was Porsche DeVille.

"Is this a joke?" Eve asked.

"No," he said.

Eve flipped the picture over and, out of curiosity, looked at Porsche's credits on the back. It was a list of bit parts in TV shows and low-budget movies. Waitress. Dog Walker #1. Angry Lady. Stewardess #2. Except for the role of Topless Bather, it was like looking at her mom's IMDb. com listing, only from a different era.

"There's no point in giving me this," Eve said. "If there was a movie being made about me, and there isn't, I wouldn't have anything to do with it."

"Why not? You could make a fortune," Biddle said. "What do you need this job for?"

My sanity, Eve thought.

"Nice try. You just want me out of here," she said. "You have from the day I walked in. It's not going to be that easy."

"You don't know how lucky you are to have Hollywood knocking on your door. If someone wanted to make a movie about me, I'd quit this job in a nanosecond, move to Hawaii, and spend my days on the beach."

"That's not who I am," Eve said, handing the photo back to Biddle. "Neither is she."

"That's tragic." He shook his head and walked away.

Eve didn't see what was so tragic. She lived for her job, for the satisfaction of restoring order. Working in Hollywood, or lying on a beach, couldn't give her that same sense of balance. It was a kind of peace that she knew she wouldn't find doing anything else.

But she wasn't feeling that peace now, not with Sabrina's disappearance a mystery and her rape unsolved. Eve turned back to her computer and started looking for the artist who could help her set things right.

CHAPTER SIX

Nathan Holt's family used to live in the same cul-de-sac as the Mortons. But after Nathan graduated from high school, he went off to Valencia to study at Cal Arts and his parents traded their split-level empty nest for a condo in Las Vegas.

Now Nathan lived in Culver City and worked at an advertising agency in Venice that occupied a four-story building that was designed to look like a Santa Monica Beach lifeguard tower. The building had become a tourist attraction, so Eve had to weave and dodge through a forest of selfie sticks to get inside.

Eve introduced herself to the receptionist, who gave her Nathan's office number on the third floor and pointed her to the elevators. She went up, then wound her way through a maze of cubicles to his open office door.

"I'm glad you were able to find me," Nathan said from behind his standing desk. "Most people get lost somewhere between the elevators and the copying machine and are never seen again."

"I have a natural sense of direction."

Nathan was bald, with purple-framed glasses and an untucked collared shirt that looked like a quilt comprised of different swaths of fabric. His office walls were decorated with mock-ups of various advertising campaigns for Brace, a men's deodorant. Men diving out of airplanes. Men climbing mountains. Men racing cars. All under the headline: BRACE YOURSELF. BEING A MAN NEVER SMELLED SO GOOD.

"What can I do for you, Detective?" he asked.

Eve stood in front of his desk, which was like facing a podium. "I'm working a cold case, the rape of Sabrina Morton six years ago. I understand from her parents that she came to you to draw the tattoos that she saw on her attackers."

Nathan took off his glasses and rubbed his eyes. "Have you found her?"

"We recovered her remains yesterday in the Santa Monica Mountains. We don't know her cause of death yet."

He was quiet for a long moment, his head down as he cleaned his glasses with his shirttail.

"We grew up next door to each other. I had a crush on her since nursery school." Nathan raised his head, put his glasses back on, and looked at Eve. "When she told me what happened to her, we cried together for an hour. I wanted to do anything I could to help her."

"Do you still have the drawing?"

"I'm sure I do somewhere. I'll look for it when I get home tonight."

She handed him her card and wrote a phone number on the back. "You can send it to the email address on the card or text it to the number on the back. Do you remember what the tattoo looked like?"

Eve hoped that if he did, he could do a quick sketch for her right now.

"Not really, only that it had something to do with a surfboard and a gun. I sat with them for hours, tweaking the sketch until I got the tattoo exactly the way they remembered it. That was the last time I ever saw her."

"Them?" Eve said. "Who else was with her?"

"Her roommate, Josie Wallace."

Something wasn't adding up. "How could she help Sabrina describe the tattoo?"

"Because Josie was raped that night, too."

The evening rush hour on the San Diego Freeway usually began at 3:00 p.m. and continued until about 8:00 p.m. Today, the evening rush hour began two hours early, immediately after the six-hour morning rush hour, thanks to a jackknifed big rig on the Sepulveda Pass. So Eve chose a different route back, taking the Pacific Coast Highway thirteen miles west, the beaches to her left and the eroding hillsides of Santa Monica and the Palisades to her right. She called Duncan on the way and filled him in on what she'd learned from Nathan Holt.

"Now we know there were two women raped by those surfers that night," she said. "I wonder why Sabrina didn't mention her roommate when she gave her report to Nakamura."

"Maybe Josie Wallace didn't want to get involved. Or maybe Josie didn't share Sabrina's belief that they were both raped," Duncan said. "I'll run Josie's name through the system and see what comes up."

Eve let him go and slowed as she neared Topanga Beach, where Sabrina Morton and Josie Wallace were raped. It was part of Topanga State Park, so there wasn't a row of multimillion-dollar oceanfront houses to block the view of the beach and the bay.

The beach was below the highway, separated by a boulder-lined embankment. It was a rocky shoreline, with bathrooms, a lifeguard tower, a long parking lot, and not much else. At night, even with traffic on PCH, nobody would have been able to see the assault or hear Sabrina and Josie even if they'd been able to scream. The gas station where Sabrina reported her rape had been partially destroyed years ago by a landslide and was now abandoned, boarded up with plywood, and covered with graffiti.

A few miles west, Eve took a right onto Malibu Canyon and headed north toward Calabasas. She was halfway through the fire-ravaged canyon, and about to hit a notorious cellular dead zone, when she got a call from Nan.

"How far are you from the station?" Nan asked.

"About fifteen minutes," Eve said. "Why?"

"Stop by the mobile lab with Duncan when you get here. I've got something to show you both."

Eve resisted the urge to put on her light and siren, settling instead for driving ten miles over the speed limit, cutting a few minutes from her drive.

Duncan was waiting in the parking lot with his Patagonia coat on when Eve arrived. She wished it had occurred to her to call ahead and ask him to grab her coat, too. It was too late now. He joined her as she got out of the Explorer and walked with her to the lab.

"I hope they keep this trailer here until I retire," he said. "I hate driving to Monterey Park."

Nan buzzed them in and escorted them over to the exam table, where there were a lot more bones now, some like bits of charcoal. "We've recovered almost all of Sabrina Morton's bones, enough to know what happened to her."

Eve was surprised that Daniel wasn't there, too. "Where's Daniel?"

Nan and Duncan looked at her with curiosity.

"Daniel?" Duncan said.

"Dr. Brooks, the forensic anthropologist," Eve said. "I thought he'd want to be here for this."

"He went back to the scene to search for more bones," Nan said. "He wants to collect as much of her body as he can before I release the scene, which will be right after this conversation."

Eve admired him for wanting to find every last shard of bone. She would, too, if she had his job. "How did she die?"

"Someone broke her neck," Nan said. "Her C3 and C4 vertebrae are fractured."

"How do you know she didn't break her neck in a fall?"

"Because there would be blunt force trauma to the skull as well as injuries to other parts of the body. There aren't any."

Duncan gestured to the bones. "How can you tell? It looks like someone drove a steamroller over the bones and set 'em on fire."

"That's where Dr. Brooks' expertise comes in," Nan said. "Those other breaks are all postmortem and consistent with fracturing caused by fire and environmental factors. This is definitely a homicide."

Duncan nodded and looked at Eve. "There's your leverage."

Eve was thinking the same thing. She turned to Nan. "A few weeks before her murder, Sabrina reported that she was gang-raped. Her rape kit hasn't been tested."

"It will be now," Nan said.

◆ ◆ ◆

"It's sad that Sabrina had to be murdered to get her rape kit tested," Eve said to Duncan when they stepped out of the lab.

Duncan took off his coat and began to jam it into its own inside pocket. "That's a cynical way to put it and you haven't been at this long enough to be so jaded."

"I jade fast," she said and wondered if she was now one step closer to losing the idealism that Duncan had teased her about.

"I checked out Josie Wallace. She has no arrest record and has never reported the sexual assault, or any other crime. She's living and working up in San Luis Obispo now." Duncan had managed to reduce the coat into a tiny zippered pouch that wasn't much bigger than his hand. It could fit easily in a purse. She decided she had to get one of those coats. "I've got some more details about her life. Mundane background stuff. I've printed it all out, stuck it in a folder, and put it on your desk."

"Thanks," she said. "I'll go through it before I talk to her."

He gave her a look. "Is talking to her really necessary?"

"What's that supposed to mean?"

"Josie didn't want to report the rape six years ago and I doubt the passage of time has changed her reasons. Why do we need her to tell us about it today and relive the worst night of her life?"

"Because now we're investigating a homicide."

"We don't know that the rape had anything to do with Sabrina's murder."

"So far, it's the only lead we've got."

"We've only been investigating the homicide for thirty seconds."

Her stomach growled loud enough to sound like an angry reaction to his gentle rebuke. She put a hand on her stomach, as if that would silence it. "I'm going to grab a late lunch. Can I bring you back anything?"

"Something with lots of meat and grease."

"You're not going to have a very long retirement if you keep eating like that."

"That's what Lipitor is for," he said as they reached the Explorer.

She opened the driver's-side door. "I'll be sure to remember that line for your eulogy. It will get a big laugh."

Eve slipped some disposable booties over her shoes—she wasn't going to ruin another pair—before getting out of the Explorer in front of Sherwood Mintner's house. She was bringing Daniel lunch from In-N-Out to reward him for going beyond the call of duty in his efforts to collect every last bone fragment that he could.

Only two CSU techs were left behind, and they were packing up. All the yellow tape that had marked the crime scene and all the string that had defined the search quadrants were already gone.

At first, she didn't see Daniel, then she spotted him far beyond the parameters of what had been the crime scene. She felt a tug when she saw him, like a rope pulling her to him. The tug also came with a jolt of excitement that she felt inside her chest. The reaction surprised her. She hadn't felt a tug like that in a long time.

Eve trooped through the backyards of three destroyed homes to reach him. Daniel turned and gave her a big smile as she approached. She wasn't sure if the smile was for her or the bag of burgers from In-N-Out and the two Cokes that she was carrying.

"I'm so glad to see you," he said.

Eve was surprised how good that made her feel. She offered him the bag and the drink. "I thought you might be hungry. I hope you aren't a vegan."

"It's not a meal if there isn't meat in it," Daniel said, but he didn't take the bag from her yet. "Do you have a little wire flag? I found a metacarpal."

"I appreciate your dedication, but I don't think even Sabrina's family expects you to find every last bone."

"It's part of a finger."

"We already know she was murdered, Daniel. We don't need a finger now unless it's pointing at the killer."

"You don't understand," he said. "We've already recovered all of Sabrina Morton's fingers."

Eve understood now. *There was a second body.*

"I don't have a flag," she said. "Will a straw do?"

Eve called Nan to get the CSU unit back—then she called Duncan, who told her that after he ate his very late lunch, the two of them needed to brief Captain Moffett. *Duncan's priorities never change,* she thought. *Food first, law and order later.*

She'd swung through the In-N-Out Burger in Westlake again on her way back to the station to get Duncan his lunch. He wolfed down his burger at his cubicle so quickly his burp afterward might as well have been a sonic boom.

They walked down the hall together to Captain Moffett's office. He was a square-shouldered man in his forties who wore his pressed uniform like a second skin and somehow exuded a military bearing at all times, no matter how he was dressed or what he was doing. Eve was sure he was saluted at birth by the obstetrician instead of spanked.

Moffett saw them at his door and waved them into his office without rising from behind a neatly organized desk.

"What's the story on those bones out in Hueso Canyon, Donuts?" He asked Duncan the question without so much as a glance at Eve, a detail that wasn't lost on her. Ever since she'd arrived at Lost Hills, Moffett had tried his best to pretend she wasn't there. She hadn't made that easy, especially the way her first homicide case went down. It was hard to ignore a Ford Explorer in flames.

"It keeps changing," Duncan said and quickly briefed the captain on what they knew about Sabrina Morton and the discovery an hour ago of a second set of remains in the same ravine. Moffett listened without asking a question or shifting his attention from Duncan.

"We're lucky the finger was discovered today," Moffett said, "and not two months from now by some grandma planting roses."

"I'm beginning to think that news lady was right," Duncan said. "The mountains are a graveyard."

So Duncan saw her on the news last night, too. Eve was tempted to ask him if he also thought she looked fat.

"Search the whole damn ravine if necessary," Moffett said. "We'll look like fools if any bodies turn up out there after we're gone."

"We'll need more manpower to secure the wider scene," Duncan said.

"You'll get whatever you need," Moffett said. "I'll approve the overtime."

Eve wondered if the answer would have been the same, or as swift, if she'd made the request. "That's going to draw a crowd."

Moffett glanced at her like she'd farted in church. "You mean your friends in the media. You must be getting itchy, Ronin. You haven't had a viral video in weeks."

"She's right, Captain," Duncan said. "The press will come like flies to shit. What do we tell them?"

"That we've identified the remains as Sabrina Morton, but let's keep the homicide determination and the discovery of more bones to ourselves for as long as we can," Moffett said. "Let them think we're still collecting Morton's bones. I don't want to give the press anything that will fuel irresponsible speculation."

Eve wondered what sort of speculation that would be, and if any of the possible reasons running through her head for two bodies being in the same canyon would qualify. But she didn't ask. She turned toward the door, sensing that the meeting was over, but Duncan didn't move. He had one more thing to say.

"Maybe Crockett and Tubbs should handle these new remains."

Eve couldn't believe what she'd heard. Even Captain Moffett seemed startled, enough to actually glance at her to gauge her reaction before he responded.

"It's your case, Donuts," Moffett said. "The bones were found on your crime scene."

"Technically, they were found *outside* of it," Duncan said.

"It's your case," Moffett repeated firmly. "If you need help, I'll get it for you. Keep me informed. I'll brief the sheriff."

That was definitely a dismissal. Duncan and Eve walked out. As soon as they were away from the captain's view, Eve pulled Duncan into an interrogation room and slammed the door.

"What the hell was that all about? Why were you trying to give away our case? Have you decided to retire early?"

"The new bones could belong to some Cherokee," Duncan said.

"I don't think there were any Cherokees in the Santa Monica Mountains."

"Or they could belong to another executed gangbanger. Or to another senile old coot who wandered off."

"What's your point?" she asked.

"Just because the bones were found in the same ravine as Sabrina Morton's, that doesn't mean there's any connection. It could be a big time-sucking distraction that takes us away from her case."

"Or there is a connection," Eve said.

Duncan waved the notion away. "I'll go to Hueso Canyon and stay on top of the new search while you start the investigation of Sabrina Morton's murder. I don't want to lose momentum."

"What *momentum*? She's been dead for six years."

"That doesn't matter."

Eve was confused. "You're supposed to be the voice of reason. Why do I feel like we've switched roles?"

"If I've learned anything in this job, it's that once an investigation starts, it generates its own heat. You have to chase the case now, while it's hot. If you put on the brakes, the case will go cold and stay that way," he said. "We can't do that to Sabrina Morton, not after she spent six years lost in the weeds."

Eve was ashamed of herself. She'd completely misjudged Duncan, and not for the first time, either.

She smiled at him. "You never stopped being a junior crossing guard."

"What job do you think I've got lined up for my retirement?"

Since San Luis Obispo was 160 miles north of Calabasas, Eve decided to make the two-hour-plus trip to see Josie Wallace before her shift early the next morning. So she spent the rest of the afternoon updating the Sabrina Morton case file, which was now a murder book, the official record of their homicide investigation that would become a key piece of evidence in any eventual prosecution. Duncan went out to the new crime scene, even though she reminded him he'd be as useful as makeup on a mule.

"Have you looked at a mule lately?" Duncan said. "Some lip gloss couldn't hurt."

She rode her bike home at the end of the day, got into her car, and went to the Walmart in Canoga Park to search for a birthday present for her niece. Nothing excited her. She drifted over to the garden section, found the irrigation aisle, and bought a pack of one hundred wire marker flags for Daniel and a hundred more for herself. On the way home, she asked herself if that was the real reason she'd gone to Walmart to start with, but she didn't trust herself to answer truthfully.

CHAPTER SEVEN

When Eve was in high school, her class took a field trip to San Luis Obispo and learned that the quaint college town got its name from the Mission San Luis Obispo de Tolosa, which was built in 1772 and was widely known for having a beautiful red-tiled roof that was the architectural inspiration for countless California homes to this day. The mission was less known for entertaining parishioners with bear-baiting shows, a blood sport where a bear with one leg chained to a post had to fend off a pack of ravenous dogs. But that was the fact that had stuck with Eve, and that was on her mind at 9:00 a.m. Wednesday morning when she parked in front of Josie Wallace's office on Monterey Street, around the corner from the mission.

Josie worked in an insurance brokerage on the second floor of an ornate old building. Eve took the stairs and approached the young receptionist at the front desk.

"May I help you?" the woman asked. Eve guessed, by the open agricultural sciences textbook on the desk, that she was a Cal Poly student working part-time.

"Yes, I'm looking for Josie Wallace. A friend of mine recommended that I talk to her about my insurance needs." Eve didn't want Josie's coworkers to wonder why a Los Angeles County sheriff's detective was there to see her. She was also worried that if she revealed that she was a sheriff's detective from LA, Josie would find some excuse not to talk with her.

"May I get your name?"

"Eve Ronin."

The receptionist picked up the phone, dialed an extension, and repeated what Eve had told her. She listened for a moment, hung up, and flashed a polite smile at Eve. "She'll be out in a moment."

Eve's phone vibrated in her pocket. She pulled it out and saw that she'd received a text from Nathan Holt. His timing was impeccable. The text read:

> I found the original drawing. Please let me know if there is anything else I can do to help.

The drawing depicted two surfboards, a gun, and a great white shark, arranged together so that the pointed tips of the surfboards, the front sight of the gun barrel, and the fins and tail of the shark created the six points of a star set against the backdrop of a monster wave.

Eve was trying to figure out what it all meant when a woman stepped out of the office behind the receptionist. She was in her thirties, with her Vietnamese mother's eyes and coal-black hair, and her father's pale skin and tall, slender build. She wore a sleeveless blouse that accentuated her strong arms and shoulders.

"Hello, I'm Josie," she said with a bright smile. "What can I do for you?"

Eve slipped the phone back into her pocket and took a furtive glance at the receptionist for Josie's benefit. "It's a very personal matter. Can we talk in your office?"

"Of course," Josie said, beckoning her to the door with a sweep of her arm. "Please come in." Eve walked past her and Josie closed the door. "Do you mind if I ask who recommended me?"

"Actually, nobody did. I wanted to speak with you privately and I didn't want to put you in an awkward situation with your coworkers." Eve parted her blazer to show Josie the badge clipped to her belt. "I'm a detective with the Los Angeles County Sheriff's Department. We've found Sabrina Morton's bones in Hueso Canyon, not far from where the two of you shared a guesthouse."

Josie's pleasant, upbeat demeanor evaporated. She sat down in one of two guest chairs in front of her desk. "How did she die?"

Eve positioned the other chair so it faced Josie and took a seat. "We don't know yet."

"I'm very sorry to hear that she's dead, but I don't understand why you came all the way here to tell me in person."

"I'm wondering if her death might have something to do with her rape," Eve said. "And yours."

There was a brief flash of anger in Josie's eyes. "I thought Sabrina kept my name out of it. She'd promised that she would."

"She kept her word, but you went with her to meet an artist. She wanted him to draw a sketch of the tattoo you saw on your attackers. He mentioned your name to me."

Josie shook her head with a grimace of regret. "I knew that going with her to see him was a mistake, but Sabrina pleaded with me to help her remember. I just wanted to forget."

And now Eve was here, making her relive it again. She felt a stab of guilt but pushed it down. She had a job to do. "Is that why you didn't report the sexual assault on you?"

Josie stood up, walked around her desk, and took a seat behind it. Eve saw it for what it was, an unconscious defensive move, using the desk for protection, something for Josie to hide behind while she was vulnerable. It took a moment for Josie to collect her thoughts, or perhaps to wrestle with her emotions, before she spoke.

"I went with Sabrina to the beach to watch the surfers. We met some guys on the beach. I don't remember how. I suppose we drank, smoked some pot, and did a few lines of coke with them before we blacked out."

"You suppose?" It came out sounding like an accusation and Eve immediately wished she'd found another way to pose her question.

"Because I don't remember what actually happened but that's what we were into back then. That's why I didn't want to report the rape. I knew the police would take blood and urine samples from us and our partying would come out," she said. "We'd be trashed in court as a couple of drunken druggie sluts. Nobody would believe that we were raped. Even if they did, by some miracle, and the men were convicted, I'd still lose. Everything that was said about us would haunt me on Google for the rest of my life. I was thinking about going to medical school at the time . . . and no school would have accepted me if they found out about my partying."

Eve didn't blame her for staying quiet. She thought Josie's fears were entirely justified. It was a cruel, painful decision that Josie had to make and then had to live with ever since. But it raised a question. "Sabrina wasn't worried about any of that?"

"All she cared about was nailing those men," Josie said. "So Sabrina was crushed when the detective told her the same thing I did, that even if he caught them, they'd never be convicted. He said she should be thankful that she couldn't remember the worst of it . . . and just go on with her life. But Sabrina wouldn't do that."

Eve tried to keep her expression blank although she felt her anger rising. How could any detective say that to a possible rape victim? That was assuming, of course, that what Sabrina told Josie was true. Eve knew that she should give Nakamura the benefit of the doubt. But she believed what she was hearing.

"So that's when Sabrina decided to find an artist to draw the tattoo," Eve said. Josie nodded. "What do you remember about the rape?"

"Their faces were a blur, thanks to whatever they put in our drinks, but they all had that same calf tattoo."

"How do you know they all did?"

"I was pinned on the sand, my head turned to one side . . . that tattoo is what I saw as each man stood, waiting his turn with me . . . that's why I remember it so clearly and so did she."

Eve took out her phone and showed Josie the drawing Nathan had texted to her. "Is this it?"

The look of revulsion on Josie's face was the only answer Eve needed.

"I've never forgotten it," Josie said.

Eve put the phone away. "What did Sabrina do with the drawing?"

"She went to Topanga Beach, Surfrider Beach, Zuma . . . showing the tattoo to every surfer she could find, hoping somebody would give her a name. She was only at it an hour or so before a deputy got word somehow, pulled her over, and told her what she was doing was stupid and dangerous. Sabrina told him to fuck off, that if the cops weren't going to do anything about it, she would," Josie said, smiling at the memory. "That was Sabrina. But it was all bravado. She came home and cried for three hours. She felt helpless."

Sabrina wasn't helpless, Eve thought. Far from it. She was unwilling to be a silent victim and fought for herself, loud and strong, not just against her attackers, but against the detective who didn't believe her.

Eve admired Sabrina's tenacity and was even more determined now to continue the woman's fight and get her the justice that she'd been denied. She'd start by finding the deputy who'd pulled Sabrina over and tried to shut down her efforts to expose her attackers. "What did Sabrina do after that?"

"She walked out the door the next day and never came back," Josie said. "I thought she'd killed herself."

"Did she have any enemies? A bitter ex-boyfriend, maybe? A rival at work?"

"The only enemies she had were the men who raped us," Josie said. "Is that what you think happened? That they found out what she was doing and killed her?"

It seemed a lot more likely to Eve now than it had before she made the trip to see Josie, but she couldn't say that. She couldn't even admit that they already knew that Sabrina was murdered.

"I don't know if they were involved in her death, directly or indirectly."

"You mean if they murdered her or if she killed herself because of what they did to her."

And to you, too, Eve thought. "No matter how Sabrina died, I'm going to find the men who raped you."

"Oh no, keep me out of it." Josie stood up, holding her hands out in front of her, palms out, as if pushing Eve away. "Nobody knows what happened to me and I want it to stay that way."

"I understand," Eve said, rising from her seat. "I'll do what I can to keep your name out of it."

Eve knew it would be impossible to keep Josie's name from being revealed if her investigation established a connection between the rapes and Sabrina's murder. But that was a big *if* for now.

"Thank you," Josie said.

"I appreciate the help you've given me. I know how painful it must be for you." Eve placed her card on Josie's desk. "But if anything else occurs to you, please give me a call."

Josie nodded, but Eve doubted that she'd hear from her again.

Eve walked out of the office, her heart racing. Duncan was right—there was momentum to this case. She could feel it now.

CHAPTER EIGHT

Eve was passing through Ventura on her way back, and wondering if she was a bad daughter for not stopping by to see her mom, when her phone rang. It startled her. Could it be her mom? Did she sense Eve was nearby? Did she see her car somehow?

She looked at her phone and didn't recognize the number on the screen. But she took the call anyway, hoping it wasn't a robocaller offering her a deal on carpet cleaning or warning her that the IRS was about to arrest her for unpaid taxes.

"Ronin."

"It's Mitch Sawyer, your physical therapist. You missed our appointment."

She would have preferred her mom or the robocaller.

"Oh crap, I forgot all about it," Eve said. She'd also forgotten to do her home exercises, but she wasn't going to admit that, too. "I'm sorry, Mitch, but this is a bad time for me to be doing physical therapy. I'm busy working a case right now."

"Of course you are, because that's your job," he said. "But if you don't want to be doing it from a desk, you'll make time to see me."

She didn't like being threatened and she felt her cheeks get hot with anger. "Why are you being such a prick about this?"

"A prick would charge you for the missed appointment, but I'm not," he said lightheartedly. "I can see you tomorrow morning at seven thirty. How's that work for you?"

"I can't wait."

She broke the connection and immediately called her sister, Lisa, something she should have done two nights ago.

"Hey, Eve," Lisa answered, groggy. "Make it quick. I worked an all-nighter and I'm asleep."

"You've got to call Mitch and tell him to back off."

"Why?"

"Because I'm in the middle of working a case and he's threatening to disqualify me for active duty unless I go to every useless PT session."

Lisa yawned. "That's exactly why I recommended him."

"I asked you for a good physical therapist, somebody close to my home and the Lost Hills station who'd understand what I do and what I need."

"And that's what you got," Lisa said. "Calabasas is a very small town. There aren't that many physical therapists and he's the best. He looks like a beach bum but he's a drill sergeant as a therapist. He will make you do rehab even when you try to wriggle out of it, which I knew you'd try to do."

There was no point pressing Lisa on this. Eve knew her sister was as stubborn as she was. "Why are you doing this to me?"

"Because I love you," Lisa said. "See you Saturday."

"Wait," Eve said. "What should I get Cassidy for her birthday?"

"Anything but toy handcuffs and a gun," she said. "Try something fluffy. Good night."

Lisa hung up before Eve could tell her that it was *day*.

The CSU was back in force in Hueso Canyon, working in the back-yards of all the torched homes along the steep, fire-denuded hillside below Latigo Canyon Road. The LASD was also there in force, with uniformed deputies controlling traffic on both roads and keeping the media at a distance.

A deputy that Eve didn't know was manning the entry point to the crime scene and was responsible for keeping the log of everyone who came and went. He was barrel chested, flat nosed, and had an extreme buzz cut that left a mere shadow of stubble on his bullet head. She approached him, holding a Walmart bag in her hand.

"I'm Detective Ronin."

"I know who you are." He offered her the clipboard and a pen. She took them and glanced at the name tag on his chest: Charles Towler.

"Have you seen Detective Pavone?" she asked as she signed in.

"Under the tent at the far end of the canyon."

"Thanks," Eve said, handed him the clipboard, and walked past him.

She'd changed into her boots in the car, but it turned out that it wasn't necessary. The CSU team had laid a plywood path through the field of tiny flags and numbered cones. She followed the path to the last tent, where Duncan sat in a folding camp chair watching Daniel, who was farther off, advancing the leading edge of the search, unmistakable in his Australian bush hat and cargo pants. Duncan's jacket was draped over the back of the chair and his shirt was soaked with sweat.

"Did you fall in a swimming pool?" Eve asked.

"I wish." Duncan wiped sweat from his brow with the back of his hand. "I'm already on my second shirt and the day isn't over yet."

"Any action here besides your wardrobe changes?"

"Indiana Jones has found more bones. I'll let him give you the details."

"Indiana Jones is an archaeologist," she said. "Daniel is an anthropologist."

Duncan looked up at her. "Is that what *Daniel* is? Thanks for the reminder."

"Has he found anything else?"

"A belt buckle. Levi buttons. Some rivets."

"Rivets?" she asked.

"The metal thingies that hold a pair of jeans together where there's the most strain," he said.

"I thought the rivets were there for fashion, not function."

"They are," Duncan said. "Until your gut is as big as mine."

"I learn something every day," she said and walked out to Daniel, careful to stay on the plywood path.

Daniel was crouched beside the bones on the white sheet. One of the bones was a blackened pelvis. It was one of the few human bones besides a skull that she could identify. He rose to his feet as she approached. There were dark circles under his eyes, which were bloodshot.

"You look tired," she said.

"I am," he said. "But I can't stop now."

He felt the momentum in his case, too.

"I know the feeling," she said. "What have you found?"

"For starters, I can tell you her bones were on the hillside before the fire, just like Sabrina Morton's, maybe for months, maybe for years, and that she was white, middle-aged, and somebody's mother."

"Is that all?" Eve said with a grin. "How do you know all of that about her?"

He crouched beside the sheet again and pointed to the pelvis. "Well, the pelvis reveals her sex and the sacral anterior breadth indicates that she was Caucasian."

She squatted next to him. "What is a sacral interior breadth?"

Daniel cocked his head, looking at her in a new light. "You really want to know?"

"Of course I do," she said.

"No cop has ever asked me to define my terms before. They either pretend they already know or they don't want to look dumb or they just don't care."

"I'm dumb," she said. "But I don't mind admitting it. I want to know what I'm talking about, especially if I am going to build a case on a pile of bones."

He pointed to the arrowhead-shaped bone in the top center of the pelvis. "This is the sacrum, the bone between the spine and the tailbone. The sacral breadth is the distance across the front of the sacrum at its widest point. It's typically 112 millimeters in a Caucasian woman versus, for example, 103 millimeters in someone of African American descent."

"And what told you that she was in her fifties and had given birth?"

"The pubic symphysis is where the pelvis joins in the front. It's a jagged line when a woman is young, but it smooths out and straightens by the time you're fifty," he said. "Hers is straight. Pregnancy and birthing can strain the pelvic bones and cause them to appear scarred, particularly along the pelvic opening. Hers are scarred."

Men have it so easy, Eve thought. "For your next trick, can you tell me how she died?"

"I'll need to find a lot more bones before I can pull that rabbit out of my bush hat."

"Then you'll be needing these."

Eve handed him the Walmart bag. Daniel looked inside, broke into a smile, and pulled out the wire flags.

"That was very thoughtful of you."

Eve shrugged. "I ran out of pens and straws."

She headed back to Duncan, who'd watched the exchange between Eve and Daniel.

"He knows his stuff," Duncan said.

"It was nice of you to let him impress me."

"He earned it." Duncan got up from the chair. "I need to change my shirt again. Walk me back to the car and tell me how it went with Josie Wallace."

She did. They were nearly at the Explorer when Duncan asked to see Nathan Holt's drawing of the tattoo. She took out her phone, held it up to him, and showed him the picture.

"Shit." Duncan forced her hand down and looked around to see if anyone was watching them.

"What's wrong?" Eve asked.

Duncan opened the car door. "Get in. Now."

Eve got into the passenger seat and she watched him walk around the car and get into the driver's seat. She studied him. "You've seen the tattoo before."

He met her gaze. "Every fucking day. Half the deputies at Lost Hills station have it on their calves."

CHAPTER NINE

For years, the LASD was rocked repeatedly by revelations that deputies and detectives charged in beatings, drug dealing, sex trafficking, and murder were also members of secret cliques tied to individual patrol stations or elite, special units. The cliques had names like the Grim Reapers, the Death Merchants, the Regulators, and the Vikings. Their members all had tattoos on their calves. It was rumored that they "earned their ink," and were sent to a secret tattoo artist, either by beating inmates or shooting felons. One exasperated federal judge called these deputies and detectives "gang members with badges." After a dozen tattooed deputies were imprisoned or fired for their conduct, and $17.5 million was paid out by the county in settlements to victims of their abuses, the previous sheriff promised to wipe out cliques in the department.

Eve knew that history and shook her head in disgust. She could see how the old tattoos might have lingered among the deputies who'd remained with the department and weren't outed, but not how the cliques could have survived. "I thought all the secret cliques were shut down fifteen years ago."

"They didn't end," Duncan said. "They just went deeper underground."

Eve hadn't seen any of the tattoos, because women weren't invited into cliques or men's locker rooms. But it meant the tattoos had to be common knowledge among the brass.

"And the department tolerates it?"

"The cliques aren't all bad," Duncan said. "It's a bonding thing, a brotherhood. It gives a deputy a sense of belonging to something bigger than himself."

"The badge should be enough," she said. "Do you have a tattoo?"

"I didn't start out at Lost Hills. I started in patrol in Compton. And no, I don't have a tattoo from there, either."

"What do the Lost Hills deputies call themselves?"

"The Great Whites," Duncan said.

It was worse than she thought. "Are they white supremacists, too?"

"No, no, there are black, Asian, and Hispanic deputies who wear that tattoo. We're the station that patrols the beaches, so they just picked the scariest shark in the sea as their name without considering the racist meaning. But it's only a bit more stupid than deputies calling themselves the Grim Reapers or the Death Merchants and implying they are only interested in inflicting violence on the people they are supposed to serve and protect."

Eve nodded, though she wasn't as certain as Duncan was that the double meaning of the Great Whites wasn't intentional. She took a deep breath. It was time to confront the obvious, ugly facts.

"This means that the men who raped Sabrina Morton and Josie Wallace were deputies. That's why there's no mention of the tattoos in Ted Nakamura's report and why he didn't do shit on Sabrina's rape or disappearance. He was protecting them."

"We don't know that Sabrina ever told Teddy about the tattoo," Duncan said. "When you are in a life-or-death situation, your brain doesn't process things the same way it usually does. It can be two or three days before memories rise to the surface. She may not have remembered the tattoos in her first interview and there may never have been a second."

"There was," Eve said.

"Says who? Her parents? Josie Wallace? It's been six years. Did it occur to you that over time their memories of the days leading up to

Sabrina's disappearance may have faded, or got mixed together or colored by their feelings of anger, frustration, and loss? You're making some huge leaps that aren't supported by any evidence."

"They will be." She knew he was right, that memories weren't reliable, but she was certain that she was right, too, even if she didn't have the admissible evidence yet to back up her conclusions.

Duncan sighed. "Keep this up, and you'll be an ex-cop before I am."

She glared at him. "Are you suggesting that I bury this for the good of the department and my career?"

"I'm suggesting that you don't run blindfolded into a minefield."

"Meaning?"

"Proceed with extreme caution and discretion. Think very carefully about every move you make and all of the possible consequences. Don't jump to any conclusions that you can't back up with evidence. Put justice for the victims first and your own agenda second," Duncan said. "Because if you fuck this up, there's going to be a lot of collateral damage."

"Justice for Sabrina and Josie is my agenda."

"Not if you've already decided you're leading a one-woman crusade against police corruption."

"One woman?" she said. "Does that mean you're abandoning me?"

"Eve," he said gently. "I've got your back until I retire. After that, you're on your own, which is exactly what's going to happen the way things are going."

"I'm not in this job to be loved by my fellow officers."

"Then congratulations," Duncan said. "You're succeeding brilliantly."

◆ ◆ ◆

Eve went to the station and called Josie Wallace, who didn't sound pleased to hear from her so soon.

"I'm sorry to bother you again," Eve said. "I just need to clarify something you told me. You mentioned that the day before Sabrina disappeared, she was pulled over by a deputy who warned her that it was dangerous for her to be showing the tattoo drawing around. Did Sabrina mention if he was in a patrol car?"

"He was a uniformed deputy riding a police motorcycle," Josie said. "She was on a motorcycle, too. It was on PCH. Why are you asking?"

"I'd like to dig up his report and find out how he learned about what she was doing," Eve said. "Maybe whoever called us had a motive for wanting her off the street."

"What does it matter after all of these years?"

"It matters to me," Eve said. "Sabrina deserves justice and so do you."

"I've made my peace with it."

"Sabrina never got that chance," Eve said. "Maybe I can give her that peace now."

Eve thanked Josie for her help. The answer that Eve gave Josie was only partially the truth. What she was really interested in was confirming the deputy was in uniform and on duty that day. She already knew the date of the traffic stop. What she'd needed was the deputy's name.

She pulled up the duty rosters on her computer for that day to see who was on patrol on PCH. The only deputy on motorcycle patrol was Brad Pruitt. She looked him up and discovered he was working out of the Santa Clarita station now and lived in Castaic. He'd never filed a field investigation report on his encounter with Sabrina, or it would have come up when Eve did her initial in-house records search on her. Why didn't he?

Out of curiosity, Eve checked the duty roster for the next day, when Sabrina disappeared, to see which deputies were on patrol in the vicinity of Kanan Dume and Latigo Canyon Road. Pruitt's name came up again, along with Deputies David Harding and Charles Towler.

She recognized Towler's name. She'd just met him. He was the officer who was handling the crime scene log in Hueso Canyon. It gave her a shiver. Did he have a special-interest reason for watching the investigation unfold up close?

Next, she checked the duty roster again to see which deputies were off duty the day that Sabrina and Josie were raped. There were over a dozen. Pruitt wasn't on the list, but Harding and Towler were.

Eve prepared a list of all the deputies working out of Lost Hills station at the time of Sabrina's rape, downloaded their names and photos, and saved them to her personal account. It was a laborious process, since it was impossible to do in bulk, and there were sixty individuals.

When Eve was finished, she leaned back in her seat and got an idea. She accessed the station's front desk visitor logs for the day of Sabrina's disappearance and scrolled backward. She discovered that Sabrina came in to see Detective Nakamura the day before she hit the beaches with her drawing. Eve went back and looked at Nakamura's case file. He made no mention of Sabrina's last visit.

The discovery chilled Eve. Did Sabrina show him the tattoo drawing? If so, did he cover it up or did he warn the deputies? Did they kill her?

Sabrina had no idea that the tattoos were part of a sheriff's department clique and how dangerous it was for her to walk into the Lost Hills station with that drawing in her hand.

But Nakamura certainly did.

She was pondering those disturbing questions when Duncan came trudging in. He wore a different shirt and it was also soaked with sweat.

"We're done for the day," he said. "Daniel is in the lab with his bones."

"Did you make any progress?"

"We'll know who she is in the morning. They found pieces of a right knee replacement. Nan is going to trace the serial numbers."

"That certainly makes identifying a corpse a lot easier."

Duncan nodded. "It'd be nice if everybody had serial numbers on their bones."

"Are we any closer to learning the cause of death?"

"You'll have to ask Daniel. But if we don't find out soon, my cause of death is going to be homicide," he said. "My wife is going to kill me if I bring home four dirty shirts again tomorrow."

Duncan didn't ask her what progress she'd made. She figured it was either because he didn't want the other detectives in the squad room to overhear her answer or he didn't want to know, at least not yet. She didn't push him. Instead, she went to her locker, pulled out her heavy coat, and went out to the lab to see Daniel. She found him hunched over the exam table, arranging the bones. She felt that tug again and decided to do something about it.

"How's it going?" she asked him.

"I was encouraged when we found the pelvis relatively intact but the rest of the bones haven't been as easy to find and are more fragmented," he said. "How goes your investigation?"

"About the same as yours."

"Sometimes there is nothing you can do but keep digging."

"How about we both put our shovels down and take a break?" Eve said. "When was the last time you had something to eat?"

"I had a McMuffin for breakfast," he said.

"Let me take you to dinner."

He tugged at his sweat-stained khaki shirt. "I'm not sure I'm dressed for it."

"The place isn't fancy," she said.

The city of Calabasas had a split personality disorder. If you entered the city from the east end of Calabasas Road, the main thoroughfare, you went through Old Town, where the frontier storefronts and hitching posts presented Calabasas as part of California's Wild West. But if you entered from the other end, you went past the Commons, an idealized re-creation of an old rural village in the hills of Tuscany.

Until tonight, Eve thought the Commons was supposed to be a faux French village, perhaps because the property was dotted with four eighteenth-century statues, each representing a season, that were imported from a château in southern France. But as she was telling Daniel about the Commons, she was firmly corrected by the waiter serving them their entrees at Toscanova, the center's Italian restaurant. Either way, the two radically different visions the city had of itself made no sense to her.

"It's like dealing with an irrational person," she said to Daniel. "They should choose to be one or the other, a western town or a Tuscan village. I don't care which, just be consistent. It makes me anxious."

"But you live here anyway."

"I like to be close to where I work," she said. "Besides, I don't hang out here. I spend most of my free time bike riding in the hills."

"Can I ask you a personal question?"

"You'll know if my pasta is in your lap after you ask it."

"Why do the deputies call you Deathfist?"

She studied his face and he seemed honestly curious. "You really don't know?"

"Are you a martial artist or something?"

"Hardly." Eve told him the story about arresting Blake Largo and the viral YouTube video of the incident. The telling got them through their entrees. "You could have googled me and got the answer."

"I'll do that later to get everything you left out."

"What makes you think there's more to the story?" she asked.

"Because of the way the deputies say your nickname," he said. "There's a lot of resentment behind it."

"I leveraged my fame to get into Lost Hills Robbery-Homicide," Eve said. "I didn't get it on merit or experience."

Daniel shrugged. "You would have got there anyway."

"Maybe in fifteen years, but I took a shortcut. I totally understand why some people are pissed off about it," Eve said, surprised by her candor with him. "How come you didn't know about me? The video was all over social media and was big news in LA last year."

"I'm not on social media and my job takes me away a lot."

"Away where?"

"Mostly South America and Mexico the last few years. The drug cartels like to dismember their enemies, throw them in a pit, and set them on fire. The authorities hire me to help identify the dead," Daniel said. Now Eve knew what he meant when he said that he'd slept in worse places than a cot at the Lost Hills station. "I also worked that plane crash in Texas and the apartment building fire in Oakland."

"That's grim work," she said.

"No worse than yours. But that's not the way I see it. I enjoy putting together the puzzle, and that when I do, it's not just a scientific or academic pursuit. The solution is meaningful—it gives families peace and closure."

"It's like that for me, too," Eve said. "But it's also about restoring order. I don't like it when things are unsettled or uncertain. My little sister will tell you it's because I was the oldest child of a single parent who was totally irresponsible and made our lives chaos."

"You say it like it's a character flaw," he said. "I'd say it's the source of your superpowers."

"Superpowers?" Eve laughed. "You don't know if I'm even half-decent at what I do."

"I've seen the way Nan looks at you." And now Eve noticed the way he looked at her. It was brief, but she sensed his attraction. Did he feel the same tug that she did? Was he flirting with her?

"What way is that?" she asked.

"The way she looks at me, and I'm *terrific* at my job." Daniel grinned and then glanced at his watch. "This has been really nice, but I'm tired and smell like a dirty dishrag. I need to get back to the station, take a shower, and grab a cot."

"Why don't you go home?"

"I'm too tired and I'm eager to get back to work at first light," Daniel said. "I've got a detective on my ass demanding to know how this woman died."

Eve picked up the check, they got into her Subaru, and they headed west on the Ventura Freeway toward the Las Virgenes exit. She took the exit, but when she reached the intersection with Las Virgenes Road, she didn't immediately turn left and take the overpass toward the Lost Hills station. She made an impulsive decision and looked at Daniel instead.

"The station is to the left, on the other side of the overpass."

"I know," he said.

"I live right over there, real close by." She gestured to the right and the row of two-story town houses. "I've got a guest bed and a great shower. You're welcome to spend the night at my place instead."

Her heart was pounding so hard in her chest that she thought he might be able to hear it. She'd surprised herself with her offer and now she was afraid she'd crossed a line with the invitation and what else it implied.

He looked at her for a long moment, then smiled. "That's very nice of you. Are you sure it's no trouble?"

She smiled back, relieved. "It's the least I can do since I'm the one driving you to exhaustion. But if that makes you uncomfortable, I'll be glad to take you back to the station."

He shook his head. "One night in the Four Seasons Lost Hills was enough for me."

She parked on the street out front and they walked to the door. While she was unlocking the dead bolt, he kicked off his boots and left them on the front mat.

"Will they still be here in the morning?"

"Nobody in Calabasas is going to steal dirty boots," she said.

Daniel stepped inside. "I see we have the same decorator."

"IKEA," Eve said.

"I feel at home already."

She led him to the bathroom upstairs. "The towel is fresh and you can use my bathrobe. It's hanging on the door. I'll wash your clothes."

"That's not necessary," he said.

"Trust me, it is. The guest room is straight across the hall."

Daniel went into the bathroom, closed the door, and after a moment opened it again. He had a towel wrapped around his waist and his dirty clothes in his arms. She greeted him with her hands in a pair of rubber gloves. He broke into laughter and so did she.

"Okay, you made your point," he said, still smiling, and handed her his clothes. "You're washing them, not burning them, right?"

"We'll see," she said, meeting his gaze and feeling an almost electric charge crackle between them.

"Yes, well, I'd better get cleaned up," he said and began to close the bathroom door.

Eve went downstairs to the laundry room, which was actually just a closet in the kitchen. She put his clothes in the washer, poured in the detergent, and was about to start the load when she heard the shower running. This wouldn't be a good time to run the load, not if he wanted a long hot shower.

She went back upstairs and saw that the bathroom door was ajar. She could hear the shower running.

Eve felt that tug again, only this time it was more like a hard shove. Without thinking, she stripped off her clothes and walked naked into the bathroom.

"Daniel?" she said. It wasn't until that instant that she realized the risk she was taking. He had to know she was offering him more than her spare bed when she invited him to stay at her place. Wasn't that why he hadn't closed the bathroom door? Or was it an accident? What if the spark between them was entirely in her imagination? What if she was the only one feeling an attraction?

She was about to turn around and leave when he peeked out from behind the shower curtain and smiled at her. There wasn't shock in his eyes. There was excitement.

"How tired are you?" Eve asked.

"I'm suddenly wide awake."

She stepped into the shower with him and pulled the curtain closed behind her.

CHAPTER TEN

They didn't get much sleep.

Eve was awakened on Thursday by the touch of his fingertips, lightly tracing her collarbone. She opened her eyes to see him on his side, leaning over her. Sunlight was beginning to come through her window shades.

"You have good bones," Daniel said.

She didn't know it could feel so good to have her collarbone caressed. "I'm surprised you can tell. My mom says I'm getting fat."

"Your mom is insane."

"You're a doctor. Could I get that opinion in writing?"

"I'm not that kind of doctor." Daniel let his fingers trail down between her breasts.

That felt even better than his fingers along her collarbone. "Mom won't know the difference."

He ran his fingers around her nipples, then down her belly. "Thank you for inviting me over. This was much better than the cot at the station."

"I'm sorry you didn't get more sleep."

"I'm not."

Daniel's fingers reached her hip bone and he began to trace it. Her breath caught in her throat and she instinctively lifted her hips, eager for his touch. It amazed her that she had any desire left after everything they did last night.

And that reminded her of how the night began.

"Oh crap!" She sat up in bed. "I forgot to run the washing machine last night. There's still time."

"You're thinking about laundry *now*?"

She trooped naked to the bathroom, snatched her pink bathrobe off the hook on the door, and tossed it on the bed. "I'll make breakfast while we wait on your clothes."

Eve ran down the stairs, started the washing machine, and pulled a bra and panties from a basket of clean underwear on the dryer. She put the underwear on, for a little modesty, then got out two bowls and two spoons and took them to the table.

Daniel came down in her bathrobe. It was way too small for him but she thought he looked adorable in it.

She took a box of granola out of the cupboard. "Do you like your cereal dry or with milk?"

"I don't care." He stared at her. "God, you look great."

"So do you. Hot pink must be your color." She put the cereal box on the table. "Your clothes will be ready in an hour or so."

"Forget them," Daniel said. "I'd rather wear this today."

Eve laughed. She liked how relaxed they were together. No morning-after awkwardness. It was sweet. She felt that damn tug again.

"You must be very comfortable in your masculinity." Eve walked up close to him. "Or sexually fluid."

"I'm sexually exhausted."

She pushed him into a seat at the table and climbed onto his lap, straddling him. "Are you sure?"

"It couldn't hurt to check."

"It might." She kissed him hard, nearly tipping them over.

Eve drove Daniel to the Lost Hills station at 7:25 a.m. He leaned over and gave her a hug and a tender kiss on the cheek. His clothes were still warm from the dryer. Being in his arms felt like being in a warm bed. It made her want to turn around and go home with him.

"I'd like to see you again," he said.

"You will."

"I mean outside of these cases."

"I do, too, though when I am working a case, there usually isn't time for anything else in my life." And that was when she remembered what else she didn't have time for. "Damn! I've got a PT appointment. I've got to go."

Daniel grinned at her. "Haven't you already exercised your wrist enough today?"

She grinned back. "Get out."

"I'm a doctor. I could write a note."

"Out!"

He slid out of the seat, closed the door, and she sped off to Old Town.

The hour-long physical therapy session felt like six hours. It was also monotonous and painful.

Mitch frowned at her from across the table as she squeezed a rubber ball. "Have you been doing your exercises?"

Nope, not once. "Yes. Diligently."

"If that were true, your wrist wouldn't be so stiff and weak."

"It feels fine to me," she said.

"It won't if you have to wield a baton."

"I'm a detective, not a patrol officer," she said. "I don't have a baton."

"Good, because you couldn't wield a turkey sandwich with that hand."

"A turkey sandwich?"

He smiled and gave her a shrug. "It was the best I could come up with off the top of my head."

Maybe he isn't such a prick after all, she thought. "Well, as it turns out, I'm more likely to swing a sandwich today than a baton, so I guess you're right. I need these exercises."

"Let's get you some ice," Mitch said.

This time she didn't refuse. But there was more involved than just an ice pack. First, he placed some electrodes on her wrist that were plugged in to a small device the size of a garage door opener.

"What's this?" she asked.

"TENS treatment. A low electrical charge that stimulates the muscles, easing pain and swelling." He turned a tiny dial. "Let me know when it gets uncomfortable." It felt like a lot of ants scrambling around under her skin. It felt surprisingly good, until it didn't.

"Down a touch," she said.

Mitch adjusted the intensity, then wrapped the ice packs around her wrist. "We'll give it ten minutes and then you can go."

He walked off to greet another patient. Eve sat and stared at the poster on the wall of Kendra Leigh, who was still missing. She wondered if there was a poster out there somewhere for the unknown woman they'd found in Hueso Canyon. It gave her an idea that she kicked herself for not having yesterday: they should look through the missing person reports filed in the last few years for a white woman in her fifties. At the same time she was having that thought, her phone vibrated in her pants pocket.

Eve reached into her right pocket with her left hand, which wasn't easy, and extracted the phone. There was a text from Nan:

We've identified the second woman. Her name is Debbie Crawford, age 57. I'll email you and Duncan the details we got from her orthopedic surgeon.

Eve texted her back with her left hand, which was even harder than taking the phone out of her pocket.

Thanks. How are you doing on Sabrina Morton's rape kit?

There was a long delay. Three dots, indicating that she was writing a reply. Then the dots were gone. Then three dots. Then gone. Then three dots. Finally, a reply:

We haven't been able to find the kit yet.

Why did it take her so long to write that simple sentence? Eve thought, although she knew the answer. Nan was obviously trying to come up with the best way to minimize that the kit was lost. Eve wrote:

How is that possible?

Nan replied, quickly this time:

There's a backlog of thousands of rape kits and all it takes is one transposed number or letter in the case number for it to get misplaced. We're on it.

Eve was sure it wasn't an accident that the kit was missing. Nakamura didn't want it found. She caught Mitch's eye as he passed with another patient, a man in his fifties with a bad knee.

"Mitch, I have to go. Can you get me out of this thing?"

He led his other patient to a chair, then came over to Eve, turned off the TENS, and began peeling the electrodes from her wrist. "I'll see you on Monday. Same time?"

"I don't know yet."

"Let's not play this game again. As I said before, I can come to you, to your home or office or in the field," he said. "We can even do it on your lunch hour and work on your sandwich-wielding skills."

She smiled, despite herself. "Okay, okay. Monday."

Eve felt a tug again, which was odd, since she'd already been tugged pretty good. *It must be the hormones in my bloodstream,* she thought. This was exactly why she shouldn't screw around while she was on a case. It was a distraction.

But on her way back to Lost Hills, she wondered if her momentary attraction to Mitch was a clue to another possible motive behind Lisa recommending him to her as her therapist.

Was Lisa trying to set them up?

Duncan was at his cubicle when she came in, making notes on his legal pad, though it looked more like random doodling to the untrained eye.

"Did you get a text from Nan?" he asked.

"Yeah."

"Pull up a chair," he said. She did. "I've done a complete rundown on Debbie Crawford. She's a widow. A missing person report was filed on her two years ago by her daughter Celeste, who is twenty-three. Debbie lived up on Latigo, a mile or two south of Hueso Canyon. I checked and her house is one of the lucky ones that survived the fire. Our deputies have been out there a lot over the years, responding to her complaints about her neighbor, Nick Egan."

He was the TV star of one hit drama series after another, starting when he was a kid. *He has to be in his fifties now,* Eve thought.

"Let me guess," Eve said. "Stan Garvey's name is on every report and Egan has never been cited for anything."

"That's not a guess," Duncan said. "You can see the star-fucker's cubicle from here and the five pictures of Garvey with his arm around Egan's shoulder. They're besties."

He was right, she could.

"So all Sabrina Morton and Debbie Crawford appear to have in common is that they both lived near Hueso Canyon and their bodies ended up in the same ravine, sixty yards and four years apart," she said. "A tragic coincidence?"

"Looks that way to me," he said.

"Unless it turns out that Crawford was raped, too."

"We don't know that Sabrina Morton's rape and her murder are connected," Duncan said.

"We need to talk about her rape kit."

Duncan shushed her, even though the only other detective around was on the phone. "Not here. Let's get some breakfast."

Eve and Duncan went to their usual breakfast stop, the Manhattan Donuts & Bagels in the sprawling shopping center at the intersection of Calabasas Road and Mulholland Drive, across the street from the entrance to Old Town Calabasas and the eastern flank of the Motion Picture and Television Country House and Hospital campus. They were in the city of Woodland Hills now, in the LAPD's jurisdiction, so perhaps on some level Duncan felt more comfortable talking here about possible LASD corruption. *Or perhaps,* Eve thought, *he just really wanted a donut.*

On the way there, she told Duncan what she'd learned yesterday afternoon from the Lost Hills' duty rosters and visitor logs—the names of the deputies who were off duty when Sabrina was raped, and Sabrina's visit to the station two days before her disappearance that Nakamura didn't write up in his report.

They got a table in the far corner, by the front window, where one of the missing person posters of Kendra Leigh had been taped. Duncan didn't speak until he had his first bite of apple fritter, followed by his first sip of coffee, and then it was in a near whisper, not that any of the customers could hear him. Most of them were retirees from the Motion Picture home, wore hearing aids, and were yelling at each other to be heard.

"You think three deputies raped a woman and killed her and that a Lost Hills detective helped them cover it up."

"Yes." Eve picked at her glazed old-fashioned. She liked to slowly eat the edges first and then devour the middle.

"You have zero evidence," he said.

"But it all fits."

"Only if you can prove it . . . and how the hell do you intend to do that?"

"I'll start by getting DNA samples from the deputies who were on patrol when Sabrina went missing."

"Even if you can pull that off," Duncan said, "their DNA is useless without the rape kit and it's lost."

"I'm not ready to give up on it yet," she said, popping the tab on her Diet Coke and taking a sip. "I'll go down to Monterey Park and sort through every rape kit there is until I find it."

Duncan sighed, shook his head, and took another bite of his fritter before speaking again. "I'll do it."

"You're 115 days from retirement. You don't have to get involved in this."

"That's exactly why I have to. Nobody can intimidate or hurt me. My career is already over," he said and pointed a sticky finger at her. "Yours isn't, though you're trying hard to change that."

"Is this how you want to go out? Branded as a traitor to the department?"

Duncan waved off her concern. "It won't come to that. If you're right about this conspiracy, that rape kit was tossed in a dumpster six years ago."

"Then I'll find another way to nail them," she said and finished her donut.

"It's not an issue," Duncan said. "Let's swap cases. While I'm looking for the rape kit, you get to work figuring out what happened to Debbie Crawford."

"Sounds like a plan," Eve said and then sensed someone approaching behind her.

"Well, hello, Hardnose," a man said. "This is a nice surprise."

She cringed at the sound of the man's familiar voice even before he appeared beside her and she could see his face.

"No, it's not, Vince," she said. "Someone called and told you I was here."

Eve glared at the clerk behind the counter, who went wide eyed with guilt and immediately found something to do in the kitchen. Duncan saw it, too.

"That's it," Duncan said. "We're taking our business to Winchell's from now on."

The man who came up to their table was well into his seventies, with a full head of white hair and a matching bushy mustache that somehow softened his craggy face. He wore a paisley red silk ascot in his open-necked white Oxford shirt and a dark-navy-blue blazer. Smiling broadly, he offered his hand to Duncan.

"I'm Vince Nyby, Eve's father."

"Strictly biological," she said, feeling herself begin to tremble with rage. She was determined not to show it.

Duncan shook Vince's hand. "I'm Duncan Pavone, her partner."

"I'm a television director," Vince said. "Did you know I live right across the street at the Motion Picture home?"

"No, I didn't," Duncan said.

"Eve has a bagel or donut with you here three or four times a week but she's never invited me to join her for breakfast."

"Or talked to you in ten years," Eve said, fighting to keep her voice even. "Maybe you should have taken the hint, Vince."

He smiled at her, then gave Duncan a sideways glance. "Now you know why I call her Hardnose."

"I already figured that out for myself," Duncan said. "I've got some calls to make. Excuse me."

Duncan picked up his coffee, stood, and walked away.

Vince eased himself into the empty seat. "You look good, Eve. You have my cheekbones. Has anyone ever told you that?"

"How could they? Nobody knows that you're my father."

"I've told everyone. I'm proud of you."

"Let's get to the point, Vince." She leaned toward him, her arms on the table. "You want to use me. I'm not interested in a TV series or movie about me, and if I was, I certainly wouldn't involve you."

"That's stupid and self-destructive, Hardnose."

"Call me that again and I'll shoot you." Eve hated his white hair, his lined face, and his fucking ascot. Who was he kidding with that thing?

"I know this business, I've succeeded in it, and I'm good at it. You know that. A TV series or movie is going to get made, with or without you. You know that, too. You need someone who will protect your character and your story."

"You sound like Linwood Taggert."

Vince grinned, amused. "Who do you think was my agent when I was at my peak?"

"And then he dropped you when your career fell off a cliff."

He raised an eyebrow. "I didn't know that you followed my career."

"I don't. It was a lucky guess." Eve leaned back in her chair and crossed her arms under her chest, hoping it would contain her rage and hide the trembling. "You're ancient history, Vince. A has-been lining up for four p.m. dinner at the retirement home. You're not employable as a director anymore."

He leaned back, too. "That's ageism and it's beneath you. Clint Eastwood is still directing and he's in his nineties."

"You're not Clint Eastwood. Show me your Oscar." Eve saw him wince, and it pleased her to know that she'd hurt him. "What do I need you for? And don't give me that shit about watching my back."

"A baby writer I worked with on *Hollywood & the Vine* is now a red-hot showrunner with an output deal at Netflix," he said. "She wants to do this. With her on board, you go straight to series, no pilot. That's what I bring."

"And what do you get out of the deal?"

"I'll direct the first episode," he said.

"Forget it," Eve said and stood up.

"Why?" he asked.

The question stung deep, and the trembling rage she'd been trying to hold back burst free. She leaned over him.

"Why? Because you seduced my mother into bed with empty promises of big acting jobs, got her pregnant, and walked away without paying a dime of child support, leaving her to struggle as a single parent, just like you did to seven or eight or God knows how many other women. That's why."

"When you were a kid, I was there for every birthday with a nice gift for you and a nice check for your mother."

And nothing afterward. Eve saw him only when her mother brought her to court as a prop to try to get more child support out of the judge. Seeing him only revived the old anger and pain, making it feel fresh again, even though she was an adult now.

"The best gift would have been if you didn't show up at all. You didn't want me in your life then, and that's the way it's going to stay now."

By the time Eve was done talking, she was right in his face, nearly nose to nose. But Vince didn't pull back or even flinch. She saw herself in the expression of stubborn determination on his face, and it was jarring. She'd never thought of herself as even remotely like him.

"Your mom called me after your wildfire rescue video went viral," Vince said. "She is the one who brought me into this. If she's not bitter, why are you?"

"Because she didn't grow up without a father, you fucking idiot."

Eve turned her back on him and stormed out to the car. Duncan was in the passenger seat. She got in, started the car, and backed out, peeling rubber, the tires squealing like an injured animal.

"Eve," Duncan said gently. "Maybe I should drive."

"Why?" she said, jamming the car into drive and speeding off. "My wrist is fine."

"You're crying," he said.

Eve was shocked to realize that he was right. She wiped the tears away with the back of her hand. "It's my allergies."

"Now that you mention it, mine are acting up, too," Duncan said. "We're spending too much time out in the hills with all that pollen."

"That must be it," she said, except the hills were burned as black as the final fade-out in one of Vince's TV shows.

CHAPTER ELEVEN

Debbie Crawford's house was a rambling two-story Craftsman with flower boxes under the windows and a wide wraparound porch stuffed with wicker furniture and decorated with wind chimes, bird feeders, and strings of Christmas lights. Small, arched wooden bridges crossed the man-made, plant-lined creek that weaved through the two-acre property filled with trees, birdhouses, and birdbaths. A vintage Airstream trailer sat gleaming in the middle of a vibrant flower garden. Ceramic rabbits, deer, squirrels, and other animal statuary nestled amid the vegetable and herb gardens and sipped water from the creek.

Eve parked her Explorer between a 1970s-era Volvo wagon, its paint oxidized, and a new Prius in the gravel driveway. She got out and couldn't help noticing Nick Egan's massive, fifteen-thousand-square-foot mansion next door. It was like an aircraft carrier parked next to a dinghy, blocking the sun and casting a shadow over the house.

Celeste Crawford stepped off the porch to greet Eve, who had called earlier to say her mother's body had been found but that they didn't know anything about the circumstances of her death.

"You have a lovely home," Eve said. The air was alive with the sound of wind chimes and birdsong. It was one of the few places around for the birds to go that hadn't been ravaged by the wildfire. It was a miracle that the hilltop had survived. "It's so peaceful."

It was true and Eve felt the last embers of her anger beginning to cool from the unwelcome encounter with her estranged father.

"Thank you," Celeste replied. Her long red hair was tied in a ponytail and her face was flecked with freckles. She wore a tank top, shorts, and flip-flops. "My father built it with his own hands."

"Was he in the construction business?"

"No, he was an engineer at Rocketdyne," she said, referring to the massive plant in Canoga Park that had manufactured rocket engines for sixty years and had once employed thousands of people before shuttering. Now it was gone, a forty-six-acre patch of weedy, toxic soil next to the Westfield Topanga Mall. "He bought this land for next to nothing in the 1970s and lived in that Airstream trailer until the house was finished, which was the same day he met Mom."

"That's romantic," Eve said, understanding now why the trailer was surrounded by flowers and kept in such fine shape. It was like a headstone. *Maybe,* she thought, *it actually is.*

"Dad liked to say he built the house for her, he just didn't know that when he started," Celeste said, leading her around to the back of the house. "They were completely devoted to each other, even though they were so different. He was ten years older than her, very straight, very grounded, all about engineering and science. She was loose and carefree, all about nature, poetry, music, pot, and nudity."

Eve wasn't going to ask for specifics. "I'm guessing your mom was responsible for the landscaping."

"Oh yes, that's all her. She never stopped tinkering with it, especially after my dad died ten years ago of Rocketdyne cancer. Now I'm beginning to put my own touches on the place, starting with decent Wi-Fi."

"How long have you been living here?"

"Since I graduated from UC Berkeley last year," Celeste said. "It's going to sound silly, but I guess I've been waiting for Mom to come home." They climbed up to the back porch, where a table had been set with a pitcher of iced tea and two glasses. "Would you like some iced tea? It's our own blend from my mom's leaves."

"You're in the tea business?" Eve asked, taking a seat. She had a spectacular view of the blackened hills and canyons that stretched to Santa Monica Bay.

"She was, in a small way," Celeste said as she poured them each a tall glass. "She'd sell the tea, along with her homemade soap, candles, incense, that kind of thing, to make a few extra dollars on top of what she got from Dad's pension."

Now that she had a sense of who Debbie Crawford was, it felt to Eve like the right time to ask the painful questions. "What can you tell me about the day she disappeared?"

"That morning, a few of Mom's friends came by to do yoga with her and she wasn't around, even though her Volvo was here. They waited a half hour or so, then started to worry. They looked all over for her, inside and out, thinking she might have fallen or something. Then they called me in Berkeley to see if I knew where she might be. I didn't, so I called Lost Hills and reported her missing."

Eve sipped her tea. It tasted like drinking wet grass, not that she'd had any personal experience doing that. "Did she take her keys, wallet, or cell phone with her?"

"No, but that wasn't unusual," Celeste said. "She never locked the door and she hated cell phones. Reception here is terrible anyway."

"Do you have any idea what she might have been doing down by Hueso Canyon?"

"The Backbone Trail is down that way. She liked to hike, and after her knee replacement, she was determined to get back in shape as fast as possible," Celeste said. "She pushed herself too hard. Maybe her knee gave out and she fell off the cliff. Or somebody pushed her."

That got Eve's attention. "Why would you say that?"

"She was overdoing her physical therapy. Even her surgeon told her to slow down."

"No, I mean the part about being pushed," Eve said. "Did she have any enemies?"

"Just one." Celeste looked at her neighbor's massive house.

"Nick Egan," Eve said.

"One of the things that makes this hilltop so special is the peace and solitude. That was shattered the day he started constructing that monstrosity, a monument to building code violations and government corruption."

"Did your mom file a lot of complaints with the city during construction?"

"Oh yeah, almost every day, but it made no difference. The star-struck inspectors ignored the code violations or granted him waivers because he was 'Nick Egan.' Things got even worse once he moved in. Loud music, constant partying," she said. "I have to admit, I loved it at first, a teenager being invited to hang out with stars by the pool. It caused some big fights between me and Mom . . . until I realized that he was just using me as leverage to stop her from calling the cops on him all the time. Not that they ever did anything. They were as starstruck as the building inspectors, especially one detective."

Eve knew who that was. "Do you really think Egan might have killed her?"

"It was the first thing I thought of when she disappeared. I know it sounds silly, but Mom was relentless. For her, it was war and she was determined to make his life hell. She was driving him crazy mad. He'd scream profanities at her from his window and piss into our yard from his balcony."

"Did she report that to the police?"

"She reported everything. I didn't keep up on her feud while I was up in Berkeley, but I know he even tried to buy our house, offering her way more than it was worth, just to get her off his back. But she refused."

"Has he offered to buy it from you since she disappeared?"

Celeste shook her head. "The war is over. She's gone and I haven't been complaining."

"The noise doesn't bother you?"

"I've learned to live with it," she said. "Besides, if it wasn't for him calling every politician in California during the wildfire, demanding that they bombard this hill with retardant, our houses wouldn't be here."

So much for believing in miracles, Eve thought.

Eve promised that she'd keep Celeste updated on the investigation and then she headed back to the station. She wasn't going to bother talking with Egan unless it turned out that Debbie Crawford's death wasn't natural or accidental.

She was walking down the hall to the squad room when Captain Moffett stepped out of his office in front of her, followed by Assistant Sheriff Ted Nakamura in his perfectly pressed LASD uniform. Nakamura was in his fifties, graying at the temples, and had a tiny scar that split his left eyebrow in half, like two parallel lines.

"Detective Ronin," Nakamura said. "Just the person I hoped to see. I got Duncan's call about Sabrina Morton but haven't had a chance to respond."

Eve forced a polite smile. "You didn't have to come all the way out here, sir. We could have spoken on the phone."

"I had business to discuss with Captain Moffett and I like any excuse to get out of Monterey Park and back to my old stomping ground." Nakamura turned to Moffett. "Are we good?"

"I'll get back to you tomorrow with the numbers."

"Excellent," Nakamura said, and turned back to Eve as the captain went back in his office. "Is Donuts around?"

"Actually, Duncan is out in Monterey Park," she said, "trying to run down Sabrina Morton's rape kit."

Nakamura appeared confused. "That's not his job. We have evidence specialists for that."

"Well, the specialists have lost the kit, so he's making it his job."

Nakamura arched his bifurcated eyebrow. "Let me buy you a cup of coffee."

They headed to the break room, where he poured himself and Eve each a Styrofoam cup of coffee and tossed a dollar into the empty Kirkland cashew jar on the counter. The money was used to buy better coffee than the Folgers the county was willing to pay for.

"I don't see why the rape kit matters," Nakamura said. "The captain tells me it's a murder investigation now."

He led her to one of the four empty tables in the room and they sat down.

"Her murder could be connected to the rape," she said.

Nakamura took a sip of his coffee. She was surprised he didn't gag. It had probably been days since anyone had made a fresh pot. "Do you have any evidence to support that belief?"

"No." She wasn't ready to tell him about the tattoos or Josie. As far as she was concerned, he was a suspect, not a colleague. "But I don't have any evidence to the contrary, either."

"To be honest, I wasn't convinced that a rape even occurred."

"Why was that?"

"Sabrina admitted that she'd been drinking and doing drugs with some guys, partying so hard that she blacked out. When she sobered up, she remembered doing some things under the influence that she was deeply ashamed of." He got up, grabbed a half dozen packets of sugar, and came back to the table. "Sometimes the only way a person can reconcile that conduct with how they see themselves is to say it happened against their will." He tore open two packets at once and emptied the sugar into his coffee. "So she says someone must have slipped a roofie into her drink. I've seen it dozens of times before."

"Or she was raped," Eve said. "I'm sure that's happened dozens of times before, too."

He took another sip of his coffee but she was sure that it still tasted lousy. "I dutifully investigated it as a rape. But the fact is, even if I'd been able to find the guys that she partied with, we wouldn't have been able to make the charge stick. It was a very weak case."

"The rapists didn't know that," Eve said.

Nakamura set the coffee aside and looked at Eve. "For the sake of argument, let's say she wasn't raped a few weeks before her killing. Let's say instead that her car was stolen."

"Okay."

"Would your first investigative step in her homicide today, six years later, be to hunt down the car thief?"

"No, sir, it probably wouldn't," Eve said. "But car theft and rape are two very different crimes."

"Yes, they are, and that's precisely my point. You're outraged that her rape wasn't solved, I get that. But your emotions are muddying your thinking," Nakamura said. "Your job now is to find her killer, not her rapist."

It was hard for her not to toss her coffee in his face.

Her emotions were clouding her judgment? Did he really just use that old sexist trope? At least he didn't ask her if she was menstruating. But Eve kept those thoughts to herself and said: "It may be the same person."

Nakamura frowned—this wasn't going the way he wanted it to. He took a deep breath and then a new approach.

"When you buy a puzzle, there's a picture on the box of what you're putting together. That's handy, because it tells you how the hundreds of pieces are supposed to fit together. In your job, you just get the pieces without the box. You have to put the pieces together without the picture to guide you. Are you following me?"

No, I'm too emotional. "Yes, I am."

"The worst thing you can do is come up with the picture yourself. Because then your pride and ego get involved . . . and you'll make the pieces fit your picture even if they don't. The physical evidence dictates the theory, not the other way around." Nakamura wagged his index finger at her. "You don't have any evidence that the rape and the murder are connected, but you sure as hell want it to be, don't you?"

"I hear what you're saying, sir," Eve said. "Let the evidence dictate the theory, not the other way around, or I won't solve the murder."

"That's right. Let that be your golden rule." Nakamura smiled and leaned back in his seat. "I'm a big fan of yours, Eve. I think you've got a brilliant future in the department. I'd hate to see your career derailed by a bad decision made on your second murder case."

"I appreciate that, sir."

Nakamura looked around, as if worried about eavesdroppers, even though they had the room to themselves. "There are people in the department who resent you for using that viral video to get yourself my old desk."

"Do you?"

"I see a woman with political savvy. Then you solved a triple murder. Some people in the department say it was a lucky break. I see a talented detective with great instincts," Nakamura said. "I believe in you. But you're still green. Donuts will be retiring soon and when that happens, you're going to need a new mentor, someone in your corner with the experience to help you avoid the kind of mistakes you almost made in this case. I want you to know I'll be here for you."

"Thank you, sir."

"I'm glad we had this talk."

"So am I," Eve said. "I think it set me straight."

He smiled, stood up, and placed a firm, reassuring hand on her shoulder. "Call me any time. I mean that. I'm glad to be a sounding board for you on this case, or any others down the road."

"I'll try not to abuse the courtesy," Eve said and watched him go. She sat still for a long moment, trying to control her anger at his patronizing effort to shift her focus away from him and the deputies. Her gaze rested on his coffee cup. *Did he have a tattoo on his leg? Did he toss Sabrina's rape kit in the trash?*

She took a napkin from the dispenser on the table, picked up his cup with it, walked over to the sink, and poured the remaining coffee in the drain.

But she kept the cup.

Eve brought Nakamura's cup to her desk as if it were her own and, when she was certain none of the detectives in the room were paying any attention to her, she pulled a transparent plastic evidence bag out of a drawer, used a Sharpie to fill out the case number and collection details on the form printed on the front, put the cup inside, and sealed it.

She dropped the evidence bag in her drawer and locked it.

CHAPTER TWELVE

Deputy Chuck Towler was on duty again at the Hueso Canyon scene, handling the log and keeping a wary eye on the press vehicles on the street. Eve pulled up in her Explorer, grabbed two bottles of water from the passenger seat, and peeled the edge of the label off one of them.

Eve got out of the car with both bottles, approached Towler, and offered him the water with the altered label. "I'll trade you this for the log."

"Deal," he said, taking the water and handing her the log to fill out.

She gestured to the media as she signed in. "How long have they been here?"

"An hour or so." He twisted the cap and took a long sip.

"You're putting in a lot of overtime here. You must like standing around in the hot sun." She handed the clipboard back to him.

"I like the extra money, except now it's my shift, and when I'm on the clock, I'd rather be on patrol. But I got assigned here. Ironic, huh?"

Was it a coincidence that Towler was assigned here or did he angle for it somehow? Was he trying to keep tabs on the investigation? Did he know that Eve was onto him?

"You can't have it all," she said.

Eve took a drink from her bottle and looked back at the reporters. Kate Darrow and her cameraman were here again, which meant it must be a slow news day or else she suspected something was up. Otherwise, there would be other TV reporters at the scene.

The other two reporters present were Scott Peck from the *Acorn*, the free local newspaper, and Zena Faust, a blogger from the Malibu Beat. Of the three, Eve thought that Zena was the one most plugged in to what was happening in the communities between PCH and the Ventura Freeway. Her sources were usually nosy residents with agendas.

Eve headed over to the reporters and they gathered around her like ducks to someone tossing bits of bread on the water.

"Have you got anything for us?" asked Peck, who was Eve's age. This was his first newspaper job, one he'd hoped would be a stepping-stone on his way to the *Los Angeles Times*, which kept cutting back their staff. He'd been standing on his stepping-stone for five years.

"I do, Scott." Eve gave them a second to get their cameras fired up and their audio-recording apps set up.

"We're rolling," Darrow said.

Eve took that as her cue to begin. "We've identified the remains that we recovered on Monday. They belong to Sabrina Morton, age twenty-four, of Malibu, who was reported missing by her parents six years ago." Eve stole a glance at Towler to see if he showed any reaction, but his face was impassive.

"How was she killed?" asked Zena. She was covered with piercings and tattoos, so some people thought she wasn't serious about her work and underestimated her reporting skills. Eve was sure Zena knew that and used it.

"We don't know yet how she died."

"Was she buried?" asked Darrow.

"No, she wasn't. We believe her bones were on the hillside and fell into the yards below as a result of the wildfire burning away vegetation," Eve said. "The bones have been up there a long time, they've been charred, and they've been scattered by firefighters, rain, and animals. It's a difficult case."

"But you've found two bodies, haven't you?" Darrow said. "Or perhaps more?"

So Darrow did get a tip, Eve thought. "In the course of gathering the bones of Ms. Morton, which were dispersed over a wide area, we discovered the remains of another person, who has been identified as Debbie Crawford, age fifty-seven, also of Malibu. She disappeared two years ago."

Eve saw the name register on Zena's face and wondered what that meant.

"How did she die?" Zena asked.

"We don't know that yet, either," Eve said. "But we believe her body was also tangled in vegetation on the hillside before the fires."

"Is this the work of a serial killer?" Peck asked, obviously hopeful that this could be the local story that would get him out of Calabasas. *This must be the speculation that Captain Moffett was worried about,* Eve thought.

"That's reckless speculation, Scott. I'm surprised at you. We don't even know how both of these women died yet," Eve said, not quite lying but not being exactly truthful, either. "As far as we can tell, there's nothing connecting these two women."

"Except they were both found in Bone Canyon within a hundred yards of each other," Darrow said. Eve assumed she was calling Hueso Canyon by its English translation because it sounded more sensational. It was as if Darrow was practicing, seeing how it sounded to her ear before using it in her news report.

"A few weeks ago, we found the bodies of Aurelio Rojas, an MS-13 gang member, and later Ezra Wilkins, an eighty-year-old Alzheimer's patient, in Malibu Canyon below Las Virgenes Road. Rojas had seventy-seven stab wounds and a gunshot to the head. He was executed by a rival gang. Wilkins died from injuries sustained in a fall," Eve said. "What those two cases, and now these two, have in common is that they died years apart and their bodies were found in deep canyons below a well-traveled road, in this case Latigo Canyon Road, after the fire."

"Were either of these women stabbed, shot, or suffering from Alzheimer's?" Darrow asked.

Eve didn't fall for the trick question. If she answered no, she would be admitting that they knew something about their causes of death. "What I can tell you is that Latigo Canyon Road was used by countless drivers, joggers, hikers, and bicyclists every day before the fires. There's also a popular hiking trail that runs through here, the Backbone Trail. Both women lived nearby and were active outdoors. There are lots of ways a person walking on a ridgeline road or trail in these mountains, over a very steep gorge, could accidentally fall, land in the thick brush, and go unseen for years."

"That'd be a horrible way to die," Peck said.

"There aren't many nice ones. That's it for me today," Eve said and started to walk away.

But Zena chased after her, waiting to speak until they were out of earshot of the others. "I knew Debbie."

Eve stopped. "I'm sorry for your loss."

"We weren't close. She used to bombard me with emails, recordings, and photos of Nick Egan harassing her."

"What kind of recordings and photos?"

"Photos of protected oak trees he cut down and audio recordings of all his noisy parties and hot tub orgies. We posted it all online. Have you talked with him?"

"Why would I?"

"He threatened to sue me out of existence, and blanket social media with the pics of my pierced labia that I texted to my girlfriend, if I didn't pull everything off the blog. So I did. I can't imagine what he threatened Debbie with."

"I don't investigate things that people imagine," Eve said, though she couldn't help imagining Zena's labia piercing, which made her cringe.

Eve walked up to Towler. "We're going to see more media out here and make sure they stay away from the crime scene, especially up along Latigo, where they can get a bird's-eye view of what we're doing."

"Roger that," he said. "I'll spread the word among the troops."

She walked past Towler and out on the plywood path to Daniel, who was in a tent, photographing some items on the white sheet on the ground. He smiled and got to his feet when he saw her.

"How was PT?" he asked.

"A waste of time. I could have slept in."

"No you couldn't," he said with a grin.

She glanced back at Towler. He tossed his empty water bottle into the trash box that the CSU team placed beside their van so no outside objects would contaminate the crime scene. She looked back at Daniel. "Have you had any luck here?"

"We've found more bone fragments, but nothing that immediately suggests a cause of death. That might change once Nan and I put the pieces together at the lab."

"Have you found any personal effects?"

"We found some buttons from a blouse, part of a zipper. It's all being cataloged."

So a dead end. "Okay, I'll catch you later."

"I hope so," he said.

She walked back to her car, pausing by the trash can at the CSU truck. Towler was signing in a newly arrived CSU tech, so Eve used the opportunity to snatch the doctored water bottle out of the trash. When she got back to her Explorer, she dropped Towler's empty water bottle into an evidence baggie and sealed it.

At the station, Eve went straight to her desk, unlocked her bottom drawer, and placed the new evidence bag inside, next to the bag with Nakamura's cup.

"Hey!"

The man's voice startled her and she slammed the drawer shut. She looked up to see Garvey leaning over the partition of her cubicle.

"What?" she said.

"Sorry, did I startle you?"

"My mind was on a case I'm working on."

"Yeah, I heard the pile of bones you found was Debbie Crawford," Garvey said. "What a batshit crazy, hippie-dippie psycho she was."

"I know she filed a lot of disturbing-the-peace complaints against Nick Egan, but how does that make her batshit crazy? Was she hearing things?"

"No, Nick partied hard, that's true, and sure, maybe he cranked up the volume too high sometimes, and maybe he pleasured a few girls who loudly expressed their delight, but what she did was worse."

"Nick? You're on a first-name basis with the guy?"

"That tells you how often he called me out there to deal with her," Garvey said. "She was constantly harassing him, screaming at his guests, throwing dead rats over the fence into his pool, and blasting harpsichord music when he was entertaining."

"Can you blast harpsichord music?"

"You wouldn't believe the stuff she was doing."

Eve nodded at her computer. "I don't see any reports about that in the system."

"Because there aren't any. Nick asked me to handle it, to smooth things out with the batshit crazy, hippie-dippie psycho." Garvey twirled a finger beside his head in case Eve didn't get the subtle message that he thought Crawford was nuts. "He didn't want his domestic troubles getting into the press, where it would be blown all out of proportion. I honestly thought I had it handled."

"You say that like something went wrong."

"Crawford went nuclear. She shot a video of him getting a blow job from Bootilicious Ramos, the lucky bastard, and told him she'd release it on the net if he didn't move out."

"Bootilicious Ramos?"

"The singer, the one with tits out to here and fish lips." He held his hands out in front of him and puckered his lips. When that didn't spark recognition, he leaned into his cubicle, snatched a photo off the partition, and showed it to her. Naturally, it was signed.

"I recognize her now," Eve said.

"When Nick told Crawford to fuck herself, she followed through on her threat and posted the video everywhere."

"That must have pissed him off."

"Hell yes, he's a family man, divorced three times, but he has kids. He didn't want his kids seeing a blow job video of their dad," Garvey said. "He was preparing to file a restraining order against her when she disappeared."

"Convenient timing," Eve said.

"I know what you're thinking, but Nick wouldn't hurt the batshit crazy, hippie-dippie psycho."

"He'd just pee in her yard from his balcony."

"That story is bullshit," Garvey said. "Nick's not that kind of guy."

What kind of guy would *do that,* Eve wondered, *and how would you know when you met him?* But the question she asked Garvey was: "So what did you think happened when Crawford disappeared?"

"Maybe she was kidnapped by space aliens," Garvey said with a grin. "For real this time."

Garvey went back to his cubicle and Eve thought how odd it was that both the women found in Hueso Canyon had connections to Lost Hills detectives who may have covered up for men who'd behaved very badly. It suggested that it was common practice at Lost Hills.

That made her angry.

There was nothing more she could do for Debbie Crawford right now, but there was something she could do for Sabrina Morton.

CHAPTER THIRTEEN

On a map, the city of West Hollywood was shaped like the silhouette of a gun. The grip was North Doheny Drive to the west, La Cienega Boulevard to the east, and Beverly Boulevard to the south. The barrel was Fountain Avenue to the north, Willoughby to the south, and La Brea to the east. Eve was seated at the eye of the barrel, at a window table at Jersey Mike's on Santa Monica Boulevard, where she had a view of the patio of Hot N Juicy Crawfish next door, where Deputy David Harding was eating dinner with his patrol partner. She'd tracked them here by monitoring their radio calls and by following them from a safe distance.

Eve took a few pictures with her phone of Harding eating his crawfish po'boy and sipping his large drink. The pictures had no real evidentiary value, but she wanted something to establish where and when she'd retrieved his DNA. Nakamura's DNA sample was taken at the Lost Hills station, and Towler's at a crime scene, both locations that were under LASD control, so she didn't feel photos were necessary to establish the circumstances in those situations.

She didn't let Harding's drink, or the fork he used to eat the overflowing contents of his po'boy, out of her sight, while she ate her own dinner, a chipotle cheesesteak sandwich and a Diet Coke.

Harding was tall, blond, and broad shouldered. *He could have made a good high school basketball or football player,* she thought. He might have been both. Her phone vibrated on the table and the screen lit up. Caller ID: DONUTS.

"Did you find the rape kit?" she answered.

"Hello to you, too. No, not yet," Duncan said. "But I bumped into Teddy Nakamura."

"So did I," she said.

"Teddy mentioned that. He thought I should go back to the station and forget about the rape kit because I am not doing you or your career any favors with this investigation."

"What did you say?"

"I said I was doing myself a favor. That I was out here for the food. Monterey Park has the best Chinese cuisine in Southern California," he said. She knew it was true. It was because the Chinese population of Monterey Park was 45 percent, the highest percentage of any city in the United States. She'd made the trip out there a few times herself just to eat.

"Did he buy it?"

"He wished me a wonderful retirement, meaning he couldn't wait to see my fat ass go out the door," Duncan said. "He'll be thrilled when he sees me back out here tomorrow. Tell me about your day."

Eve kept her eyes on Deputy Harding's progress on his sandwich while she briefed Duncan on what she'd learned about Debbie Crawford and what Nakamura told her.

"Teddy actually gave you some very good advice," Duncan said. "You ought to think about it."

"It sounded like a threat and a bribe to me," she said.

"Then it's a good thing you're concentrating on what happened to Debbie Crawford right now and leaving Sabrina Morton to me."

"Yes it is," Eve said, watching Harding. The deputy had finished his sandwich and was laughing at something his partner was telling him. "I have a quick question for you, drawing on your experience as a father. What would you buy a five-year-old girl for her birthday?"

"A doll, a makeup kit, or a cooking set."

"How about something that isn't socially conditioning her to fit into a sexist female stereotype?"

"Sure," Duncan said. "How about a jockstrap and a tin of chewing tobacco?"

"Good night, Donuts."

"Good night, Deathfist."

She ended the call and watched Harding carry his tray to the trash can, drop his plate inside, take one last sip of his drink, and drop it in afterward. The two deputies went to their patrol car, which was parked in a red zone at the street. Eve divided her attention between their car and the trash, hoping nobody came along to put anything else in before the deputies left.

Harding drove off and, the instant the car turned the corner south on La Brea, she dashed out of the Jersey Mike's, putting on her rubber gloves while in motion. The trash can was full and, thankfully, Harding's plate and cup were right at the top.

She took an evidence bag out of her pocket, carefully plucked Harding's fork and cup from the trash, placed the items in the bag, and sealed it.

Eve went home, sat down at her kitchen table with her MacBook, and watched the video of Nick Egan sitting on the edge of his Jacuzzi, getting a blow job from a topless Bootilicious Ramos, who was in the bubbling water. Her head and enormous breasts mostly blocked the view of Egan's crotch. The camera angle was from high above, and from the side of the property where Crawford's house stood. The image was slightly grainy because it was zoomed in. The content aside, something about the video didn't feel right to her, but she couldn't figure out what it was.

She went to bed before 9:00 p.m., exhausted from her long day and lack of sleep the night before. As she lay in bed, she thought about her day, and it occurred to her that Sabrina Morton never had the opportunity to identify her attackers.

But Josie still could.

Eve woke up at 4:00 a.m. on Friday, showered, and rode her bike to the Lost Hills station. She was surprised to see Daniel's Ford Fusion in the lot. She was careful to be quiet going inside the station and stopped outside the sleep room to peek inside. Daniel was curled up on a cot in his underwear and T-shirt. She felt guilty for not inviting him home again, but she didn't want to give him the wrong idea about their relationship, which wasn't one yet. It was a friendly hookup and nothing more, at least for now.

The squad room was empty. She'd have to work fast. Eve went straight to her computer and spent forty-five minutes putting together a photo array, using DMV records, of the deputies who were off duty the night Sabrina was raped, and some convicted rapists who were active in the area six years ago. She put a number on each photo that corresponded to a separate list of names, so she'd know who was being identified when the array was shown.

She placed the photo array in a manila envelope and rushed out, nearly colliding with Daniel as he emerged, still groggy, from the sleep room.

He smiled when he saw her. "Do you live here?"

"I could ask you the same question."

"And the answer would be yes, at least lately. Could I buy you breakfast?"

"I wish you could, but I have to make a long drive," Eve said. "Can I get a rain check?"

"Absolutely."

"Can I ask you another question?"

"Sure," he said.

"What would you buy a five-year-old girl for her birthday?"

He answered instantly. "A kid's pirate treasure-hunting kit."

"What's that?"

"A plastic shovel, a rake, a bucket, and sieve," he said. "It also comes with fake bones, gems, and doubloons, all kinds of stuff that you can bury and the kids have to dig up."

"Sounds like fun," she said.

"It is, but I have to warn you, it's a gateway drug. Look what it did to me."

◆ ◆ ◆

San Luis Obispo was covered in a blanket of thick fog when Eve arrived outside of Josie's office building. She got out of her car as soon as she saw the light go on in the upstairs windows and went up to the office.

The receptionist hadn't arrived yet, but Josie was there, her office door open, reviewing a file and sipping a Starbucks coffee. Josie looked up when she saw Eve come in and the color seemed to drain from her face.

"I'm so sorry to bother you again," Eve said. "But there has been a development in the case and I need your help."

"What kind of development?"

Eve pulled the stack of numbered photos out of the envelope and set them in front of Josie on the desk. "Do you recognize any of these men?"

Josie set her file aside, picked up the stack, and began to browse through them. Eve sat down in a guest chair and watched her. Josie hesitated over three of the photos, set the stack down, and then looked at Eve across the desk.

"Are you sure you want to know?"

Eve thought it was a strange question for Josie to ask, but it revealed so much. There was only one reason that Josie would wonder if Eve, a Los Angeles Sheriff's Department detective, really wanted to know the answer and was prepared for the consequences knowing it might bring.

"Yes, I'm sure."

Josie went through the stack, pulled out three photos, and laid them out in front of Eve, faceup like she was dealing blackjack. Two of the men were Deputies Charles Towler and David Harding. The third man, according to Eve's list, was Deputy Jimmy Frankel.

Eve met Josie's gaze. "How long have you known that they were sheriff's deputies?"

"A year or so after Sabrina disappeared, I saw this one at Trancas Market on PCH. He was in uniform." Josie tapped Towler's photo.

"Did he recognize you?"

"I don't think so," Josie said. "But it terrified me. That's why I moved away. I didn't want to get killed."

"You think Sabrina was murdered."

"I wasn't sure until that moment," she said. "But yes, I know she was."

"Have you always remembered their faces?"

She shook her head. "It didn't happen until I saw him in the grocery store. Then it all came back in high definition. It was horrifying. I ran outside and vomited in the parking lot."

"Why didn't you tell me this when I was up here before or when I called you?"

"I wasn't sure I could trust you," Josie said. "Or that I wanted to risk getting involved."

"And now?" Eve asked.

Josie studied her for a long moment, then pulled her purse out of a drawer in her desk, and stood up. "Follow me."

Eve followed Josie's BMW to a storage unit facility in an industrial area south of town. Josie typed a code that opened the gate and led Eve to a long cinder block bunker of storage units, each with a bright-orange roll-up garage door secured by a fat padlock.

Josie stopped in front of one of the units, got out of her car, unlocked the unit, and rolled up the door to reveal a narrow space, the three walls lined with stacked office file boxes. There were also some covered furniture, a few small appliances, and two tall cardboard wardrobe boxes. Josie crouched in the corner, found a small, unmarked box, and brought it back to Eve, presenting it to her like a gift.

"What's this?" Eve asked.

"My Monica Lewinsky insurance policy."

Eve put on a pair of rubber gloves, carefully lifted the flaps while Josie held the box, and looked inside.

It contained a sandy bikini and a sundress.

Eve got back to Lost Hills before eleven by breaking every speed limit in San Luis Obispo, Santa Barbara, and Ventura Counties. She went straight to her desk, sat down at her computer, and ran Deputy Jimmy Frankel's name through the system and what she discovered shocked her. He was in prison at Soledad, serving nine years for rape.

A year after Sabrina's disappearance, Frankel pulled over a woman in City of Industry for erratic driving. He ran her plates and discovered her license was yanked for prior DUIs and that she was wanted on an outstanding warrant for shoplifting. So he gave her a choice—she could go to prison or she could have sex with him. She gave in, so they drove to an empty lot and had sex in the back of his patrol car. Two days later, Frankel showed up at her home, demanding more sex and, when she refused, he raped her. Afterward, he fell asleep and she called the police, who arrested him while he was still in her bed. Two other rape victims, also pulled over in traffic stops, also came forward after his arrest.

Nakamura was responsible for this, Eve thought, and so was Brad Pruitt, the deputy who'd pulled Sabrina over in Malibu. If they hadn't covered up for the deputies, Frankel would have been put in prison a year earlier and these rapes wouldn't have happened. What rapes or other crimes had Towler and Harding committed over the last six years?

It's time to end this outrage.

Eve unlocked her desk drawer, grabbed the three evidence bags, and headed for her Explorer. She opened the trunk and put the evidence bags in the back with Josie's bagged box, when Daniel called out to her from the lab. She turned to see him leaning out the door.

"Perfect timing," he said. "There's something here you need to see."

Eve hated to leave the evidence in the trunk, but she didn't see much choice. She locked the Explorer and dashed into the lab, where Daniel had Crawford's bones spread out on the table. It was cold inside, but it helped cool Eve's anger at Nakamura and Pruitt. Daniel led her to the table.

"Debbie Crawford's skull was in pieces, but I've reconstructed it." The skull looked like a shattered ceramic model that had been glued back together. "Much of the fragmentation was caused by the flames, the tumble down the hill, maybe even firefighters inadvertently stomping on the pieces, but not this." He turned the skull around and pointed to a jagged hole in the back. "Blunt force trauma leaves a unique signature that fire, and even smashing the skull with a sledgehammer, can't hide, such as these tiny radiating fractures around the hole."

"You're saying that Debbie Crawford was murdered."

"That's Nan's determination to officially make but, since you seduced me into talking, yes, she was murdered," Daniel said. "Someone hit her with an ice pick or a garden tool of some kind, but I'm just guessing. Nan might be able to pinpoint the exact weapon from the shape of the puncture."

Eve grimaced. Now she had two murder cases on her hands, both with ties to Lost Hills detectives. It sucked.

"Do you have any more bones left to find?"

"Found 'em all," Daniel said.

"So you're done here?"

"I have a report to write, but yes, I'm checking out of the Four Seasons Lost Hills." Daniel reached into his pocket and handed her his card. "I hope you'll give me a call sometime."

"I will," Eve said and started to walk away. But then, on impulse, she came back and kissed him hard on the mouth, which evolved into some frenzied groping between them, and just when it felt like he might sweep the bones off the table and push her on top of it, her good sense prevailed and she let go of him.

"To be continued," Eve said, catching her breath. It was the first time she'd felt warm in that trailer. "I promise. But preferably not in a morgue."

He grinned. "I think that can be arranged."

She straightened her clothing, ran a hand through her hair, and hurried out the door before she changed her mind.

CHAPTER FOURTEEN

If the San Fernando Valley were to secede from Los Angeles, then Van Nuys would be its capital. Not only was Van Nuys the first town founded in the valley, a master-planned community established in 1911, but it had its own civic center comprised of numerous federal, state, county, and city government buildings, including the monolithic superior courthouse where Eve sat outside, waiting.

She was on a bench facing the building, which looked like an enormous single cinder block with a window in the middle, and was showing enormous willpower by not devouring the contents of the In-N-Out bag in her lap. It wouldn't be good if she ate her bribe before she had the chance to offer it.

Eve had to wait only five minutes before Rebecca Burnside, an assistant district attorney, came out of the courthouse on a lunch break from the trial she was prosecuting. Burnside was beautiful and knew it. She carefully chose her makeup, suits, and hairstyle to dim her fashion-model wattage just enough to appear professional, serious, and determined but not so much as to blunt the potential positive impact of her attractiveness on jurors.

Burnside spotted Eve immediately and came over to her. "Is this an ambush?"

"You might say that," Eve said. "Your office told me you were here. I need a word in private."

"I only have a few minutes. It's lunch recess and I'm starving."

"So am I." Eve held up her bribe. "I know where we can eat and have some privacy."

Five minutes later, they were in the parking structure behind the courthouse, sitting in the front seat of Eve's Explorer with the air conditioner running. Burnside took a Double-Double with Cheese out of the bag, holding it as if it were nitroglycerin that could explode at any moment.

"This better be important, Detective," Burnside said. "And if I dribble anything on my blouse, I'm sending you the dry-cleaning bill."

"Fair enough," Eve said. She took a bite of her own Double-Double for energy and launched into the story of Sabrina Morton's death, the tattoos, the lost rape kit, the IDs by Josie Wallace, and the DNA evidence in the trunk of the car.

"I don't know if we'll ever find the rape kit," Eve said in conclusion, "but in the meantime, I want to run the DNA that I've collected against whatever is on Josie Wallace's sundress and bikini."

Burnside dabbed her lips delicately with a napkin. She managed to finish her burger and her fries without damaging her wardrobe at all. "Why are you telling me this? Why not your captain or someone else in your chain of command at LASD?"

"Because I don't know who I can trust or who else has the tattoo," Eve said. "The detective on the Sabrina Morton case six years ago is now assistant sheriff and he warned me not to pursue the rape angle in my murder investigation. I don't want this buried with Sabrina Morton's bones."

"So you're going outside the department to cover your ass."

"That's about it," Eve said and took a few bites of her burger.

"The DA's office might not be enough cover."

Eve waited to swallow her mouthful of food before speaking. "Are you saying I have a gigantic ass?"

"This could still cost you your career in law enforcement, tainting you as a traitor, regardless of whether you are right about those deputies being guilty of rape, and possibly murder." Burnside checked her watch. "Not that you have any evidence to support that."

"Yet," Eve said.

"It's a big evidentiary mountain to climb and you could take a big fall on your way up."

"I'm doing this, Counselor, with or without you."

Burnside took a sip of her drink, put it back in the cup holder, then reached into her briefcase for a yellow legal pad. "Okay, I'll memorialize this conversation in writing, so when this comes out nobody can say you went rogue." She started making notes, and another thought occurred to her. "In fact, I'll say we spoke yesterday and I authorized you to collect the DNA samples from the deputies."

"You don't need to do that for me."

"I think I do," she said.

"In that case, you should know I also took a DNA sample from Assistant Sheriff Nakamura," Eve said.

"You did?"

Eve nodded.

"You really are Deathfist," Burnside said and went back to making notes. "I'll call the lab before I go back into court and let them know you're walking the evidence in and that it's a rush. We should have the results on Monday or Tuesday."

"What about your career?"

"This is what I do. Besides, it won't hurt me to take on the sheriff's department, even if you're wrong about everything," Burnside said. "It makes me look tough and incorruptible."

"Sounds like you're planning to run for DA someday."

"You're not the only one with ambition, Eve."

"I don't play politics."

Burnside laughed. "Oh please. You wouldn't be in homicide, and we wouldn't be having this conversation, if you didn't play politics and play it well." The prosecutor put her pad back in her briefcase, opened the door, and started to get out of the car, when she had another thought. "By the way, I see Cobie Smulders playing me in the TV series."

Eve had no idea who that actress was, not that it mattered. "There isn't going to be one."

"Don't blow it off," Burnside said. "You're probably going to need the paycheck."

The crime labs for the Los Angeles County Sheriff's Department and Los Angeles Police Department, and nearly fifty other local law enforcement agencies, were housed at the Hertzberg-Davis Forensic Science Center on the Los Angeles campus of California State University in Monterey Park. Eve checked in the evidence with the clerk, filled out the forms, and was walking away from the counter when Duncan emerged from one of the doors leading to the back rooms.

"I heard you were out here," Duncan said. "Did you come to give me a hand?"

"I'll tell you outside."

They walked through the lobby in silence, out to the parking lot, and kept going along the fenced perimeter.

"I've just delivered the sundress and bikini that Josie Wallace was wearing when she was raped," Eve said as they walked. "She's been saving it as an insurance policy."

"No wonder she's in the insurance business," he said. "But that won't do us much good without Sabrina Morton's rape kit."

"There's more," Eve said. "I put together a photo array of deputies who were off duty the day of the rape and I showed it to her. She identified three of them. Charles Towler, David Harding, and Jimmy Frankel, who is in Soledad, doing nine years for raping three women he pulled over on traffic stops. I got a full statement from her."

"Good work," Duncan said. "Now we need DNA samples from the deputies."

"It's done. I also submitted samples from Towler and Harding today. I didn't know about Frankel until this morning, but his DNA must already be in the system."

Duncan stopped walking and stared at her. "I'm assuming you didn't ask Towler and Harding to give you cheek swabs or hair follicles."

"I collected samples from them yesterday without their knowledge," she said. "But I cleared it with ADA Burnside."

Eve surprised herself by how easily she adopted the lie. It wasn't something she was proud of.

"But you didn't say a word to me about it," Duncan said. "I'm your partner, damn it. You should have told me what you were doing and let me be the one to talk to Burnside."

"I can't hide behind you forever."

"You could have for another 114 days. I have nothing to lose."

"Only your legacy," she said, walking on, not that she had anywhere to go. "You deserve to retire without me staining your record."

Duncan kept pace beside her. "I don't give a shit about my record."

"Well, I do," Eve said. "Have you made any progress finding the rape kit?"

"No, but there's still a chance it was misfiled."

"I think it never got here," she said.

"You better hope that it did, because Josie Wallace's clothing is far from a slam dunk, even if it's soaked with DNA."

"What do you mean?"

They reached the far end of the parking lot and started to circle back toward the building.

"A good defense attorney will argue that we have no idea when those samples were actually left on Josie Wallace's clothing, that it could have come from consensual encounters days, weeks, or even years after Sabrina Morton was allegedly raped," Duncan said. "They'll say all her semen-stained clothes prove is that Josie was a party girl who likes fucking cops."

"That's ridiculous," Eve said. "I think a jury, given the context under which Josie's clothing was recovered and the totality of the evidence in the case, would reject that argument."

"That's because you were still in nursery school during the O.J. trial," Duncan said.

◆ ◆ ◆

It took Eve ninety minutes to get back to Lost Hills station, which was fast for a Friday night.

At the station, she turned in the Explorer, rode her bike home, and got into her Subaru Outback to go searching for a children's pirate treasure-hunting kit for her niece's birthday party tomorrow afternoon.

Her first stop was the Walmart in Canoga Park, because they had an in-store McDonald's and she could eat dinner while she was shopping. Unfortunately, they didn't have the kit, so she ate her Big Mac, fries, and Diet Coke at a table and then went to the Target on the other side of the same shopping center.

She didn't find the pirate treasure-hunting kit there, either, but they did have all the elements for her to create one herself. Target stocked a toy pirate chest, stuffed with plastic doubloons and fake jewels, and they also sold a metal detector's tool kit that came with a plastic hand shovel, trowel, and sifter. She bought both products and a camouflaged shoulder bag for them to go in.

The gift shopping was a nice distraction, but as soon as the task was complete, and she was on her way home, her mind drifted to the

Sabrina Morton case again and what Duncan had said. She knew he was right, that she would need more than the tattoo drawing, the DNA, and Josie Wallace's testimony to make the rape case against the deputies and establish the motive for Sabrina's murder.

What she needed was another witness, someone who could add credibility to Josie's claims, and establish that the deputies knew Sabrina was coming after them.

Nakamura would be perfect, but there was no way he'd step up.

That left only one person.

There was a white picket fence around the front lawn of Deputy Brad Pruitt's tract home in Castaic, an unincorporated area in the northwest corner of Los Angeles County that was once the battleground in one of the bloodiest, and longest lasting, range wars in US history. Now Castaic was mostly known, if it was known at all, for the giant reservoir that had submerged most of the disputed land. If the earthen Castaic dam ever collapsed, then Pruitt's house, on the western ridge of the floodplain above Interstate 5, would become riverfront property.

Pruitt was in his driveway, wearing shorts and a T-shirt, washing his Ford F-150 truck with his five-year-old son, when Eve pulled up across the street in her Subaru on Saturday morning. They were scrubbing the car with soap sponges.

She was dressed in a tank top and jeans, but she could see from the expression on Pruitt's face that he'd pegged her as a cop. Perhaps he detected the ankle holster on her right leg. He dropped his sponge in a bucket of water and turned to face her as she approached.

"Deputy Pruitt," Eve said. "I'm Detective Eve Ronin. I work homicide out of Lost Hills."

"I know who you are. I've seen the videos," Pruitt said. "You don't look the same without your cape and golden lasso."

His son whirled around, excited and soaking wet. "She has a cape?"

"She thinks she's Wonder Woman," Pruitt told the boy.

"I'm Batman!" the boy told Eve, poking himself in the chest with his thumb.

"You are?" Eve said. "You don't look like Batman."

Pruitt nodded toward the house. "Why don't you show her, Jake?"

Jake wagged a finger at Eve. "Don't go anywhere."

Pruitt watched his son run to the front door and go inside. Eve stole a glance at Pruitt's calf and saw the Great White tattoo. He turned back to her.

"He's cute," Eve said.

"What are you doing here, Detective?"

"I'm investigating the murder of Sabrina Morton."

"I don't know her."

"She was raped six years ago on the beach in Malibu," Eve said, "back when you were working patrol at Lost Hills."

"Still doesn't ring any bells."

"She went around showing people a drawing of the rapist's tattoo, hoping someone would recognize it," Eve said. "You pulled her over and told her she was putting herself in danger. Does that refresh your memory?"

Pruitt studied her for a long moment, perhaps wondering exactly how much she knew or could prove, before making a decision. "Yeah, I remember her now. Some surfers told me what she was doing. It was reckless. I was concerned that she might get hurt."

"Was that why you were concerned?" Eve asked. "Or were you worried about your friends?"

"What is that supposed to mean?"

Eve reached into her back pocket, took out a piece of paper, and unfolded it. "This is the drawing she was showing around." She held it up in front of her. "It's the same tattoo you've got on your leg."

Pruitt didn't flinch. "So do dozens of other deputies and detectives."

"Which brings me back to my question. Who were you really concerned about getting hurt, Brad?"

That got under his skin. He took a step toward her. "I didn't rape her."

Eve stood her ground. "I didn't say you did."

That was when Jake bolted out of the house, dressed in a Batman costume, followed by his very pregnant mother. Eve put the drawing back in her pocket and Pruitt took a step back from her.

"I'm the Batman!" Jake said, affecting the Affleck growl.

His mother duckwalked out toward them. Her belly seemed far too big for the woman's tiny frame. She eyed Eve with a wary gaze. "Hello. Jake said Wonder Woman was outside. I had to see for myself."

"I don't have any superpowers," Eve said to her, then smiled at Jake. "But you do. It's a pleasure to meet you, Batman."

"My superpower is that I'm rich," Jake said, still in character.

"That's not a superpower," his mother said to him. "I've told you that."

"Terri, this is Eve Ronin, a detective from Calabasas," Pruitt said.

Eve offered her a polite smile. "I'm following up on a case your husband worked on a few years ago."

"It's a Saturday," Terri said, sensing the tension between Eve and her husband. Her words were a rebuke aimed at Eve. "It's his day off."

"She won't be long," Pruitt said.

Terri gave Eve a cold look, then held her hand out to her son. "How would Batman like a juice box?"

"Batjuice," Jake growled and took his mom's hand, gladly letting himself be taken back inside. Pruitt watched his family go and turned to Eve the instant the front door was closed.

"How dare you come to my home with this shit," he said. Now he was growling like the Batman.

"You may not have raped her, but you know who did, and instead of helping her, you chose them."

"I'm loyal to the badge," he said.

"So am I. To me, that means loyalty to what the badge represents, not to the people who wear it. One of the deputies that you protected went on to rape two other women." Now she got in his face, staring him in the eye, letting him see her anger. "That's on you."

He shook his head.

"Oh yes, it is. You're also an accessory after the fact in the rape and murder of Sabrina Morton, for keeping your mouth shut about what you knew."

"Murder? What murder?"

"The day after you warned her to stop asking questions about the rapists with that tattoo"—she pointed to his leg—"someone broke her neck and tossed her body off a cliff. But she wasn't silenced. The truth is coming out, Brad. All of it. Every sordid detail. I'm giving you the opportunity to get on the right side of this, or go down with the rest of them."

Pruitt couldn't look at her. "I've got a family."

"We've all got families," Eve said and walked away to see hers.

CHAPTER FIFTEEN

There was something creepy to Eve about her younger brother, Kenny, living a block away from the house they grew up in. Going to visit him was like driving into the past, and not in a good way. She wondered why, out of all the places to live in Los Angeles with his wife and daughter, he had to pick this neighborhood. She didn't have fond memories of her time here, she thought, so how could he?

The actual house Jen rented was gone now, torn down to build a McMansion that was way too big for the narrow lot, and even though it was brick and mortar and not a living thing, it still looked to Eve as she drove past like it was sucking in its walls to fit and might suddenly explode into its true size. If it ever did, the wreckage would probably hit Kenny's place on the next street.

His house was a tiny two-bedroom, one-bath ranch-style house on a long, narrow lot, with a detached garage in the backyard. Eve knocked on the front door promptly at noon, holding her present for Cassidy in the Walmart bag.

Kenny opened the door, wearing a stained apron and smelling of hickory smoke. Even though he was married, and a father, she couldn't get over the feeling that he was a little kid playing house. He hadn't outgrown his boyishness and she hoped he never did.

"Noon on the button, I knew it." Kenny stepped out and gave Eve a kiss. "Have you ever been fashionably late for anything?"

"There's nothing fashionable about being late," Eve said as she stepped inside. "Besides, I wanted to prep Cassie's gift." She held up the Walmart bag.

"Great," Kenny said, closing the door. "Because I hate assembling toys."

The house was recently renovated by someone who'd watched a lot of HGTV fixer-upper shows, so Eve stepped inside an open-concept living room / kitchen that opened out to the awning-covered backyard, where there was an outdoor dining set, making the outside like another room.

"No assembly required," Eve said. "I have to bury some things in the garden for Cassie to dig up."

"I hope it's not bodies," said Rachel, Kenny's apron-clad wife, as she walked around the kitchen's peninsula to greet her. "Even if they are dolls."

"Of course not," Eve said, giving Rachel a hug. "What kind of aunt do you think I am?"

"You gave Cassie a badge and a gun last year," Rachel said. "I thought you might be moving on to crime scene investigation."

"It's a treasure-hunting kit," she said and decided it was better if they never knew that the gift was suggested by a forensic anthropologist at a crime scene.

Cassidy came bounding down the hall, shrieking, "Auntie Eve!"

She wrapped herself tightly around Eve, who hugged her back and gave her a kiss.

"I can't believe how old you are," Eve said. "Pretty soon you'll be driving."

"Did you know I'm having two birthdays?" Cassidy said, holding up two fingers.

"No, I didn't."

"One today with you and one tomorrow with my friends at a Chuck E. Cheese," Cassidy said. "Want to come?"

Eve would have rather had a colonoscopy. "I wish I could, but it's for kids only."

Rachel held her hand out to Cassidy. "Do you want to help me decorate the cookies?"

Of course Cassidy did, because she knew it meant eating half of them and licking all the frosting in the bowl. Eve went outside with Kenny, who was firing up the grill for smoked spareribs, and buried the treasure chest in the flower garden behind the garage. She came back just as the doorbell rang and Kenny went to answer it.

Lisa stepped in, carrying a wrapped birthday present, and kissed her brother. She had curly black hair and was shorter, and plumper, than Eve, thanks to having different fathers, but they both shared their mother's piercing blue eyes. "I hope you don't mind, but I brought a date."

"Of course not," Kenny said.

Lisa stepped aside to let her date in. "This is my friend, Mitch Sawyer."

He came in wearing a vintage bowling shirt, shorts, and flip-flops, a gym bag slung over his shoulder.

"Aha!" Eve said, marching into the house, a playful grin on her face. "Now the whole evil plot becomes clear."

"There is no plot," Lisa said. "It's totally innocent."

Kenny looked back and forth between his sisters. "You've lost me. What's going on?"

Eve pointed to Mitch. "He's my torturer."

"Physical therapist," Mitch said, then looked at Eve. "I assure you none of this was premeditated."

"Notice the choice of words," Eve said. "He clearly knows he's talking to a cop."

"He really is the best therapist for you and he works in Calabasas," Lisa said. "Close to your home and office, just like I said."

"But you didn't tell me you were dating."

"We aren't," she said.

"I bumped into Lisa at the hospital yesterday," Mitch said. "When she mentioned the party, and that you'd be here, I sort of invited myself along. I figured it was the only way to be sure I'd see you for another session. I brought my stuff . . ."

He slipped his gym bag off his shoulder. The truth, Eve assumed, was that Mitch and Lisa were either already romantically involved or he wanted them to be. Or perhaps it was the other way around: Lisa was interested in Mitch and using her sister as an excuse to bring them together. Either way, Eve was being used, which wouldn't have bothered her if there wasn't physical therapy involved.

"Oh joy," Eve said, and gave her sister a nasty look. "I'm going to get you for this."

But before she could, Cassidy came running over, covered in frosting, to give her aunt Lisa a hug and stain her clothes. *Thank you, Cassie, I owe you one,* Eve thought.

Mitch ran Eve through her wrist exercises at the outdoor table while Lisa watched him work. Kenny was busy at the grill with his ribs, while Rachel and Cassidy were preparing a salad in the kitchen.

"I saw on the news that you found another body in the hills," Mitch said.

"The fire wiped the hills clean, exposing everything that's been hidden in the brush and ravines for years," Eve said, doing curls with only her wrist, the rubber ball in her hand. It might as well have been a fifty-pound barbell. "Cars, furniture, even the wreckage of a small plane from thirty years ago."

"Wow," Lisa said. "It must be hard to figure out what's happened to those two women when all you've got to work with is charred bones."

"You'd be surprised what even burned bones can reveal," Eve said, letting go of the ball, her wrist weak. "I met a guy who can look at a bone fragment and tell you amazing details about the person it came from."

"Amazing details, huh?" Lisa shot a smile at Mitch, who smiled back.

"What?" Eve said.

"You like him," Lisa said.

"He's very good at his job," Eve said.

Lisa's smile got bigger. "What else is he good at?"

Eve didn't like where this conversation was going, especially not in front of her physical therapist. That was when the front door burst open and Jen Ronin blew in, carrying two identical bags from Sephora. Jen was on her third set of breast implants (these were, in Jen's own words, "downsized"), her face had been stretched tight enough for Ringo Starr to play "Here Comes the Sun" on her cheeks, her hair was colored black, and her eyebrows had been plucked into an expression of permanent bemusement by a Vulcan stylist. She wore a colorful Chico's three-quarter-sleeve blouse that looked like it had been worn by a painter at work, and a pair of pink Lululemon capris that showed off her butt-lift and excellent legs.

Kenny set down his BBQ tongs and glanced at Eve. "This is fashionably late."

"No, it's just late," Eve said. "Like always."

"Where is the birthday girl!" Jen declared.

Cassidy came running out of the kitchen and hugged her grandmother. Jen handed her one of the Sephora bags. "Happy birthday, this is for you."

"What is it?" Cassidy asked as Eve, Lisa, Kenny, and Rachel gathered around.

"Concealer. Foundation. Blush. Mascara. Eye shadow. Lipstick. Eyeliner. Nail polish and sticky boobs," Jen said.

"Sticky boobs?" Cassidy asked, confused.

"She's five, Jen," Rachel said. "She doesn't have boobs."

"Now she can pretend that she does," Jen said, then smiled at Cassidy. "You're going to get a big-girl makeover."

"I am a big girl now!" Cassidy said.

"Yes, you are," Jen said and handed the other Sephora bag to Eve. "I got the same present for you."

"It's not my birthday," Eve said.

"I saw you on TV. You need a big-girl makeover, too."

"Nothing for me, Mom?" Lisa asked.

"You're perfect as you are," Jen said and spotted Mitch. "Well, hello. Who is this?"

"Mitch Sawyer," he said.

"Eve's physical therapist," Lisa said.

Jen nodded in approval. "It's about time she got some physical therapy."

"It's for my wrist," Eve said. "And he came with Lisa, not me."

"Actually, I'm just leaving," Mitch said, slinging his bag over his shoulder. "It was a pleasure meeting you all." He looked at Eve. "See you on Tuesday."

As Mitch went out, he had to squeeze past a woman coming in. She was black, in her thirties, wearing a blouse and slacks, as if she were heading to a boardroom rather than a five-year-old's birthday party.

"I also brought a guest," Jen said. "This is my friend Simone Harper."

"It's wonderful to finally meet you," Simone said, a slight Southern twang to her voice. "I've heard so much about y'all from Jen."

Eve smelled a setup. "How do you and Mom know each other?"

"Actually, your father introduced us," Simone said. "Vince and I worked together on *Hollywood & the Vine*."

Eve felt her anger rising. "You're a TV writer."

"Oh, she's much more than that," Jen said. "She's the creator of *Playing Doctor*."

Eve knew the show. It was a big hit about a headstrong woman, Tessa Goode, who took over her father's medical practice in a remote corner of Alaska after he died . . . even though she wasn't actually a trained, licensed doctor. Tessa learned everything she knew about medicine by growing up at his side. But without her, there would be no health care for the townspeople. So the town helped Dr. Goode maintain the charade because they trusted her and needed her.

"She wanted to get a feel for our family and bring that reality to your show," Jen said.

"You have a show?" Lisa asked.

"No, I don't," Eve said. She was getting very, very tired of this.

"You do if you want," Jen said.

"Half-woman, half-plant, all cop," Kenny said, doing the announcer voice from the opening of *Hollywood & the Vine*. "That could be you."

"Yes, it could," Simone said to Eve. "Unless you take charge of your story."

How many times had Eve heard that line this week? It was like everybody had teamed up to work on her, hammering the same points over and over.

"She's right," Jen said. "And she's got three Emmys, a Peabody, a Humanitas, and a WGA award to prove it."

Simone smiled. "Your mom left out my thirty-two patches and forty-three badges I earned in Girl Scouts."

Eve turned to Simone. "Could I have a word with you out front?"

The two women went outside, Eve closing the door behind them. She walked Simone to the sidewalk. "Mom made a mistake bringing you here."

"I thought I might be crossing a line, and I apologize if I've offended you, but it was a risk I was willing to take," Simone said. "That's how passionate I am about your show."

"There is no show," Eve stated, hoping it would finally stick.

"There will be, Eve, and I think I am the best person to write it . . . because I understand your character."

"We just met," Eve said. "You don't know me at all."

"I'd like to," Simone said, undeterred. "That's why I've been talking to your parents."

"They don't know me, either."

"So tell me who you are," Simone said.

"I'm sorry, but that's not going to happen."

Simone gave her an appraising, appreciative look. "I see a lot of Dr. Goode in you."

"I'm not pretending to be a cop. I am one."

"But you have so many of her qualities. You're stubborn, daring, and determined to do whatever it takes to get the job done, even if you aren't entirely sure you know what you are doing. You fought hard to get where you are, but you're not sure you deserve it, even if you've already proven yourself with a big success. That's all me, too," Simone said. "I can do your story justice. Ultimately, isn't that what you want?"

"I'm interested in an entirely different kind of justice and it has nothing to do with me or some TV show," Eve said.

"You can have both," Simone said. "Your story will be told, Eve, and I am the best person to tell it. I'm glad I finally met you. I hope we can talk again."

Simone smiled and went to the Porsche Cayenne parked behind her mom's red Miata convertible. Eve went back inside and was immediately confronted by her mother.

"That was the rudest thing I've ever seen in my life," Jen said. "Now Simone is going to think you're a racist."

"What?" Eve was used to her mom's irrational outbursts, but this one took her by surprise. "Why?"

"You just threw a black woman out of the house."

"I didn't throw anybody out."

"She's not here, is she?" Jen said.

"Don't make this about me. You used Cassie's birthday as an excuse to ambush me with a writer I didn't want to meet. That's what was rude."

Jen smirked. "But it's okay for your sister to bring a physical therapist you didn't want to see."

Eve shot an angry glance at Lisa. "I'm not wild about that, either."

"Wait," Lisa said, looking at Jen. "How did you know Eve was avoiding her physical therapy?"

"Because I know my children," Jen said.

"Enough," Rachel said, coming out of the kitchen and facing Eve, Jen, and Lisa. "This is Cassie's birthday, remember? Are you here for her? Or is it all about Eve?"

Eve felt unfairly targeted, since she had nothing to do with Mitch or Simone being brought over. But she took ownership of the situation anyway.

"I'm sorry," Eve said. "You're absolutely right."

So they spent the next hour eating ribs, and chips, and cake, and cookies, and completely ignoring the salad. Then Cassidy opened her presents. Eve spent a half hour helping her find and dig up the treasure. Cassidy couldn't believe there was treasure in her own backyard and insisted on wearing most of the jewelry she discovered. Finally, the women spent another hour or so letting Jen put makeup on their faces. Cassidy absolutely loved the big-girl experience and the big-girl look.

Eve wanted to wipe the makeup off her face the instant her mom was done, despite the oohs and aahs she got from everyone. But she'd wait until she got home out of consideration to the others. It was true, Eve did look great with the makeup, and she knew it, but it made her very uncomfortable. It felt like she was wearing a mask and yet, at the same time, asking to be noticed.

"This is how you should look every day," Jen said. "Take a picture so you won't forget."

"We aren't allowed to wear this much makeup at work."

"There's a rule against detectives looking gorgeous?"

"Yes," Eve said.

Her mother stroked Eve's hair and gave her a kiss on the cheek. "You're not fooling anybody. Beauty isn't a weakness or a disguise, honey. It's a strength. You should start using it, too."

It was early evening. Jen had headed back to Ventura and Rachel was giving Cassidy a bath before bed. Eve, Lisa, and Kenny were sitting around the table outside, eating what was left of the cake and frosting with their hands. These were the moments Eve truly loved and missed the most, the time alone with her siblings, just being together. That was what their nights were like so often when they were growing up, their mom off spending the night with some guy she met. Now that Eve thought about it, maybe not all her memories of living in this neighborhood were so bad.

Kenny licked some frosting off his finger. "Why are you fighting so hard against a TV show being made about you?"

"I don't want my life turned into entertainment," Eve said.

"Those YouTube videos didn't bother you," Kenny said. "We must have watched them a hundred times together."

"Because that was me, doing my job. This would be fiction."

Lisa said, "You don't think people can tell the difference?"

"They will if Brie Larson is playing her," Kenny said.

"That would be so great," Lisa said.

"No it wouldn't," Eve said. "I want to be taken seriously as a cop. If there's a TV show about me, my life won't be my own anymore. It will be a character I'm supposed to play. People will expect me to be Brie Larson."

"That sounds to me like an argument for being involved in the show," Lisa said.

Eve shook her head. "If I'm not a part of it, I can disavow it. I can honestly say it's not me, and has nothing to do with me. My life will be my own."

Kenny said, "Like that distinction will matter to anybody."

"It will to me."

"What a bunch of bullshit," Lisa said. "This isn't about you, your image, or your career. It's all about Mom . . . and Vince."

Kenny nodded. "You're right."

Eve felt her anger flash at the mere mention of Vince's name. "This has nothing to do with them."

"Of course it does," Lisa said. "You're opposed to the show because Mom and Vince will benefit from your success, and you'll be damned if you're going to let them."

"Why should I?" Eve said. The idea was outrageous. No, it was more than that. It was offensive. "Vince knocked Mom up, abandoned her, and wouldn't pay a dime of child support . . . but now she's willing to forget all that if he'll help her take advantage of me . . . because it's not enough that she stole my childhood using me as her live-in babysitter, cook, maid, and driver. Is she insane? And what about Vince? He didn't want to spend a penny supporting me, or a minute seeing me, but now that ascot-wearing shitbag wants to make money off my back. Well, fuck them both."

There was a long moment of silence and Eve became aware of her flushed face and the smug expressions on her siblings.

"I rest my case," Lisa said.

"You didn't make a case."

"I didn't have to," she said. "You confessed."

Kenny laughed and scooped up a gob of frosting with his finger. "Maybe you should be a cop, too."

Eve knew Lisa was right but would be damned if she'd admit it. So she stole a bite of cake instead.

"So what if Mom gets a part and Vince gets to direct?" Lisa said. "How does that hurt you?"

"It rewards their bad behavior."

"You have to let go of the past," she said.

"Like I have," Kenny said. "Instead of resenting Mom for the woman she was, I love her for the great grandmother she is today."

She was wonderful with Cassidy, Eve thought. But that was easy for Jen. It came with no responsibility.

"I have a lot of fun with her now that we're adults," Lisa said. "Nobody makes me laugh as much as Mom does."

"That's because she doesn't want anything from you," Eve said. "Or tell you how awful you look on TV."

"You do look awful on TV," Kenny said.

"Thanks."

"You're forgetting the most important thing about Hollywood calling," he said. "The big money."

"I don't need the money."

"So put it all in a college fund for Cassie. We're working two jobs and barely getting by."

"You could pay off my student loans, so I could have something called"—Lisa used air quotes now—"a savings account."

"I've heard of those," Kenny said.

Eve smiled at her siblings. "You're as bad as Mom and Vince. Is there anybody who doesn't want something out of this show?"

"You," Kenny said. "At least not that you'll admit. You should think about how you can use the show to get what you want at work."

"I have what I want."

"For now," Lisa said. "But what about tomorrow?"

CHAPTER SIXTEEN

On Sunday, Eve decided to clear her head, and get the rust out of her joints, by going on her first real bike ride since she broke her wrist. Within only a few minutes, Eve was lost in the motion, becoming one with the road and the wind, and felt freed from herself. The sense of absolute, natural balance, of being centered and true, was something she wished she could feel all the time. She came home at the end of the day exhausted and yet somehow revitalized.

Monday started with a call from Nan, officially notifying Duncan and Eve that Debbie Crawford was murdered, most likely struck in the head with some sort of gardening implement. Eve didn't reveal that Daniel had already given her a heads-up on Friday.

There was nothing Eve and Duncan could do on the Sabrina Morton case until the DNA results came back, so they drove out in an unmarked Explorer to see Nick Egan, who was the only person they knew of so far with a hate for Crawford.

Eve and Duncan drove up to the front gate of Egan's mansion, rolled down the driver's-side window, and pressed the button on the intercom mounted on a freestanding brick pillar with a stone lion on top.

"Who are you?" a voice asked.

"I'm Detective Eve Ronin with the Los Angeles Sheriff's Department. I'm here with my partner, Duncan Pavone. We're here to talk with Nick Egan about his missing neighbor."

"Can you please hold up your ID to the camera?"

Eve took out her badge and held it up to the camera lens embedded in the pillar. An instant later, the ornate iron gates swung open and she drove along a curving driveway into a wide cobblestone motor court. There was a tall manicured hedge and several oak trees separating Egan's property from Crawford's.

"This reminds me of my house," Duncan said. "Only fifteen thousand square feet bigger."

They got out of the car just as Nick Egan emerged from his front door. He wore a faded, untucked denim work shirt and jeans and cowboy boots, as if he were in Montana and getting ready to break a horse.

"Stan mentioned you two might be coming up," Nick said, not bothering to introduce himself, since he assumed everybody already knew who he was.

"Did Stan say why?" Duncan asked.

"No, but I can make an educated guess. I was FBI Special Agent Mack Bennett on three seasons of *G-Girls*, you know."

"Of course I do," Eve said. He'd played the handler of three female FBI agents who worked undercover as Las Vegas strippers. Vince directed an episode entitled "Tassels of Terror." "It's the show that empowered women and made me want to become a cop."

Nick wagged a finger at her. "You're teasing me."

Eve smiled. "Yes I am."

"You two came here because you're wondering if I strangled my crazy neighbor and tossed her in the canyon."

"Did you?" Duncan asked.

"I didn't, but God knows I was tempted." Nick waved his arm, gesturing for them to follow him.

He led them around the side of the house to the backyard, where there was a huge infinity pool with a swim-up bar in a stone grotto that was under a waterfall and slide, all against the backdrop of a spectacular view of the blackened mountains. There was a hot tub with a firepit in the center, an outdoor kitchen with a pizza oven, and a gazebo with another bar and a huge flat-screen television. The landscaping was lush and tropical, with mature palm trees everywhere. A big-boned, big-breasted, broad-shouldered blonde woman in a bikini was sunbathing on one of the many chaise longues around the yard.

"What did she do that made you so angry?" Eve asked.

"I'm sure Stan must've told you," Nick said. "She was on my ass from the day I broke ground on this place, calling the city every time we hammered a nail, and it got worse as time went on. If I grilled a hamburger, she'd call the fire department. If I pulled a weed, she'd call the coastal commission. She was determined to drive me off."

"I think what she really wanted was the opposite," the blonde woman said. "She wanted to fuck you."

"Detectives," Nick said, waving an arm in the woman's direction. "This is Inga, my publicist."

"I majored in psychology in Sweden before I got into PR," Inga said.

"I don't see how constantly calling building inspectors, the forestry service, and the police on me would get me to fuck her."

"She was sublimating," Inga said. "She knew she couldn't have you, so she fought her desire by trying to drive you away. As her lust increased, so did her counterresponse."

"That would explain why she filmed me getting a blow job," Nick said. "It wasn't to extort me into moving away. She got off on it."

Eve glanced at the hot tub where the blow job occurred, then over her shoulder toward Crawford's property. There was an oak tree and, beyond that, she could see the roof of Crawford's house. She also saw that a security camera was mounted in one of Egan's eaves and aimed at the pool.

"She put the video on the internet to obfuscate her real reason for watching you," Inga said. "Erotic obsession."

"Sublimate and obfuscate," Nick said. "That's Inga's degree talking."

He smiled at the detectives. Eve guessed that meant their little performance was over. It was a nice scene, with a cute button at the end. She wondered if they'd written and rehearsed it.

Duncan spoke up. "That's certainly an interesting explanation of Mrs. Crawford's behavior."

"But you don't buy it," Nick said.

"Nope."

"You think she was just crazy."

"Or maybe she was genuinely irritated about her peace being disturbed."

"Well, it all worked out for the best," Nick said.

"How do you figure that?" Eve asked. "She's dead."

"Yes, but she's at peace," Nick said somberly. "And so am I."

"That's very touching," Duncan said. "Can you account for your whereabouts the day she disappeared?"

"Not offhand. I'd have to go back and check my calendar," Nick said. "Why do you ask? Was she murdered?"

"We don't know yet," Duncan said. "We're just covering all the bases."

"That's a cliché," Nick said. "I've used that line a hundred times on *G-Girls*, and each time I did, the audience knew that Mack Bennett was really saying: 'We know you're the killer, you sick bastard, and we're gonna take you down.'"

Eve said, "What about the guy who says he has to go back and check his calendar?"

Nick gave her a sheepish grin. "He was always guilty."

Eve and Duncan left Egan's place, got in their Explorer, drove out the gate, and made a sharp U-turn into Celeste Crawford's driveway. She didn't have a gate, or a motor court, and was waiting for them on her porch, as if she was expecting them. The detectives got out of the car.

"Ms. Crawford, this is my partner, Duncan Pavone," Eve said.

Duncan said, "I'm sorry for your loss."

"Thank you. I saw you drive up next door and thought you might stop by. Why did you want to talk to Nick?"

Before Eve could answer, Duncan spoke up. "You have a gorgeous garden. Do you mind if I look around? My wife is always looking for landscaping ideas."

They lived in a condo. Eve knew that the only landscaping she did was water her potted plants.

"Not at all," Celeste said, and turned back to Eve, expecting an answer to her question.

"Your mom's death is still an open investigation, and I wanted to get his side of the feud," Eve said. "May I go upstairs? I'd like to see what his house looks like from here."

"It looks like the Berlin Wall, without the guard towers. But sure, go ahead." Celeste brought her inside, up the wooden staircase, to the master bedroom, which looked as if it hadn't been touched since her mother disappeared, except to dust and keep the cobwebs out.

Eve peered out the window. One of Egan's windows was directly across from hers. Crawford had a view of Egan's backyard, if she twisted her body and craned her neck, but most of it was blocked by an oak tree.

"Has that tree always been there?" Eve asked.

"It's one of the few oaks Nick didn't cut down before Mom got the forestry service on his ass."

Eve checked out the view from the other windows on the second floor. Along the way, she said: "You didn't mention to me that your mom took a video of him engaged in a sex act with a rap star and that she threatened to release it publicly if he didn't move away."

"Because that's a lie. If she was going to threaten him with anything, it would have been the picture she took of him watching her through his bedroom window and jerking off."

"You didn't mention that, either."

Celeste shrugged. "It's ancient history."

The revelations about the feud between the two neighbors were getting uglier every day and it seemed to Eve that violence would have been a likely escalation in their dispute. "Did Egan know she had the photo?"

"I have no idea," Celeste said.

"What did your mother do with the photo? Did she show it to anybody?"

"I don't know and I don't care. I certainly don't want to start a war over it now." Celeste went downstairs and Eve followed.

"Because you want to live in harmony with your neighbor?"

Celeste crossed to the front door and opened it for Eve. "Actually, it's not an issue anymore."

"Why not?" Eve asked as she stepped outside.

Celeste went out with her. "I agreed to sell him the house yesterday."

"Why did you change your mind?"

"Mom is never coming back. It's time to get on with my life, and it's not here. This is the past."

Duncan came around from behind the house. "It's so beautiful here. A little piece of paradise."

"You missed your chance to buy it," Eve said. "Ms. Crawford just sold it to Nick Egan."

"Congratulations," Duncan said to Celeste. "Will you be taking anything with you?"

Celeste nodded toward the flower garden. "Just the Airstream." Duncan followed her gaze to the flower garden. "And my dad's urn, which is underneath it."

Score one for my instincts, Eve thought.

As soon as Eve steered them onto Latigo Canyon Road, and they were heading toward Kanan Dume, Eve filled him in on everything else that she'd learned from Celeste and then asked: "What were you up to, Columbo?"

"I checked out the garden shed. It was full of dust, cobwebs, and rat droppings. There's a chance the hand tools haven't been used since Debbie Crawford's death. I'm going to call a judge, get a warrant, and send CSU out here to check 'em out."

"You really think we'll find the murder weapon in there?" she asked.

Duncan shrugged.

"That's a long shot," Eve said as she steered them around the tight curves. It surprised her there weren't more cars, motorcycles, and people going off the side of the road. But it would be fun to ride on her bike.

"I don't think the killer brought a weeding fork with her," Duncan said. "I think the murder was a spontaneous act and she grabbed whatever was within reach as a weapon."

"*Her?* You think Celeste killed her mom?"

"I was being sex neutral. I used *her* as I would *him* in deference to you and your sensitivities. That said, sure, why not? We should check out Celeste's story. She's pointing us real hard at her neighbor."

"I can see why. Because he's a creep who had plenty of motive. I don't see Celeste's motive."

"Greed. She wanted to sell the place and her mother wouldn't," Duncan said.

"How do you know that was an issue between them?"

"I don't, but two days after we find her mom's body, Celeste unloads the place. Seems awfully fast to me. We should also look into the women who came to see her mom the morning she disappeared. Maybe they killed her."

"Why would they do that?"

"Maybe she slept with all of their husbands and they teamed up for vengeance. I like to keep an open mind to all possibilities."

"I'm glad to hear that," Eve said and tossed her phone into his lap. "Check out the video I downloaded into my photo library."

He fumbled around with the phone for a minute, then started playing the Nick Egan blow job video. Eve couldn't see it, but she could hear it.

"It's like an episode of *G-Girls*," Duncan said. "If it was done for Cinemax."

"There is no way Debbie Crawford could have shot that video from the high angle you're seeing. Either someone was in the tree or it came from the security camera on Egan's house."

"Maybe she climbed up the tree."

"She just had a knee replacement, remember?" Eve said. "It was a setup, and a lame one, to discredit her."

"How come she never fought it?"

"Because she disappeared the day it went viral," Eve said.

"That doesn't mean Egan killed her," he said.

Eve made a sharp right turn onto Kanan and headed north toward the freeway. "Why are you still watching that?"

"I'm invested in the story now. I want to see how it ends."

"Stop it. You know how it ends," Eve said. "I went out to Egan's place for the first time today and I knew right away the video was bogus. Garvey has been out there a dozen times. He had to know the instant he saw the video that it was staged, that there was no way Crawford shot it. But he kept his mouth shut."

"Maybe Tubbs isn't as observant as you are."

"What about that picture Crawford had of Egan masturbating while peeking into her bedroom?"

"We don't know if that picture ever existed."

"What if it did? Did she tell Garvey about it? And if she did, why didn't he file a report? I'll tell you why. Because he was protecting Egan. How far did that protection go?"

Duncan rubbed his temples. "Are you on a crusade against every officer in the sheriff's department or only the ones at Lost Hills?"

"I'm just following the evidence where it leads, and it keeps coming right back to our squad room."

Eve's phone rang and the caller ID read: Burnside.

"Put it on speaker," Eve said. Duncan did as she asked and held the phone up between them. "This is Eve, Counselor. I've got Duncan with me."

"I've got the DNA results from Josie Wallace's bikini and sundress," Burnside said.

"That was fast."

"It's possible to get DNA in twenty-four hours if it's high priority."

Isn't a rape, any rape, a high priority? Eve thought. *How many more women get raped by the same perpetrator while detectives wait months, years, or even decades for DNA results?* But that wasn't an argument Eve was going to pick with Burnside, who wasn't responsible for the systemic problems.

Duncan said, "I didn't know you had that kind of juice."

"I don't," Burnside said. "But the DA does."

The district attorney had a very public grudge against Sheriff Lansing for reinstating a deputy the previous sheriff had fired for stalking his ex-wife. Eve thought perhaps the DA sensed an opportunity for a takedown. The case was already political. *That didn't take long,* she thought.

"We got positive matches on Towler, Harding, and Frankel," Burnside said. "But nothing on Nakamura."

Duncan stared at Eve in disbelief. "You took a DNA sample from Nakamura?"

Eve shrugged. "I wondered if preventing a scandal was his only reason for covering up for the deputies."

"You've got balls."

"I know Frankel has the Great White tattoo," Burnside said. "I just looked it up in the file on his previous prosecution for sexual assault. There's a picture of the tattoo as one of his identifying features. But do we know Towler and Harding have the tattoo?"

"I've seen it on Towler," Duncan said. "But we're gambling on Harding."

"I'll bet my badge that he does," Eve said.

"It's too late for that. You've bet your badge already. But I'll take the gamble," Burnside said. "It's time to bring Lansing into this. We need to arrest Towler and Harding as soon as possible."

"What about arresting Nakamura?" Eve asked. "We know he sabotaged the rape investigation."

"You *think* he did," Burnside said. "There's no actual evidence of wrongdoing. Any action against Nakamura will be the sheriff's call. Speaking of which, we need to brief Lansing in person. Today."

"If the three of us show up at headquarters," Eve said, "Nakamura will know what's coming and might tip off Towler and Harding."

"Lansing is out of the office this morning," Burnside said. "But I know where we can find him."

CHAPTER SEVENTEEN

On the way to the DoubleTree hotel in Culver City, where Lansing was speaking at a luncheon for the Southern California Association of Collegiate Women Entrepreneurs, Duncan called a judge he knew and managed to smooth-talk a search warrant out of him. Then Duncan called Nan to get a CSU unit out to Crawford's place. He finished his calls as Eve pulled into the DoubleTree parking lot. The hotel was wedged between the San Diego Freeway, Sepulveda Boulevard, and Dinah's Fried Chicken, a couple of miles north of LAX.

"Shouldn't we notify Celeste that her mother was murdered before we send a crime scene team out to her place?" Eve said.

"I have a more important and pressing question to consider," Duncan said. "Do you think we have time to grab some fried chicken before we talk to Lansing?"

Eve and Duncan decided the answer to both questions was no. If they told Celeste a crime scene unit was coming, and she was the killer, it would give her time to get rid of any evidence she hadn't ditched before. And if they got some chicken, they risked missing Lansing before he headed back to Monterey Park.

They met Burnside in the lobby and went upstairs to the meeting rooms. The sheriff's talk was in the main banquet room and they slipped in the back, unnoticed by the five hundred collegiate women entrepreneurs but not by Sheriff Richard Lansing, who was in uniform at the dais, giving a speech about how small business investment in a community can deter crime. He spotted the ADA, Eve, and Duncan immediately and looked like he was swallowing back acid reflux.

Lansing was at home on the stage. He was the son of a preacher who had his own church out in Beaumont. But when the time came for Lansing to choose between divinity school and the sheriff's academy, he picked wearing a badge over a collar. Even so, he still liked to deliver a sermon.

When the speech was over, Lansing took some photographs with the organizers, then gave some excuse for having to go. Burnside, Eve, and Duncan slipped outside to wait for his arrival.

The sheriff emerged a few moments later, his driver/bodyguard right behind him. Lansing had a grim look on his face. "You didn't come here to rescue me from eating another rubber chicken breast."

The mere mention of chicken made Duncan glance longingly out the window at the Dinah's sign across the street.

"I'm afraid not," Burnside said. "Is there somewhere private we can talk?"

"This way." Lansing led them to a small meeting room and told his driver to stand outside the door and keep people out. Once they were inside, he studied the three of them. "You didn't call ahead and neither did Captain Moffett, so whatever you're bringing me must be a steaming pile of shit involving the Lost Hills station. And whatever it is, it's going to draw the media like flies." He rested his gaze on Eve. "Or you wouldn't be here."

It sounded like an accusation, and since he'd put her on the spot, she decided to be the one to break the bad news.

"Six years ago, three off-duty Lost Hills deputies raped two women on the beach and we believe that the detective investigating the case covered it up."

"Does this have something to do with the woman's bones that were found a few days ago in Calabasas?" Lansing asked. Eve nodded. "So what you're actually saying is that you think these deputies raped *and* murdered her."

Duncan said, "We're still investigating the murder and cover-up, but we can prove the rape."

Lansing looked at Burnside. "How strong is the evidence?"

He knew the prosecutor wouldn't be there if there wasn't a case she thought she could win. But he needed to hear Burnside say it anyway.

"The surviving rape victim can ID the deputies and their tattoo, and we have DNA from their semen on her clothing," she said.

"Tattoo?" Lansing said. "They have the same one?"

"The deputies are inked to show their membership in the Great Whites, a secret society within the ranks of the Lost Hills Patrol Division," Burnside said, leaving out the fact they weren't actually certain that Harding had the tattoo.

"Your boss just loves that 'secret society' bullshit, doesn't he?" Lansing said, well aware that the DA made his name prosecuting the tattooed deputies who were arrested for running a protection racket.

"The judge called it much worse," Burnside said.

Lansing looked at Duncan. "Who are the deputies?"

"Chuck Towler, Dave Harding, and Jimmy Frankel," he said.

The sheriff winced at the mention of Frankel's name. "Frankel? He's in prison for rape and we've already paid out $10 million in settlements to his victims."

"Better get ready to write another big check," Duncan said.

"Okay, so you've proved the rape," Lansing said. "What about the murder case?"

Eve told Lansing about Sabrina's efforts to use the tattoo drawing to identify the three deputies, about the other deputy in the Great Whites who tried to warn her off, and about Sabrina's disappearance the following day.

"The evidence is entirely circumstantial at this point," Lansing said.

"That's true," Burnside said. "But I believe once we get these deputies into an interrogation room, one of them will crack. Even if that doesn't happen, I'm still feeling good about the case. I've won murder convictions with less than we've got now."

"There's one fact you still haven't told me," Lansing said. "Who is the detective that you think covered up for the deputies?"

Eve answered him. "It's Assistant Sheriff Ted Nakamura."

"Shit." Lansing walked across the room, his back to the three of them, and looked out the window at the traffic on the freeway. It couldn't feel good to know that one of his top lieutenants, the man charged with overseeing patrol operations countywide, let some deputies get away with rape. After a moment, Lansing turned and said, "I need a few words alone with Ronin. Could you give us the room?"

Duncan and Burnside went out. Eve wondered what kind of lashing she was in for and why he was excluding Duncan from it.

"Why didn't you come to me with this before going to the DA?"

That answered her question about why he'd singled her out for a chat. He'd guessed that she'd made the decision on her own, without including Duncan. But how did he know? It made no difference. She owned this.

"I don't know how close you and Nakamura are," Eve said. "I was afraid you'd cover it up to protect him and save the department from another scandal."

If he was offended, he didn't show it.

"Don't take me for a fool, Eve. That's not why you did it. You made a political calculation. You know that the DA hates me and wants to be the next mayor. You figured that aligning yourself with him would benefit you more than being tied to a sheriff who is already smeared by a prison-beating scandal."

None of that had occurred to her. She didn't think that way. "All I care about is doing the right thing for the victims. I'm not interested in politics."

"Have you forgotten who you're talking to? I'm the one you used to leverage the popularity of your viral video into a promotion to Robbery-Homicide at Lost Hills."

"You made that decision, not me."

"You know damn well why I did."

"You were playing politics," she said.

"We both were. You knew the pressure I was under then and you know what I am facing now. You saw an opportunity and you took it. Now you're doing it again. That's politics. There's just one thing I want to know," Lansing said, narrowing his eyes at her. "What's your endgame?"

"I don't understand."

"Are you positioning yourself for a run for my office? Or is this all about selling a TV series?"

"I'm just doing my job."

"Your job would still be in the burglary detail in Lancaster if it wasn't for that video," Lansing said. "But I will admit that you proved yourself when you solved that triple murder. You even managed to become a media hero again."

"You got a boost from the press, too. Both times."

"Yes I did. But not this time, will I? You're going to arrest two deputies for rape and possibly murder, reveal a 'secret society' of corrupt deputies, and expose a plot by the department to cover it all up."

"Not the department," she said, "just Nakamura."

"That's not how the media will see it or package it."

"I won't talk to the media unless you tell me to, and even then I will only say what you tell me to say," Eve said. "In other words, sir, you can present the story any way you want as long as the guilty are punished for what they did. The rape, the murder, and the cover-up. That's my endgame."

Lansing looked back out at the traffic again. She could almost hear the gears grinding in his brain. "This all happened six years ago, right?"

Eve immediately knew what he was getting at. The crimes weren't committed under his watch. He was cleaning up the other guy's mess. Lansing could be the hero of this story, even though he was the one who'd promoted Nakamura to assistant sheriff.

"That's correct."

Lansing nodded to himself. He could work with this. He turned back to her. "You informed me the instant that you suspected that deputies might be involved in felonies and that a detective might have helped hide their crimes. I told you to treat this like any other case and that I would back you every step of the way. Are we clear?"

"We are."

"Okay. Send in Burnside, then wait outside. This will only take a minute."

Eve stepped out of the room and waved over Burnside. "The sheriff wants a private word with you."

Burnside went in. Duncan gave Eve an inquiring look. She led him off toward the window, out of earshot of Lansing's driver, where not only could they see the Dinah's sign, but they could smell the fried chicken. Both their stomachs growled.

"The sheriff was with us on this from the get-go," she said. "He let us run with it, wherever it might lead."

"I guess that's what he's telling Burnside. She and the DA will go along with it, even if it makes it a bit harder for them to capitalize on the scandal at his expense."

"I don't care how they spin this, just as long as those deputies are taken off the street."

Lansing opened the door a moment later and waved them over. Eve and Duncan went back inside the room.

"Now that we're all on the same page," Lansing said. "Let's talk about how we arrest these two armed men without anybody getting shot."

It was almost 4:00 p.m. Eve and Duncan sat with Lansing in his black Expedition, which was parked beside their plain-wrap Explorer in an abandoned warehouse on the eastern bank of the Los Angeles River in Glendale, where the 134 freeway met Interstate 5. They waited in silence. Duncan held his jacket over the grease stain that he'd left on his shirt when the four of them were eating from a bucket of Dinah's fried chicken and strategizing at the DoubleTree. Somehow, only Duncan had managed to stain himself.

"Do you often meet people in empty warehouses?" Eve asked the sheriff, who sat in the front passenger seat. "I thought this kind of thing only happened in bad movies."

"You'd be surprised how often it's necessary for me to meet people away from the public eye."

"Or any eyes," said Duncan, who sat beside Eve in the back.

"It's a complicated job that requires unlikely alliances. There are people who don't want to be seen with me and vice versa that I still need to talk with to understand our community or maintain the peace."

Eve asked, "Do you carry around a list of empty warehouses in Los Angeles County?"

Lansing gestured to the driver beside him. The man was so silent and still that Eve almost forgot that he was there. "That's one of Rondo's jobs."

Rondo? Eve thought. What kind of name was that?

At precisely 4:00 p.m. a black Lincoln MKZ came in and parked beside the Expedition.

"Right on time," Lansing said.

Ted Nakamura got out of his car and eyed the plain-wrap Explorer suspiciously. Lansing got out of the Expedition first.

"Thank you for coming out, Ted."

It wasn't as if Nakamura really had a choice. "What's the situation?"

"You are."

Eve and Duncan emerged from the back of the Expedition and Nakamura stiffened up. He looked at Lansing and said: "I don't understand."

"Tomorrow we're arresting Deputies Charles Towler and Dave Harding for rape. Murder charges are likely to follow. The question I'm wrestling with now is whether Detectives Ronin and Pavone should also arrest you for obstruction of justice and accessory after the fact."

"If I could just have a word in private—" Nakamura began.

"Why do you think we're here and not at headquarters or in your living room?" Lansing interrupted. "If you have something to say, say it."

"You're going to humiliate yourself and the department if you arrest anybody. Ronin and Pavone don't have a case against Towler or Harding, much less me," Nakamura said. "It's all circumstantial and built on Ronin's vivid imagination. She's let her emotions run wild."

"That's what you told me," Eve said. "But we know more than you think we do. We know Sabrina Morton remembered that her rapists had the same tattoos, the ones worn by deputies at Lost Hills. We know she had an artist make a drawing of the tattoos and then she came to see you with it. We know you didn't report it and tried to discourage her. We know she showed the drawing around Malibu anyway and that a deputy warned her off."

"You don't *know* anything," Nakamura said. "It's what you *believe*. You don't have evidence to support any of it. You don't have Sabrina Morton's testimony. You don't have the DNA. You don't have anything."

"Sabrina wasn't the only one they raped that night. They also raped her roommate," Eve said. Nakamura looked bewildered. "You didn't know about her because she didn't step forward until now. She says Sabrina came to you with the drawing. She also identified the tattoos and she picked the deputies out of a photo array."

"You're making a rookie mistake," Nakamura said. "This woman, whoever she is, told you what you wanted to hear, or worse, you coached her, intentionally or not. But even if what she says is true, which I seriously doubt, it's meaningless without DNA."

"We have that, too," Eve said.

Nakamura wasn't shaken. "No you don't."

"You sound very confident, Teddy," Duncan said. "Is that because you tossed the rape kit or altered the case number so it would never be found?"

"I won't dignify that with an answer. The fact is, you don't have the DNA, end of story." Nakamura turned to Lansing. "I can't believe that you're seriously considering any of this. There's no case here against anybody. What we have is a rookie with an agenda and a fat old detective who should have retired years ago."

"We don't have the rape kit," Eve said, "but we have the bathing suit the other victim wore that night." Nakamura turned back to Eve. She could see his confidence was cracking. "The DNA matches Towler, Harding, and Jimmy Frankel."

Nakamura swallowed hard. His throat had gone dry, which Eve knew was an involuntary response to stress. A tell. He said, "I don't see how that changes anything."

"I do," Lansing said. "The only question I have is just how much you knew about the rape and murder when you covered up the crimes. So you'd better start talking, Ted, and when you do, we need to hear the truth. Because how honest you are now will determine whether you leave here in handcuffs or not."

"What does the 'or not' mean? I just drive away as if nothing happened?"

"I take your badge and gun. You go home and say nothing about this case or this conversation to anyone. You retire, effective immediately, and never work in law enforcement in any capacity again. You move out of Southern California, preferably to another state or country, where the odds of any of us ever seeing your face again are the same as encountering Bigfoot, extraterrestrials, or Elvis."

Eve hated the offer Lansing was making, but Burnside had made a convincing argument at the DoubleTree that the case against Nakamura was hardly a slam dunk. The trial would be profoundly embarrassing for the department and, rather than proving a crime, might only succeed in establishing that Nakamura was a lousy detective who'd nonetheless managed to rise to the highest ranks. On the upside, no matter how it turned out, Nakamura would be publicly shamed and professionally ruined.

He seemed to be making that same calculation as he stared at the floor and considered the sheriff's offer.

When Nakamura looked up again, his decision made, he pinned his gaze on Eve and said: "What did Sabrina Morton think was going to happen, going to the beach half-naked, drinking, and doing drugs with a bunch of guys? C'mon. We all know she wasn't raped. She simply got more of what she wanted than she'd bargained for. Girls who behave like her know the risks of their drinking, drugs, and promiscuity. They deserve whatever they get. But I did my job—I took the report and sent the rape kit in, knowing it would be years if it was ever tested. By then, she wouldn't want to pursue charges anyway. She'd be married, with two kids, and wouldn't want the reminder of what an irresponsible slut she was in her youth."

Nakamura stared at Eve as he said every word, as if checking to see if he'd managed to provoke her. But she kept her face impassive, or at least she hoped that she did. Eve didn't want to give him the satisfaction of seeing how much his words offended her, how sickened she was by his opinion of rape victims. He shifted his gaze to Duncan. "You know that's true, Donuts. We've seen it happen."

"She came back to you later with the drawing of the tattoo," Duncan said, ignoring Nakamura's comment. "You knew then, without a doubt, that it was Lost Hills deputies who'd raped her."

"They *fucked* her," Nakamura said. "There's a difference."

"Did you warn them that she remembered their tattoos?"

"Warn who? I didn't know which deputies were involved. There were probably at least thirty or forty deputies out there with that tattoo. But I knew what the result would be if her accusations came out. It would be a huge scandal for the department. I wasn't going to let that happen. Why should we all be tarnished by the conduct of a few basically good guys who partied a little too hard with loose girls? Why should their careers be destroyed by a momentary lapse in judgment? So I didn't report the tattoos and I changed the case file number so it wouldn't match the kit if the result ever came back."

"You did more than that," Eve said. "When Sabrina started showing the drawing of the tattoo around on the beach, you sent Deputy Pruitt to warn her off."

Nakamura shook his head. "This is the first time I've heard anything about her showing the tattoo to anybody but me and I don't remember any deputy named Pruitt."

Eve didn't know if that was true, but given everything else that he'd admitted, she didn't see why he'd lie about this one detail. "What did you think happened to Sabrina when her parents reported her missing?"

"That she'd run off with some guy," said Nakamura. "I really didn't care. I was just glad that she was gone."

Eve really wanted to punch him in the mouth. "It never occurred to you that she might've been murdered by the deputies who'd raped her?"

"Not for one second."

Lansing walked up to Nakamura and faced him. "What about after her bones were found? What about after you knew for a fact that she was killed? What did you think then?"

"That this is a case where the only outcome of pursuing it further would be that everybody loses."

"Not as much as Sabrina Morton did."

"That's done. She is dead and nothing will bring her back to life. Then and now, I did what I thought was best for the department."

Lansing glanced at Eve and Duncan, then shifted his gaze back to Nakamura. "You're a disgrace to the badge. Take it off."

Lansing held out his hand, palm up.

Nakamura removed his badge and put it in Lansing's hand. As Nakamura reached for his gun, both Eve and Duncan put their hands on their own weapons. He saw this and carefully took his gun out of his holster and gave it to Lansing. "Are we done here?"

"Burn the uniform when you get home," Lansing said. "So the infection doesn't spread."

Nakamura got into his car and drove away. Eve watched him go. It was wrong that he was leaving with his freedom, and with his pension, after what he'd done. It was his fault Jimmy Frankel had remained free to rape two women. It was his fault that whoever killed Sabrina Morton remained free and unpunished for so long. How many other cases did he sabotage over the years to save the department embarrassment? At least the rape kit wasn't destroyed. They still had a shot at finding it.

"I hate letting him go," she said.

"We got the truth," Duncan said. "That counts for something."

Lansing gave Nakamura's badge to Eve. "It counts for a lot. You can be proud of that. Now go get the men who raped and killed Sabrina Morton."

CHAPTER EIGHTEEN

The Explorer smelled like fried chicken. Duncan had insisted on bringing a bucket of Dinah's home for his wife, so they'd carried it in the back seat from Culver City to Glendale, and now from Glendale back to Calabasas. Eve wasn't sure the chicken would stay good, but Duncan insisted that once it was fried, it was impervious to rot.

They sat in the bumper-to-bumper traffic in a comfortable silence. They each had plenty to think about. Tomorrow morning, they would simultaneously arrest Towler and Harding, Eve leading the team on Towler and Duncan leading the one on Harding, so neither deputy could be tipped off by news of the other's arrest. The two deputies would be surprised, unless Nakamura or somebody in the department's tactical unit gave them each a call tonight, but Eve didn't think that would happen.

About forty-five minutes into the journey, as they hit the 405-and-134-freeway-interchange traffic knot in Sherman Oaks, Duncan's phone rang. It was Lou Noomis, one of Nan's CSU team members, a guy Eve thought looked like he had a tennis ball permanently lodged in his throat. He was really good at identifying whether urine was left by man or beast, simply by smell. Eve didn't want to know how he'd honed that skill.

Noomis was calling from Crawford's place, so Duncan put him on speaker.

"How's it going out there?" Duncan asked.

"We're wrapping it up. I believe we've found the murder weapon, a hand-rake, hand-hoe combo tool. There's traces of blood on the tines and the hilt."

"Was she killed in the shed?"

"The kitchen appears to be the crime scene. The floor has been cleaned countless times over the years, but luminol still brought up the stain. We collected traces of blood, bits of bone, and hair deep in the groove where the tile meets the cabinets. But it will be some time before we can match the DNA to her bones or the hairs that we retrieved today from her hairbrush."

"We'll get a rush on it," Duncan said.

"How will you do that?"

"We can be very persuasive." Duncan thanked Noomis for his work, disconnected the call, and turned to Eve. "Your turn."

Duncan called Burnside and put her on the speaker. Eve told her about the Crawford case and then asked her to do whatever she had to do to make the DNA test a high priority.

"It doesn't sound urgent to me," Burnside said. "Why should I call in a marker for this?"

"Because you owe me for the Morton case," Eve said.

"Isn't that the other way around?"

"Not the way I see it. For me, it's just about closing a case. For you, it's about your future career."

"You'll get a TV series out of this."

"I've already got a TV series if I want it. You want to be DA and this case gives you something to run on. You're gonna owe me for a long time."

"We'll see."

Eve took that as a yes that she'd push the DNA results. "We also need you to get us a warrant for Celeste Crawford's cell phone and credit card records for the week her mother was reported missing so we can double-check her alibi."

"Why can't you do that?"

"Because you went to law school and became the assistant district attorney and we didn't."

"I'm going to hang up now before you ask me to pick up your dry cleaning and wash your fucking car, too."

When Eve got home, she tossed Nakamura's badge in her junk drawer. She also texted Mitch Sawyer to tell him that she wouldn't be making her physical therapy appointment on Tuesday morning and if he didn't like it, she could bring him an excused absence note from the sheriff.

Shortly after dawn on Tuesday, a personnel carrier from the Sheriff's Department's Special Enforcement Detail, their special weapons and tactical unit, rolled into the restricted parking lot at Lost Hills station and parked behind the mobile lab. No officers ending their shift, or starting a new one, paid much if any attention to the vehicle. It was common to see many different LASD vehicles in the lot for all kinds of reasons. What they didn't know was that it contained an armed five-man team ready to deploy.

Deputy Chuck Towler arrived at 7:30 a.m. in a two-year-old black Camaro with windows tinted within a percentage point of the legal VLT limit. He got out holding a cup of Starbucks coffee in his right hand, which he'd have to drop if he wanted to reach for the legally concealed Glock in a belt holster under his loose-fitting polo shirt. That made Eve feel a lot more comfortable about stepping out of the station to face him.

"Good morning, Deputy," Eve said. "If you set your coffee down on the hood of your car, I might bring it to you later."

"After what?"

"After you're booked, processed, and locked in a cell." Eve drew her Glock and aimed it at him. "You're under arrest for rape and murder."

The instant she drew her weapon, the SED team spilled out of the personnel van, in full protective gear and their guns drawn, and took positions in the parking lot that would allow them to shoot Towler where he stood but without anybody else getting hit in the cross fire.

Towler gave a sideways glance at the tactical officers, then returned his gaze to Eve, his rage radiating with an almost palpable heat. "This is bullshit."

"This is justice, long overdue. Turn around and face the car. Place your coffee cup on the hood and put your hands above your head." He hesitated for a beat, then did as he was told. "Get down on one knee."

Towler turned and looked at her. "Are you fucking kidding me?"

"On. Your. Knees," she demanded. He glowered at her, but he went down on one knee, then the other. "Put your hands behind your head and interlace your fingers."

Towler complied. Eve holstered her weapon, held his hands in place with her left hand, and began to pat him down. The tactical officers moved forward, holding him at gunpoint while she searched him.

Eve removed his gun, gave it to one of the officers, and then removed his car keys, wallet, and a pack of Tic Tacs, which she placed on the hood of the Camaro beside his coffee. She pulled his arms behind his back and handcuffed him.

"You're going to regret this, you bitch," Towler hissed at her, his cheek pressed against the hood of his car.

Eve responded by yanking him up straight and reading him his rights as she pushed him toward the building ahead of her. One of the tactical officers opened the door for her and several other officers, weapons holstered, followed her into the station as a protective detail in case she encountered any resistance from the deputies during the booking process. Another officer collected Towler's personal belongings from the Camaro and, since Eve had mentioned it, his coffee.

As she came in, deputies and other employees peeked out of doorways and stared at her more in anger than in shock. Captain Moffett stepped out of his office, blocking Eve's path.

"What the hell is going on here?"

"Call the sheriff, sir," she said. "He will explain."

Moffett stepped aside. "I want to see you in my office in five minutes."

"Just as soon as I've finished booking the suspect."

The tactical officers remained through the booking process to ensure that there was no interference and then stood watch over Towler in his cell when she left him with his cold coffee to go talk to Moffett.

Deputies stared at her with open loathing as she walked down the hall to Moffett's office and knocked on the door. He called out to her to come in. She stepped inside and saw that Moffett was on the phone.

"Close the door. I'm talking with the sheriff," Moffett said and put Lansing on the speaker. "Detective Ronin has joined us."

Lansing said, "First of all, I'm pleased to say that Deputy Harding was arrested at his home this morning without incident and Duncan is bringing him to Lost Hills for booking and questioning."

"That's good to hear, sir," Eve said.

"I've informed the captain about the case against Towler, Harding, and Frankel . . . and that it was my decision to keep him out of the loop, not yours or Duncan's. I've reassured him that we never doubted his integrity or his trustworthiness, but that secrecy in this situation was essential."

"And I informed the sheriff of my profound disappointment that you didn't come to me first," Moffett said, drilling Eve with a cold stare.

Eve found this whole conversation stilted and awkward, especially Moffett's constrained anger, which he kept in check by balling his hands into fists on his desk. But she'd known that the time would come when she'd have to face him and justify her decision to exclude him from their investigation. The moment had arrived.

"Duncan and I didn't know to what extent the station was compromised," she said. "We still don't know how many deputies are involved in the Great Whites."

"I know exactly how many," Moffett said. "You just have to walk into the locker room."

"Not just here, sir, but spread throughout the department. We don't know where their loyalties lie."

"To the badge," Moffett said.

"That means different things to me than it might to them."

"Or to me? Is that what you're saying?" Moffett's face was reddening.

Lansing spoke up. "Of course not. It was a tactical decision. We couldn't risk any word of this investigation leaking, intentionally or inadvertently, before the arrest. That meant nobody at Lost Hills, or even here at headquarters, could know what was coming down. Until this morning, only me, Ronin, Duncan, the DA, and the commander of SED were aware of the investigation or today's arrests."

"This is going to be a major scandal that will be deeply damaging to Lost Hills and my command," Moffett said. "When word gets out, everybody is going to think this station is full of deputies who are rapists and killers and that it was run by command staff who either turn a blind eye to the corruption or actively condone it."

"Not after they've heard from me, at a press conference tonight on the steps of the station, that it was you and two of your detectives at Lost Hills who rooted out this corruption and it occurred before either you or Ronin were assigned to the station."

"We still have a lot of deputies wearing that ink."

"Of course we do, but this happened six years ago, not today. Towler and Harding reflect the past. You and Ronin are our future. That's the message we're conveying."

Moffett looked at Eve. He wasn't convinced or happy. "Understood."

Eve said, "I'd like to tell Sabrina Morton's parents about the arrests before they see it on television."

"It's my next call," Lansing said.

"Yes, sir," Eve said, though it left a bitter taste in her mouth. She wanted to be the one to tell them. She thought she briefly detected some smug satisfaction on Moffett's face over her disappointment.

"I'll be back there this afternoon to be briefed and to prep for the press conference with you," Lansing said and hung up.

Moffett set the telephone receiver back on the cradle. "You and I have a problem, Ronin. You think you're working alone, that we all exist here to shine a spotlight on you and your crusades. You've disrespected me and now, by arresting Towler at our front door, you've disrespected everybody in this building and possibly in the entire department."

"He's a rapist and killer."

"That's beside the point. You, of all people, should understand the terrible optics. You cheated to get this job, stepping over every man and woman who've spent years trying to earn their way, through experience, sacrifice, and pain, to get where you are. That's reason enough for everybody in the department to hate you. What did you do when you got here? You turned against your own. The smart move would have been to come to me when you learned that deputies were involved in the rape and murder, and then let me assign someone else to work with Donuts to take those bastards down. You still would have been a hero. Instead, you let your massive ego get in the way. You wanted center stage, the spotlight on you, over everything else, even if staying behind the curtain would have ultimately been in your best interest."

"You're wrong, sir. All I care about is doing right by Sabrina Morton, who was horribly wronged by this department when she was raped, and again when she was murdered. What achieving that means for my career, or the image of this department, doesn't matter to me."

"Maybe that's what you tell yourself, or even what you believe, but it's not the truth. It's all about you. That ends right now. I am your commanding officer and you work for me. Go behind my back or over my head again, and I will fire you on the spot, Lansing be damned. And if he fights me, I'll take it to the county board of supervisors, the media, whatever it takes, whatever the personal cost. Do you understand me?"

"Yes, sir."

"Good, now go finish what you started and don't fuck it up."

Eve went straight to her cubicle, ignoring the hard stares from Garvey, Biddle, and the other detectives in the squad room, and called Josie Wallace at her office. The sheriff hadn't said anything about calling her. Josie answered the phone. Eve identified herself and then said: "I wanted to let you know, before you see it on the news tonight, that we've arrested two Los Angeles sheriff's deputies for your rape, and for Sabrina Morton's rape and murder. Don't worry, your name will be withheld from the media. We'll also be filing the same charges against a former deputy who is already in prison for raping three other women." There was a long silence when Eve finished speaking. "Are you there, Josie?"

"Yes, yes I am," she said, her voice cracking. "I just can't believe it."

"The DNA recovered from your clothing, and your identification of the deputies, was crucial in securing the arrest, but it's just the beginning. You'll also need to testify."

This was the moment, Eve knew, when the whole case could come tumbling down. Josie was facing the prospect of her past becoming public, of enduring the cruel courtroom shaming that she was afraid of six years ago. The trial and publicity would have a profound impact on her relationships with family, friends, and coworkers. On a more intimate and personal level, it would mean reliving in excruciating detail the worst night of her life again and again for the world to hear. What if Josie refused to go through with it? Could Eve really blame her if she did?

"I made a decision, without even realizing it, when I identified those deputies for you," Josie said softly. "I'm not going to be afraid anymore. I'm not going to let them control me. That's what they've been doing. They've kept me silent for six years. I let them get away with murder. That's over, thanks to you."

Eve sighed with relief. Josie hadn't changed her mind. "I didn't do anything, Josie. You gave me the evidence that will put them away."

"It was worthless without someone willing to fight for me and Sabrina. I didn't think there would ever be anyone . . . until you came back with those photos and I saw the determination in your eyes. I saw Sabrina looking back at me. I knew you wouldn't stop unless they killed you, too. If you could have that courage, so could I."

"I won't lie to you, Josie. It's going to be an ordeal."

"It can't be worse than what they already did to me, or what I've put myself through, or what Sabrina endured," Josie said. "I'm ready to face them. They should be worried about facing me."

CHAPTER NINETEEN

Eve and Duncan decided that it would be better if he conducted the interrogations, because they agreed that Towler would likely be less defensive with him than with her. Besides, Eve knew that Duncan was a far more experienced interrogator. During her weeks of desk duty, he'd been schooling her in his techniques. This would be his final lesson, broadcast on CCTV into the captain's office, where Eve was watching with Burnside and Moffett.

Duncan had the table taken out of the interrogation room before Towler was brought in.

"The table in an interrogation room is a barrier—you can't see half of the guy's body," Duncan told Eve once. "The first, nonverbal signs of a suspect's deception will be in the lower body, what he does with his legs and feet."

Towler was escorted into the interrogation room by a deputy and placed in one of the two straight-back metal chairs, face-to-face with Duncan, who'd insisted on no handcuffs as well. He wanted to see Towler's hands for tells.

Towler was calm and quiet, which was the first tell for Eve. An innocent person, Duncan told her, is anxious and angry and eager to talk because they feel wronged and are terrified of going to jail for something they didn't do. They want out. But not Towler.

"Were you read your rights, Chuck?" Duncan asked.

"Yes, I was, which should tell you something right off."

"What would that be?"

"I'm talking to you now without a lawyer. Why would I do that if I was guilty? I'd keep my mouth shut. But I want to help you clear this bullshit up because we all want the same thing."

"What's that?"

"To get the bad guys off the street. So let's get on with it."

"Okay. Do you know why you were arrested, Chuck?"

"Ronin says I raped and murdered someone, which is fucking crazy."

"She can be a bit overzealous," Duncan said.

"I don't know how you can work with her."

"I eat Tums by the handful, that's how. And I tell myself I only have to endure her for a few more weeks and then I'm a free man."

"She's only interested in her career, everything else . . . you, me, the department . . . are collateral damage."

Does everyone *think that about me?* Eve wondered. But she was sure they didn't think that about male detectives who were laser focused on their cases. With a woman, it was different.

"That's why I pulled rank and I'm here and not her," Duncan said. "I want to get to the bottom of this. Who does she think you raped and murdered?"

"Sabrina Morton, I guess."

Eve hadn't mentioned a name when she arrested him.

"You guess?"

"That's the case you two are working, isn't it? Out in the canyon."

"It's one of them." Duncan snapped his fingers, as if just remembering something. "That's right, you were out there, securing the scene. What do you know about the Sabrina Morton case?"

Towler rubbed his chin, even though Duncan didn't ask a question that required deep thinking. What he was thinking about, Eve knew, was what lie to tell next. The stall was another sign of deception.

"Only that she disappeared six years ago and now her bones have turned up."

Duncan pulled his chair up close, invading Towler's personal space, and casually slid his bent leg between Towler's knees, forcing Towler to keep his legs spread, leaving his groin unprotected. It instinctively made Towler uncomfortable.

"Here's the thing, Chuck. Before Sabrina disappeared, she reported that she was raped by three guys that she'd partied with on Topanga Beach. She says they slipped her a roofie, gang-raped her, and left her on the sand. She staggered to a gas station the next morning and called us."

Towler bounced his right knee. Anxious. "News to me."

"She didn't remember the names or faces of the guys who raped her. All she could recall was that they all had the same tattoo. It's the one you have. The Great White."

Towler laughed, way too hard. Inappropriate, forced reactions were another sign of dishonesty and the body's attempt to relieve anxiety. "That's it? There are dozens of guys with the same ink. Maybe more."

"You're right, Chuck." Duncan kept repeating his name, to reassure him and establish a false sense of concern and friendship. "There are a lot of guys with that tattoo. She had a drawing of it that she was show-ing to surfers around the beach, hoping somebody would recognize it and give her a name. You never heard about it?"

Another laugh over something not remotely funny, underlining the lie to come. "No."

"Well, a deputy named Pruitt did, pulled her over, and told her to stop. Do you know him?"

"Yeah, sure, he worked here back then, but he never said anything about the traffic stop to me."

"Here's the thing, Chuck. The next day somebody broke her neck and tossed her body in a ravine."

"So are you arresting every deputy with Great White ink or just me?"

"Only the ones who left DNA behind. Tell me, Chuck, is there any reason your DNA would be in her or on her?"

"What?" Towler scratched his arm. He was feeling the pressure.

"We got a hit on your DNA."

"You got a hit on my DNA." Another tell. Repeating what the interrogator says to buy time while you think of what to say next.

"She was swabbed at the hospital after she reported the rape. We also have DNA from Dave Harding and Jimmy Frankel."

"How do you know it's my DNA?"

"Remember the water bottle Detective Ronin gave you out at the crime scene? That's how."

Towler scratched his arm again. "That bitch."

Duncan didn't say Towler's DNA came from Sabrina's rape kit, but he'd heavily implied it. He could have come right out and said that they did. There was no law that he had to tell the truth in an interrogation.

Towler licked his lips, because his mouth had gone dry, an involuntary response to high anxiety. Another tell.

Duncan leaned closer. "Look, Chuck, I haven't always been a fat old man. I sowed my wild oats, but there were some girls, after they got what they wanted, who were ashamed of what they did and wanted to forget that they couldn't wait to get their hands on my plow. You know what I mean? They'd say some crazy things."

Eve remembered another lesson Duncan taught her: You have to become the person the suspect needs you to be in order to get what you want. You need to be a chameleon in the interrogation room, changing your colors to match his.

Towler nodded. "I remember her now."

"Who?"

"Sabrina Morton."

"Describe her."

Towler did, accurately, then said: "She watched us surf, said she liked the way we moved. We invited her to party with us. We had a few drinks, passed around some weed, and the higher she got, the wilder she became."

"What do you mean by that?"

"She took off her top and started doing lap dances on us. Squeezing her tits and grinding against us. We're only human, you know? She was all over us but she said she couldn't choose which one she should fuck. So one of us, I don't remember who, says why not fuck all three of us? And she did."

"You didn't force her in any way?"

"Hell, we were the ones who were attacked. She was in heat. Some women get drunk or high and all they want to do is fuck."

"I know what you mean. Did you all have sex with her and then just leave her on the sand? I've gotta say, that's cold."

Towler bounced his knee again. "I'm not proud of that, but what else were we supposed to do? She was out cold, it was late, and we didn't know who she was or where she lived or nothing like that. We couldn't camp out with her all night and we couldn't take her with us. So we made sure she was covered and all, figured she'd wake up in an hour or two and go home. I didn't know until right now that she was the woman who disappeared. She was just some drunken party girl who got a good time from us. You know how it is."

Duncan nodded. "Is that all? There's nothing else you want to add? Nothing else you remember now that it's all coming back?"

"That's the whole story. There wasn't any rape. She couldn't control herself, you know? And since she's dead, who's to say different anyway?"

"Well," Duncan said. "There's the other woman."

◆ ◆ ◆

"Towler looks like he just shit himself," Moffett said, shaking his head at the monitor on the wall. "Duncan's the best damn interrogator in the station."

Burnside nodded. "He missed his calling. He should have been a prosecutor."

Eve leaned close to the screen. "Duncan's not done yet."

Towler instinctively tried to close his knees, a defensive act to protect his groin, but Duncan's leg was in the way. It was another show of guilt, especially in sex crimes cases. He swallowed hard. "What other woman?"

"Sabrina's roommate was with her. She not only corroborates her story, but she also remembered the tattoo, identified the three of you from a photo array, and provided her bathing suit. She kept it all these years. Your DNA is all over it, too. Same goes for Dave Harding and Jimmy Frankel. How do you explain that?"

"She's lying or confused. We must have had sex with her on another night."

Duncan nodded. "Did you, Dave, and Jimmy often party on the beach and share the same woman?"

"Is that a crime?"

Duncan grinned. "Are you kidding? It's an achievement. You were living the dream. Look, Chuck, I'm trying to help you. You understand that, right?"

Towler nodded, more than he had to, relieving more of his anxiety and revealing more of his deception. "Yeah, yeah, sure. It's just that it was six years ago."

"I get it. I can't remember what I did this morning. But I vividly remember every time I ever had sex with multiple partners."

"How many times was that?"

"Not enough, especially now that it's never going to happen for me again. It sucks getting old and fat. Now I have to live vicariously through guys like you."

"I could tell you some stories."

"Just tell me this one so I can get you out of here."

"Okay, what more do you need to know?"

"If these two girls had sex with you guys by choice, how do you explain Sabrina testing positive for Rohypnol?"

"She tested positive for a roofie?" Towler licked his lips.

No, she didn't, Eve thought, but Duncan didn't have to tell the truth.

"Yes, Chuck, she did."

"I don't know." Towler rubbed his chin again. His eyes shifted to the left, then to the right, then back to Duncan. Left to think of a lie, right to decide on it, and straight to deliver it. "Maybe Jimmy gave it to her."

"Jimmy Frankel? Why Jimmy?"

"Because a couple of years later, he was sent up to Soledad for raping a couple women he pulled over on traffic stops. We were shocked when we heard about it because that wasn't the Jimmy we knew. But now, I'm seeing things in a different light. Maybe he was always into having sex with women against their will. He was drugging them and we didn't know it."

"You mean you and Dave were innocent victims?"

"Yeah, that's right. Maybe that's how come I don't remember the other girl. Maybe I sipped the wrong drink, the one with the roofie in it, or got it from her roofied tongue in my mouth. If they were raped, it was only by Jimmy, not the two of us, because we didn't know we were screwing drugged women." Towler was smiling now, thinking he'd played Duncan and talked his way out of this nightmare.

"So who killed Sabrina?"

Towler shrugged. "Had to be Jimmy."

The point of an interrogation is not to get a confession. A successful interrogation, Duncan once told Eve, is when you walk out of the room with any information, no matter how small, that advances the investigation.

In this case, when Duncan walked out of the interrogation room, they knew that the three deputies had sex with Sabrina Morton and Josie Wallace on Topanga Beach. They knew that Towler was a liar. And they knew that even Towler believed that a deputy murdered Sabrina, perhaps because he did it himself.

It was a successful interrogation, Eve concluded. She'd have to watch the video again some time and closely study Duncan's technique.

"The 'roofied tongue defense' is a new one on me," Burnside said. "I'd like him to plead that in court just to see the judge's reaction."

"It didn't take him long to point the finger at Frankel," Eve said.

"Because he's already in prison and his criminality is a given," Burnside said. "It's a no-brainer to lay it all on him."

Duncan came into the captain's office without knocking and closed the door behind him as he faced Burnside.

"I don't see how someone that dumb got into the department," Duncan said. "Or how he's lasted this long. Surely he's had to testify in court before. How did any of his convictions stick after he was cross-examined by a defense attorney?"

"Because he never lied on the stand," Burnside said. "He did some horrible things six years ago, but that doesn't mean he hasn't been completely honest and diligent in his job."

"So, do we have a case, Counselor?"

"Hell yes," Burnside said. "Great work in there, Detective."

"It's the one thing I'm gonna miss when I retire," Duncan said.

Moffett frowned behind his desk. "I don't see a problem getting a rape conviction against these men but the murder case is entirely circumstantial."

"Two months ago, I convicted a husband of murdering his wife and I didn't have a body or a murder weapon. But I had plenty of motive, a lot of damning behavior, and a pattern of deception," Burnside said. "I've got so much more to work with here, her corpse for one thing."

"You also have three suspects," Moffett said, "any one of whom could have done it. Doesn't that create enough reasonable doubt for each individual suspect to get them all off?"

Burnside shrugged. "We just have to get one of the three to flip."

"We can't count on that," Duncan said. "Harding was smart enough to instantly lawyer up and part of wearing that tattoo on his calf is devotion to a brotherhood. They won't rat on each other."

So Harding had the tattoo, Eve thought. At least she wouldn't lose her badge on that bet.

"You'd be surprised what facing life in prison without the possibility of parole will do to weaken someone's personal convictions," Burnside said.

Eve shook her head. "I think we have more work to do."

"I certainly won't argue against giving me more evidence to strengthen my case," Burnside said. "So, where will you start?"

"With Deputy Brad Pruitt," Eve said. "How did he hear about Sabrina showing surfers the drawing of the tattoo? Why did he warn her off? And who did Pruitt tell afterwards about what happened? If we can establish, for instance, that he told Harding about it, that reinforces motive and gives us a deputy to focus on."

Duncan frowned. "Pruitt won't turn against his brothers, either."

"He's got a pregnant wife and a young son," Eve said. "I think under pressure he'll crack and choose his family over his fellow deputies."

Moffett snorted. "Not everyone places as little value on being liked, accepted, and respected by their colleagues as you do."

Moffett's phone rang. He answered it, listened for a moment, thanked the caller, and hung up before addressing his guest again. "Harding's lawyer is here. They are requesting an audience."

Duncan looked at Eve and Burnside. "Your turn."

CHAPTER TWENTY

Eve kept the table in the room for Dave Harding's interrogation. It wasn't practical to lose it since she and Burnside were sure that Kelsey Corso, Harding's lawyer, would be doing most of the talking. She was a tall fiftysomething woman with a long sinewy neck that reminded Eve of the trunk of a banyan tree.

Burnside laid out the facts that they knew from DNA evidence, the statement from a surviving victim, and Towler's admissions about the rapes committed by the three deputies. She didn't bend the truth the way Duncan had. Corso tapped her gold pen on her yellow legal pad as Burnside spoke. The only marks on the page were the dots left by her tapping.

"The only thing we don't know is which deputies are going to prison for life, and which deputy might get out a bit earlier than that," Burnside said. "I think it's going to be Towler, since we can't seem to shut him up."

"What else has he said?" Harding asked.

"Be quiet, Dave," Corso said, fixing her gaze on Burnside. "The way I see it, all you know is that my client may have engaged in an act of consensual group sex. Orgies aren't illegal."

"Rape and murder are," Eve said.

"You haven't proven that my client, or the other deputies, committed either crime."

"Well, if that's what you think, we're done here." Eve tapped Burnside on the shoulder and they stood up. "Come on, Counselor."

"Wait," Harding said. "Where are you going?"

Burnside looked down at Harding. "To make a deal with Towler or Frankel." She shifted her gaze to Corso. "See you at the arraignment."

Harding turned to his lawyer. "That's it?"

"They're bluffing," Corso said. "Relax."

Eve said, "We don't need you, Dave. Let's say Towler decides to stop running off at the mouth. Frankel is already in solitary confinement at Soledad. I'm sure he'd sell out his mother for an extra hour of sunlight in the yard each day."

Corso smirked. "You can't believe the word of a convicted rapist."

"I'll tell you what I believe," Burnside said. "It wasn't Dave or Towler or Frankel who killed Sabrina Morton. The three of them killed her together. All for one and one for all, just like the rape. That's going to be an easy sell to the jury. But if one of the defendants confesses, I'm willing to show him a little mercy for his act of contrition, whether he's a convicted rapist or a soon-to-be-convicted one."

"I didn't kill anyone," Harding said.

Eve noted that he didn't say anything about the rape.

"Convince me," Burnside said.

Kelsey Corso held a halting hand up to Harding and shook her head at Burnside. "That's not how this works, Rebecca. He's innocent until proven guilty. The burden of convincing is on you. Dave Harding is an exemplary sheriff's deputy with multiple commendations and an untarnished record of community service. His meritorious career and his fine character will speak for him against these absurd charges. He doesn't have to say a word."

"You're right," Burnside said. "Come to think of it, I'd much rather have Frankel talk, since he's a deputy already in prison for raping two women. That will demonstrate to the jury the proven character of the exemplary men that meritorious Dave likes to have at his orgies."

Harding went pale. "What are you offering me?"

"How old are you, thirtysomething?" Burnside said. "According to the actuarial tables, you've got about another fifty years to live. I'm offering you the chance to spend the last ten or fifteen of them outside of prison."

"That's a joke," Corso said. "You're right, ladies, we're done here."

Eve and Burnside walked out and conferred in the hall.

"What do you think?" Eve asked.

"One of them will crack," Burnside said. "I really don't care who it is."

"What if Towler and Harding both point at Frankel?"

Burnside shrugged. "Then we'll see who he points to."

"And if he points to one or both of them?"

"Then it gets fun," Burnside said. "Each one of 'em will offer us incriminating details about the others to convince us that he's the one telling the truth. Before you know it, the truth will be evident and they'll have tried the case for us."

"I hope you're right," Eve said.

"I know you want to do more, and I'm not discouraging you, but the hard work is done. You can concentrate on your other cases. Speaking of which, I got you the warrant for Celeste Crawford's cell phone and credit card records. You should have DNA results in a day or so."

"Thanks," Eve said. "Are you actually familiar with the actuarial tables on life expectancy?"

"Of course not, but it sure added dramatic heft to my offer, didn't it?"

Eve and Duncan spent the next few hours at their cubicles, writing up their reports and filling out all the paperwork that went along with the arrests. While they were busy doing that, local and national media began arriving at Lost Hills station in droves, filling the parking lot and lining both sides of Agoura Road in advance of the scheduled 6:00 p.m. press conference.

Lansing arrived at four thirty and Eve, Duncan, and Burnside briefed him in Moffett's office.

"Excellent work," he said. "I'd like you three, and the captain, to join me and the Mortons on stage at the press conference."

The "stage" was the front steps. Eve thought it was odd to characterize Lost Hills station as any kind of stage. Perhaps they should have concerts and plays on the steps as well. She was surprised that the Mortons were willing to be used as props, but it wasn't her decision.

"I'd rather go home and watch it on TV," Duncan said to Lansing. "I'm retiring in a few weeks and would prefer to slip away unnoticed, the same way I came in."

"You deserve recognition for what you've done."

"No, I really don't. It was just another case, like the hundreds of others I've worked in this job over the last few decades," Duncan said. "Besides, it was really Eve who ran with this while I sat on my ass, counting the days until I leave."

"I know that's not true," Lansing said. "But if you don't want to be at the press conference, Donuts, I won't force you."

Eve thought about her image in the department as a ruthlessly ambitious and publicity-hungry rookie. Grabbing the spotlight again would only reinforce the negative perceptions about her without giving her any benefits. And she didn't like the idea of being party to the exploitation of the Mortons' grief or gratitude, especially after the way Sabrina had been treated by the officers at Lost Hills.

"I'd like to sit it out, too," Eve said. "I've had enough publicity as it is. My presence will be a distraction."

Moffett and Burnside regarded her incredulously and Lansing waved off her suggestion as if she were making a bad joke.

"On the contrary," Lansing said. "The media will expect the lead detective to be there and, frankly, the public loves you. They will feel better about Lost Hills, and the department, knowing you were on the case. I want you there."

So that was that, she thought. She was a prop, just like the Mortons.

Ten minutes before the press conference, Eve slipped into the women's bathroom to mat down any wild hair with water and to make sure she didn't have some huge stain on her wrinkled blouse.

Rebecca Burnside was at one of the two sinks, putting on makeup. Eve went to the other sink and gave herself a quick appraisal. She looked tired, and her blouse could probably use a good pressing, but her hair was fine, there were no stains, there was no giant zit pulsing on her chin. Good to go.

"See you out at the circus," Eve said and started to leave.

"Wait," Burnside said. "You're not going out there like that."

"Like what?"

"Like we're shooting an episode of *The Walking Dead*. Come here."

Eve stepped over to her and Burnside began applying makeup to her face.

"This really isn't necessary," Eve said.

"Oh yes it is. You need to learn that concealer is your best friend."

"I have a hard time buying something called 'concealer.' I feel like I am doing something inherently dishonest and living a lie."

Burnside shook her head and smiled. "You are so incredibly fucked up." Eve burst into laughter, making Burnside laugh, too. "Stop! I can't do this if you're laughing."

"What can I say? You're right. I'm a complete mess."

"There's nothing wrong with you that wouldn't be cured by occasionally using some concealer and surgically removing that stick up your ass." Burnside took a step back to look at her work. "Much better."

Eve turned to the mirror, afraid of what she was going to see. She looked like herself, only now she appeared awake and refreshed. Her mom was right about the magical powers of concealer. "Wow. It's like I've had a good nap."

Burnside regarded her own reflection. She was more glammed up than Eve, but not so much that she crossed the line from professional to pinup. She unbuttoned her blouse another button so she showed just a hint of cleavage, and nodded in approval. "Okay, let's go."

Eve lingered at the mirror for a moment. She opened one more button on her blouse, nodded at herself, and walked away, but changed her mind and buttoned it back up before she'd reached the door.

Albert and Claire Morton were in the lobby with Sheriff Lansing and Captain Moffett, waiting to go outside to the podium and face the mob of reporters and camera operators. When Claire spotted Eve, she immediately came over and gave her a hug.

"I knew you were different than the other detective," Claire said. "Thank you for giving us peace."

Eve doubted they'd ever have peace. But at least now they didn't have the uncertainty. "I'm sorry it took six years."

Claire released her and Albert stepped forward. He offered Eve his hand and she shook it. She saw his gratitude but she also sensed the anger still simmering beneath the surface. There would be no peace for him.

Lansing stepped up to them. "Let's get this over with."

He said it like it was something he dreaded, but Eve could see a spark of excitement in his eyes. What was there to look forward to? It was a terrible day for the LASD.

But as they stepped outside, she realized why he was excited, and why it was so important that she and the Mortons were there, too.

He was going to reveal horrible atrocities committed by three deputies that went uninvestigated and unpunished for years. But that shameful tragedy, that failure of the department to do its job, wouldn't be the story. Instead, it would be the story of the Deathfist—the young heroine who beat up an abusive movie star, solved a triple murder, and rescued a child from an inferno—delivering justice and receiving the teary-eyed appreciation of the victim's parents.

Eve was afraid she might vomit.

Lansing stepped up to the podium and delivered the bad news with the requisite solemnity, anger, and sorrow, but then built up to the discovery of the bones, and Eve's relentless dedication to see that justice was done, with the full support of her captain, the district attorney, and himself every step of the way . . .

". . . even when the trail of blood led to this front door," he said, tipping his head to the entrance to the Lost Hills station behind him. "Since becoming sheriff, I've dedicated myself to restoring the integrity of the badge and the trust of the community. No person is above the law, especially those who are entrusted to enforce it. Today's arrests send that message and underscore our enduring commitment to let nothing stand in the way of finding the truth and delivering justice."

He took a dramatic pause to let that sink in. "Now I'll take a few questions."

"I've got one," Albert Morton shouted, startling Lansing, who turned to look behind him, where the Mortons stood with Eve, Burnside, and Moffett. "Why did it take six years for my daughter's rape and disappearance to be investigated? Why did it take the discovery of her bones before you did a thing?"

"I wish I could answer that," Lansing said.

"Don't you think you should wait until you can before you start congratulating yourself?"

Albert wasn't playing his part. He wasn't praising the department. Lansing wasn't prepared for that.

"I can assure you we share your anger and that there will be a thorough review of the department's past handling of this case. But today your daughter can rest in peace, knowing the men responsible for her rape and murder will pay for their crimes, thanks to Eve Ronin."

Lansing grabbed Eve by the arm and practically yanked her to the podium, desperate to change the subject and regain control of the narrative, to underscore today's success, not yesterday's failures.

Eve stared at the microphones and the cameras and wasn't sure what she could say that she could live with. Only one thing came to mind, but it wouldn't make her any friends at work.

She turned to Albert Morton. "You're absolutely right, Mr. Morton. This department failed Sabrina, it failed you, and it failed everyone in this county. There is no excuse. We are deeply and profoundly ashamed."

Eve faced the cameras. "What I did was my job. That's not something that should be celebrated at all—because it's the bare minimum, it's what I am expected to do every day to earn my salary and the right to wear the badge. Going forward, we need to do more than that or we don't deserve your forgiveness or your respect."

She stepped away from the podium. Lansing nodded, as if he agreed with her sentiment, but as he approached the podium, he turned his back briefly to the cameras and let her see the rage in his eyes. It was only a flash, lasting perhaps a split second, only for her to see, and disappeared in the instant it took for him to face the media again.

"Any other questions?"

There were many, but Eve didn't stay to hear them.

She went into the station, walked through the building to the back parking lot, got on her bike, and rode away while everyone's attention was on interrogating the sheriff.

CHAPTER
TWENTY-ONE

Her mother called while she was still on her bike. Eve surprised herself by answering the call.

"I just saw you on TV. You looked terrific," Jen said. "I'm glad you learned a few things from your big-girl makeover."

"I haven't washed my face since Saturday."

"Don't be a smart-ass. Congratulations on the arrests and the powerful monologue. The demand for the series is going to be even hotter now."

Answering the call, Eve realized, was a big mistake. "I didn't arrest those deputies to bolster my chances in Hollywood. I was doing my job. Didn't you hear what I said at the podium?"

"A tear would have really sold it."

"Sold what?"

"What you were saying. One tear, rolling down your cheek, to show that the emotion is real. I can teach you how to cry on cue."

"Then the emotion wouldn't be real, would it?"

"It's television, dear. Nobody expects it to be real, just convincing."

Eve was about to tell her mom that her life is real, that her cases are real, that not everything on TV is scripted and performed, but then she thought about that press conference and realized she was wrong.

One of the reasons that Eve feared a TV series about herself was that she'd be held to a fictional standard in her real life. But wasn't that happening to her now anyway? Wasn't Lansing trying to rewrite the past, and the present, into a story he liked better than the reality? Wasn't she just playing a part? Wasn't that why she was angry?

Or was she angry at herself because she was the one who suggested it to him at the DoubleTree?

You can present the story any way you want as long as the guilty are punished for what they did.

That was what she'd said. This was her fault as much as his.

"Are you still there?" Jen asked.

"I'm not sure."

"What does that mean?"

"I've already become a television character."

"You say that like it's a bad thing," Jen said.

"I have to go, Mom. I'm hitting a dead zone. Bye."

Eve ended the call, slipped the phone into her coat pocket, and headed north on Las Virgenes, across the freeway overpass, to her condo. She got off the bike at the curb, wheeled it up to her front door, unlocked it, and went inside.

The moment she stepped into the foyer, the air felt wrong. It was disturbed when it should have been still, like getting into the pool after someone has jumped in, the ripples on the surface of the water lapping against your ankles. Instinct made her let go of the bike with her right hand and start to reach for her gun.

A male voice said: "Don't move or I'll shoot."

Eve froze. Brad Pruitt stepped out of her kitchen, aiming his Glock at her in a two-handed grip. He was in his street clothes, a T-shirt and jeans. He must have picked her lock, not that it would have been too difficult, she thought. It wasn't a bank vault.

"Let go of the bike, put your hands on your head, and kick the door closed."

"This is a bad idea, Brad."

"Do it!"

Eve calmly did as she was told. Pruitt stayed where he was. "Killing me won't change anything. Towler and Harding have been arrested, Frankel has been charged. The truth is out there. It can't be silenced now."

"You saw to that."

"Yes I did. I told you that I would. But you still have a chance to do the right thing. Drop the gun and we'll forget this happened."

Brad smirked. "You won't let anything be forgotten."

"Not rape. Not murder. But nobody has to know about this. I know you're upset. I know you're scared. Put down the gun and let's talk. Tell me how you found out about Sabrina and who you told about it afterwards." She started to lower her hands from her head.

"Freeze . . . unless you want three slugs in your chest, a perfect center spread. I'm a great shot."

She put her hands back where they were. "So what are we doing here, Brad? Are you going to shoot me or what? Taking me out isn't going to make anything better for you, only worse. Same for your family. Your wife and son will have to live with the choices you make right now."

"That's your fault. I had nothing to do with that woman's rape or murder. You know that. But you dragged me and my family into this anyway."

"You pulled Sabrina over. You warned her off. You made yourself part of the crime. Now you can make it right for yourself and your family . . . but not by breaking into my house and pointing a gun at me. The way to redeem yourself, and spare your family a lot of pain and shame, is by helping me put those deputies behind bars."

Pruitt shook his head. "You're wrong. There's only one way to redeem myself after what you've done to me. You brought this to my doorstep. I'm bringing it to yours." He put the gun under his chin, aiming it at a slight right angle so he'd blow off the back of his head and not his face.

"No, don't do it!" Eve yelled.

"This is on you."

He pulled the trigger.

The gunshot wasn't as loud as she thought it would be. The sound was muffled by his head. The back of his skull exploded, splattering her kitchen cabinets and counters with brain, bone, blood, and hair. His body dropped to the floor like a puppet with cut strings.

Her first, instinctive reaction, in the instant that he pulled the trigger, was to flinch and turn away. So she didn't see the back of his head blow off. She saw the aftermath, turning back and opening her eyes as his body fell, and his brain was dripping down her cabinets. It was horrifying and grotesque, the smell of blood and gunpowder, urine and shit, hanging in the air.

She'd never seen anybody die, violently or naturally, in front of her. She'd only seen the aftermath. But Eve didn't scream and she didn't avert her gaze. She stood there, absolutely still.

She knew that she was in shock. But she also knew that her home had just become a crime scene and that she was a homicide detective. Those two facts gave her an emotional and psychological crutch, a set of procedures and duties to perform, a way to avoid dwelling on what just happened and take action instead. And action meant snapping out of her frozen state . . . *now*.

It was as if someone had snapped their fingers beside her head. Or maybe she actually did it. She wasn't sure.

The first thing she did was pull out her phone and take a bunch of photographs. She wanted to document the scene but she was careful not to take a single step farther into her condo and contaminate the scene. That task took maybe fifteen seconds.

Eve called 911. She identified herself as a homicide detective with the Los Angeles County Sheriff's Department, Lost Hills station, and gave the operator her home address. "A man has just shot himself in the head in my kitchen. I need paramedics, backup, and a supervisor immediately."

The operator wanted her to stay on the line, but Eve declined, saying that she needed to secure the scene and make other notifications. The nearest fire station was at Parkway Calabasas and Calabasas Road, one mile east of her. They would be here in two, maybe three, minutes. That didn't give her much time. Her next call was to Duncan.

"How did the press conference go?" he asked.

"I came home and Brad Pruitt was in my kitchen. He blew his brains out in front of me. I need you here."

"Jesus. Are you okay?"

"I'm dandy." She could already hear the sirens approaching.

"Don't touch anything. Secure the scene. Call the captain. Think before you speak."

"I will."

She disconnected, but before she could call Moffett, he called her.

"The emergency call just came in," Moffett said. "Are you okay?"

"Yes, sir."

"Who is the victim?"

"Brad Pruitt. The deputy who pulled over Sabrina Morton. He broke into my house and shot himself in the head."

"Shit. The press is still here. I don't think they are aware of what has happened. Don't say a word to any of them if they show up. Secure the scene. I'll be there in two minutes."

Eve ended the call and walked outside as the fire engine and the paramedic unit rolled up in front of her building.

◆　◆　◆

"You went to Pruitt's house on Saturday morning?" Lansing said, angry and incredulous, as he paced in front of Eve, Duncan, and Burnside, who were all gathered again in Moffett's office. "You actually confronted him in front of his family?"

It was nearly midnight. Eve had already given a formal statement to the captain, who'd been the first officer on the scene, and had been interviewed for hours by the Officer-Involved Shooting Team, even though her weapon was not drawn or discharged in the encounter.

"I wanted to apply pressure," Eve said. "My intention was to convince him that there was still time to align himself with the good guys instead of three rapist deputies. I went to his house because I wanted to put him on the spot, to force him to think about what the consequences would be for his family, for his relationship with his wife and son, if he made the wrong choice."

"Congratulations," Lansing said. "You succeeded."

Moffett looked at Duncan. "Did you know Eve was going to talk to Pruitt at his home?"

The question put Duncan in a terrible position. Before he could answer, Eve said: "No, he didn't. I didn't talk to anybody about it first."

Burnside said, "Or afterwards, either. Why didn't you tell us that you'd threatened Pruitt?"

"I didn't *threaten* him, I applied pressure. If he could tell us that he warned Towler, Harding, or Frankel that Sabrina was showing the tattoo drawing around, it would have established that they knew she was close to discovering that her rapists were deputies. It would have proved that they had a strong, urgent motive for killing her."

She did it because Duncan had warned her that the DNA wouldn't be enough to make the murder case. She did it because she was afraid her case would collapse without the additional information. She did it without thinking of the possible negative consequences. But even if she had, Pruitt's suicide would never have occurred to her.

"You didn't answer my question," Burnside said. "Why didn't you tell any of us that you'd confronted him at home?"

"It slipped my mind."

Burnside shook her head. "I don't buy it, Eve. You knew it was wrong, so you kept it to yourself, hoping it would all work out in the end. You gambled but this time it didn't pay off."

Maybe it was a gamble, she thought, but it wasn't something she was ashamed of, nor did she consciously decide not to tell anyone about it before she went or after she did it.

"I forgot to tell you, but I wasn't hiding what I did. It's all in writing in the case file. I reported the entire interview. Take a look now if you don't believe me. It's all there."

"That's called 'covering your ass,'" Lansing said. "It doesn't make what you did any less irresponsible."

Moffett said, "It was stupid to confront him at that point in the investigation. If you'd asked Duncan or any of us, that's what we would have told you. Because we have experience that you don't. It was a rookie mistake."

Duncan sighed, rolling his hand in front of him, indicating it was time to move things along. "Yeah, yeah, yeah, big deal."

Moffett stared at him, clearly pissed. "What did you say?"

"That's what rookies do, Captain. They make mistakes. But I've got news for you, so do old goats like us, even with all of our experience. We almost made a big one six weeks ago, remember? But the rookie here saved our asses, and a child's life. So let's put this in perspective. Let's look at what Eve got right here, which is that three deputies raped and murdered a woman. Pruitt killed himself because the coward was complicit in those crimes and ashamed of it. Fuck him."

Everyone was silent for a long moment. Eve was glad she'd called Duncan and that he was here as her advocate. She obviously needed one.

Lansing spoke first, directing his attention to Eve.

"You made a mistake, but you didn't break any rules or procedures nor did you do anything to directly precipitate what happened tonight. I don't see any grounds at this time for disciplinary action."

Of course he doesn't, Eve thought. It would send the wrong message to the public, especially after he'd just presented her as a hero. It would also call into question the integrity of the Morton case. Yet, at the same time, in front of the four of them, he was also covering his ass by saying "at this time," in case forensics showed that she'd staged the suicide in some way and murdered Pruitt.

"Thank you, sir."

"I'm also not going to place you on administrative leave, unless you want it."

"Why would I?"

Duncan gave her a look. "How about because you just saw a man kill himself in your kitchen. You should take some time off to deal with that."

"I feel fine."

"It's too soon to know how you feel, Eve. You may still be in shock."

"What I feel is tired, and pissed off that now we might never know how Pruitt heard about what Sabrina was doing or if he'd told any of the deputies about it."

Moffett said, "We've got psychological counseling available if you need it, now or down the road. There's no shame in that. I've used it myself and it helps."

"I'll keep that in mind."

"If you decide tomorrow, or next week, or next month that you need time off to get a grip on this, that's okay, too. Take the time."

"Will do, sir."

Lansing paced in front of her. "The press is going to be all over this. Avoid them if you can and don't say a word if you get cornered. Is that understood?"

"Yes, sir."

"You can't go back to your house tonight. Do you have everything you need and somewhere to stay?"

"Yeah, I'm good." She'd driven to the station in her Subaru Outback, and always kept a go-bag in the trunk with two days of clothes, several pairs of shoes, and some toiletries for stakeouts and emergencies. She also had a crime scene kit (including a Tyvek suit and work boots), an earthquake preparedness kit (which included first aid and tool kits), a case of bottled water, and a box of granola bars.

"Okay, then we're done for tonight." Lansing wagged a finger at Eve. "Get some rest and don't feel you have to rush in here tomorrow."

Duncan got up, his knees cracking. "I sure as hell won't and nobody splattered their brains all over my house tonight."

Eve drove east to the Hilton Garden Inn. It was located in an office park adjacent to the Commons and was the nicest of the three hotels in Calabasas.

She hung the Do Not Disturb placard on her doorknob as soon as she opened the door, then closed and locked it. She tossed her go-bag on the bed, turned off her iPhone, stripped off her clothes, and took a shower.

The water was scalding hot, but still not hot enough. She furiously scrubbed herself down with the tiny bar of shower soap, as if she could wash off everything that had happened that night. The soap disintegrated too soon, so she used the hand soap at the sink and the two bottles of shampoo, too. Even then, she still felt dirty.

So she just sat under the water and cried. Not for Pruitt. Not for herself. But for the pregnant wife she'd made a widow and for the little Batman who'd grow up blaming Eve for killing his father.

This is on you.

That was what Pruitt wanted her to believe. But was it true?

Maybe she did push him too hard. Maybe she shouldn't have used his family to pressure him. Maybe he would have killed himself no matter where or how she'd confronted him.

She'd never know. But regardless, she knew she'd spend the rest of her life trying to bury the memory of him looking her in the eye as he blew his brains out.

This is on you.

At about 1:30 a.m., she got into bed in a T-shirt and underwear and placed her gun within reach on her nightstand. There were a lot of Great White deputies out there and she didn't know how they might react to the arrests or the suicide.

"Sweet dreams," she said to herself and went to sleep.

CHAPTER
TWENTY-TWO

Eve woke up at noon on Wednesday, her mouth dry, her muscles stiff. She'd slept over twelve hours but didn't feel the least bit refreshed. She took another shower, but it was technically just a rinse, since there was no soap left to use.

Afterward, she got dressed and stuffed the clothes she wore the previous day into the tiny trash can. The clothes reeked of death to her and she didn't believe that could ever be washed out.

She holstered her gun and turned on her phone. A ton of text alerts and call notifications instantly appeared from her mom, Lisa, Kenny, Duncan, Burnside, Daniel Brooks, Mitch Sawyer, Josie Wallace, talent agent Linwood Taggert, TV reporter Kate Darrow, *LA Times* reporter Pete Sanchez, *Acorn* reporter Scott Peck, Malibu Beat blogger Zena Faust, and journalists from every newspaper, television station, and media outlet in Southern California. She muted her phone because she knew the calls and texts would only keep coming.

The hotel's breakfast buffet closed at 10:00 a.m., so she thought about walking over to the Commons for lunch, but she was worried that she'd run into a bunch of reporters hanging out there, waiting for some news to break at Lost Hills station on the arrest and suicide stories.

So she decided to drive to the Habit, a hamburger stand in Woodland Hills. But she had to scrap that plan, too, when she got to her car, which was parked behind the building.

Her Subaru Outback was stuffed with hundreds of full "poo bags," the distinctive plastic baggies for dog crap that were dispensed for free around Calabasas Lake and De Anza Park. The words Traitor Bitch were spray-painted in yellow on the side of her car.

Fuck you, she thought.

She wasn't a traitor to the badge. The deputies who did this were. They forgot that their sworn duty was to protect the public, not the rapists and murderers within their own ranks.

If the deputies thought this warning would scare her off, or shut her down, they didn't understand her at all. It had the opposite effect. It motivated her. It reinforced that what she was doing wasn't just the right thing, it was her responsibility.

She almost wanted to thank them for this, for dramatically shifting her attention away from Pruitt's suicide and stoking her sense of purpose.

She had a job to do . . . and she was going to do it.

Eve went back into the hotel, flashed her badge at the desk clerk, and politely asked to see the previous night's security camera footage of the rear parking lot. The frazzled clerk, a young man in his twenties, immediately complied, taking her to a back office and sitting himself down in front of a computer monitor. She had him fast-forward through the footage, starting at her arrival around one o'clock. They didn't have to wait long to see the crime.

At 3:47 a.m., a black panel van with no license plates pulled up beside her car. Four men wearing ski masks jumped out of the van with bulging trash bags. Three of the men quickly jimmied open her doors with the metal wedge tools commonly stocked in LASD patrol cars and emptied the hundreds of poo bags inside her Subaru while another man spray-painted the epithet on her car. Then all four of them unzipped their pants and urinated into her car before closing the doors, jumping back in the van, and driving off. The entire incident took less than five minutes.

"How horrible," the clerk said. "Do you know which guest owns that car?"

"Me."

"I'm so sorry. Of course, there's no charge for last night's stay and, if you are a Hilton Honors member, I would like to give you four thousand bonus points."

"That's very nice of you," Eve said. "But it's not necessary. Could you please email me a copy of the footage?"

She wrote her email address on the back of her LASD business card and gave it to him, along with her car keys.

"I'll be sending someone later to take care of the car," she said, though she had no idea who that someone might be or when it would happen. "You can give them the keys."

"I mean no offense," the clerk said, "but would you mind if we put a sheet or a tarp over your vehicle in the meantime?"

Eve could see how having a car parked in the hotel lot that was full of dog shit and painted with the words TRAITOR BITCH might not be good for business.

"Of course," she said.

Eve went outside and called Duncan.

"How would you like to take me to lunch?"

Duncan was furious when he arrived in a plain-wrap Explorer at the Hilton Garden Inn and saw what the masked deputies had done to her car. He demanded that she file a police report.

"I'm not going to do that," she said. "With my luck, the deputy that comes will be one of the assholes who did this or, at the very least, someone who sympathizes with them."

"Fair point, but you're going to need the police report to make a claim with your insurance company."

"Fine, you take my report."

"All right, but I'm not going to let this stand. You need to tell the captain about this."

"What is he going to do about it?"

"He can tell the deputies that he won't tolerate you being harassed and that whoever vandalized your car will be held accountable."

"Duncan, how do we know they were Lost Hills deputies? Those four guys could have been any of the ten thousand deputies working for the LASD."

"Then go to Lansing."

"I'm not going to run crying to the sheriff," Eve said. "Take my damn report and let's go eat."

She emailed Duncan the security camera footage while he asked her a few questions. He took photos of her car and promised to email her a copy of his report by the end of the day so she could send it to her insurance agent.

With that done, Duncan drove her to the Great China Express, a Chinese takeout in Canoga Park that was in a shopping center space formerly occupied by a Louisiana Famous Fried Chicken franchise. Remarkably, the Chinese restaurant continued serving the "real Cajun kickin' chicken" along with their Mandarin dishes.

"Fried chicken and sweet-and-sour pork together. The only thing that could possibly make this place any better is if they served pizza and donuts, too," Duncan said as they ate at one of the four tables in the place. "This is good eatin'."

Eve didn't realize until the food was in front of her that she was starving. It made sense, though, since she'd skipped dinner. She ate three pieces of chicken and a combination plate of pork fried rice, broccoli shrimp, and pork chow mein, and still felt hungry afterward. "It's delicious, but this might just kill me."

"Yeah, but what a way to go."

Her phone vibrated and so did Duncan's, so this time she didn't ignore her phone and looked at the screen. They'd received a joint text from Nan that the CSU was releasing Eve's condo and would leave the keys with the captain. She also passed along the name and contact information of a local crime scene cleaner.

"That was thoughtful," Eve said.

"You're going to keep living in the place?"

"I'm not going to move out of my home just because somebody broke in and killed himself there."

"It sounds like a damn good reason to me, in my top six with radioactivity, lead paint, asbestos contamination, built on a toxic waste dump, and formerly used as a meth lab. Besides, you're renting. Leaving would be easy. Just move to another unit in the same complex, assuming the landlord would rent to you after this."

"It would send the wrong message."

"To whom? Are you afraid it's going to encourage people to break into houses and shoot themselves to drive out tenants?"

"That I can be intimidated. That I can be driven away."

"Nobody is keeping score, Eve."

"I am," she said, ignoring her phone, which hadn't stopped vibrating since she turned it on.

"Have you given any thought to talking to a department shrink?"

"You think I'm crazy?"

"You were involved in a violent, deadly incident."

"We're cops, it's bound to happen."

"Not like this," Duncan said. "I'm retiring in 109 days and it's never happened to me."

Eve pushed her empty plate away. "I'm killing myself in front of you right now by eating this."

"It's not quite the same thing."

"What have you been up to this morning?" she asked, ungracefully changing the subject.

He sighed and let her get away with it. "I sent the search warrant over to Celeste Crawford's cellular carrier and her credit card companies to get the records for the week of her mother's disappearance. I should have it all today."

"What do you think our next move should be on the Morton case?"

"Same move we just took with Celeste Crawford. Use cell phone GPS records and credit card data to see if we can track Towler, Harding, and Frankel's movements on the day of Sabrina's disappearance. Burnside is working on getting us the search warrants."

Eve nodded and checked the time on her phone. It was almost 2:00 p.m. "Do you mind dropping me off at the Enterprise Rent-A-Car at Canoga and Sherman Way before you go back? I've got some personal stuff to do. I may not get in today."

"No one is expecting you to show up for a while. You were involved in a shooting."

"No I wasn't. I didn't fire my weapon and nobody shot at me."

"You saw a man die," Duncan said. "It's okay to be affected by it."

"How about you?"

"It didn't happen to me," Duncan said.

"But is everybody treating you like a traitor for arresting two deputies? Are they blaming you for Pruitt's suicide?"

"Of course not. It's all on you. I'm the fat old guy who has been here for decades, proven he's a stand-up guy, and is on his way out. I'm blameless. You're the young, attractive publicity whore who doesn't care how many careers you have to ruin, or deputies you have to kill, to get to the top."

"My God, is that what people are actually saying?"

"Only the ones who are being kind," he said. "You don't want to hear what the haters are saying."

That made her laugh. "I'll just look at my car."

"That about sums it up."

Duncan drove Eve to the Enterprise Rent-A-Car on Sherman Way. On the drive, she called Greta Halsey, the crime scene cleaner, who was a retired cop. Greta agreed to meet Eve at the condo at 3:00 p.m. but suggested that Eve call her insurance company first.

"You're probably covered for this," Greta said. She had a heavy Chicago accent.

"You really think so?"

"I'm ninety-nine-point-nine percent certain because I work with most of the insurance companies and they also use me as an expert adjuster in these cases."

One-stop shopping. Eve liked that.

Duncan dropped her off and went back to Lost Hills. Before Eve went inside the Enterprise office, she called her insurance company, which covered her home and car, and explained the situation. Greta was right. Eve was covered for the cleaning of her condo and her car, less her $1,000 deductible on both, and was eligible for reimbursements of $129 a day for a hotel room and $40 a day for car rental.

Eve rented a Kia Forte and got to her condo in Calabasas a little after 3:00 p.m. The crime scene tape was still stretched across her front door. She was relieved that only Greta was waiting for her and that there were no reporters staking out her house.

Greta was a hard-looking gray-haired woman in her sixties in white, wearing a Tyvek suit and black rubber boots, leaning against her van and smoking a cigarette.

Eve had brought along her crime scene kit when Duncan picked her up at the hotel. She put protective booties over her shoes, slipped on a pair of rubber gloves, and grabbed a dust mask before getting out of her car.

Greta snubbed out her cigarette on the side of her van and tossed the butt into the open passenger window. "It's not often that I get a client who comes prepared to walk the scene without getting contaminated."

"It's what I do."

"Not usually in your own home. I can do this without you, if you like, then come out and give you the lowdown."

"I'd rather see it for myself."

Greta nodded. "Let's do it."

They put on their dust masks. Eve walked up to the front door, pulled down the crime scene tape, unlocked the place, and let Greta in.

The bike had been moved to the living room, and Pruitt's body was gone, but otherwise everything looked pretty much the same as it had last night. Despite the dust mask, she could tell that the smell was the same, only now there was an additional chemical scent in the mix. She wondered if the smell would ever go away, or if it was now a permanent part of the house's scent or her own.

Greta studied Pruitt's blood, flesh, and brain matter on the kitchen cabinets, counter, and backsplash, and then the pooled blood, urine, and fecal stains on the kitchen floor.

"The good news is that most of the mess is localized to this immediate area. The solid marble countertop can be wiped, but the backsplash is going to have to be replaced. The cabinet doors can be cleaned and repainted." She turned on a little Maglite, opened the cabinets and drawers, and played the beam over dishes and utensils inside. "The blood and brain matter is like mist. It gets into every nook and crack. All the dishes, pots, and pans are going to have to be washed or tossed."

"Tossed," Eve said.

Greta examined the oven, stove, and refrigerator.

"The appliances seem fine—they were outside the spatter pattern— but we'll take a closer look, of course, and disinfect the entire condo. We'll check out the air vents, filters, everything."

She squatted and let her Maglite beam play over the tiled floor. "He bled out here. His bowels and bladder also evacuated. The fluids have seeped into the grout between the tiles and into the board underneath. This will all have to be torn out and replaced." She looked up at the ceiling and so did Eve. There was even spatter up there and on the light fixture. "The light can be cleaned, but we'll probably have to cut out that drywall and repaint."

"Do whatever you have to do," Eve said, knowing the landlord would appreciate it, and handed her the house keys. "I've got a question for you. My Subaru Outback is parked behind the Hilton in Calabasas. Four guys spray-painted a slur on my car, broke in, filled it with bags of dog shit, and then urinated all over everything. Can you clean that, too?"

Greta gave her a long look. "You're not particularly well liked, are you?"

"Not lately."

"I know the feeling. It's why I moved out here after I retired from the Chicago PD," Greta said. "Sure, I can clean the car, but you'll have to get it repainted on your own."

Eve looked at Greta and wondered if she was seeing her future, moving halfway across the country and spending her days cleaning up after death. Then again, wasn't that what she was doing now, only without the soap and sponge?

"The car keys are at the front desk. You can leave them with the clerk again when you're finished." Eve headed for the door. "Give me a call when you're all done."

"Don't you want to go up and get your valuables before you go?"

Eve stopped at the door. She had her off-duty personal Glock on her. Other than that, she couldn't think of anything that would be safer with her, or in her hotel room, than in the condo. "I don't have any valuables."

"Every woman has some jewelry that's important to her."

Like the cheap charm bracelet her mom gave her when she was a kid. Or the shark tooth necklace she bought in Hawaii with her first serious boyfriend.

"Yeah, but mine is worthless, nothing anybody would ever want to steal."

"How about packing some clothes? It might take us four or five days to clean and restore all of this."

Eve looked up the staircase. She thought of her clothes, which had been locked in with the smell of Brad Pruitt's innards for the last eighteen or twenty hours. "You can toss it all."

Greta looked at her incredulously. "You want me to throw out your clothes?"

"Everything." Her mom would be delighted that she was finally updating her wardrobe. "And the sheets, blankets, towels, and mattress, too. They're probably contaminated."

"I don't see how."

"I do," Eve said and walked out. She was half tempted to tell Greta to just burn the whole place down.

CHAPTER
TWENTY-THREE

Eve decided not to go into the station and headed to the Westfield Topanga Mall to buy a few days' worth of new clothes, some toiletries, and ten bars of soap. Her phone never stopped vibrating with calls and texts the whole time. Ignoring the media, the Hollywood agent, and her physical therapist was easy, but she felt guilty about avoiding her family. She knew they were genuinely concerned about her, and she appreciated that, but she wasn't ready to talk with them about what happened.

She took her new purchases to her rented Kia Forte and was about to drive to her hotel, but the idea of going back to her room filled her with dread. On impulse, she picked up her phone and scrolled through the dozens of notifications until she found Daniel's number.

He answered on the first ring. Before Daniel could get past hello, she asked: "Can I spend the night with you?"

"Sure, just give me a few minutes to kick out the woman who's here."

She laughed, grateful for the humor. Not everyone hated her. Not everyone thought she was a TRAITOR BITCH. "Thank you. I'll bring a pizza and a six-pack for dinner."

"You are a dream come true. I'll text you the address."

She picked up the pizza and beer at Barone's in Woodland Hills, which took thirty minutes, then spent the next hour in traffic on the southbound 405 freeway to the Santa Monica Boulevard exit, heading west.

Daniel lived in West Los Angeles in a 1960s-era, two-story apartment building with outdoor hallways around a central courtyard. The building was called Paradise Palms, written in wrought iron cursive across stacked-stone cladding, though there wasn't a single palm tree around. Perhaps there were palms once, back when there had been a pool in the courtyard instead of a planter full of gravel, ice plants, and cacti.

Eve found a parking spot on the street, where every car seemed to have a UCLA parking permit on the dashboard, and got out holding the pizza box with one hand and the six-pack with the other. She went up the courtyard staircase to Daniel's apartment and rang the bell.

He opened the door with a forced smile on his lips and deep concern in his eyes. The conflict playing out on his face, reflecting his uncertainty about how to behave and what to say given what he obviously knew she'd been through, frightened her. She was afraid of what he might say, of what he might think of her. What she needed now wasn't words. It was human warmth. Someone to hold her . . . and an escape.

So, before he could speak, she kissed him tenderly. When he tried once more to say something, she kissed him again, pushing him back into the apartment with her body pressed against his and kicking the door closed behind her.

Daniel took the pizza box from her while she was still kissing him and dropped it on his IKEA coffee table. She dropped the six-pack on his IKEA couch. Out of the corner of her eye, she noticed a short hallway that led to the bedroom.

Eve reached for the belt on his jeans and began to unbuckle it while kissing him and backing him toward the bedroom. Daniel got the message, stopped trying to say anything, and started unbuttoning her shirt as fast as he could.

◆　◆　◆

An hour or so later, Daniel walked naked out to the living room, his butt practically glowing white against his darkly tanned skin, and brought the pizza box, six-pack of beer, and some napkins back to the bed. They ate the cold pizza and lukewarm beer while sitting up, side by side, against the headboard.

"This may be the best pizza and beer I've ever had in my life," Daniel said. It was the first thing Eve had let him say besides "faster," "slow," or "stop" since she'd walked through the door.

"It's the sex. It makes everything taste great."

"I don't think you'd say that if we were eating beets right now."

"Who eats beets after sex?"

"My point exactly."

They ate some more and drank some more.

"Thank you," Eve said.

"For what?"

"This."

"I should be thanking you. It's not often I get sex, pizza, and beer delivered to my door. To be honest, this is the first time." He stole a sideways glance at her. "How are you doing?"

"Much better now."

"Have you seen the news or read the *Los Angeles Times*?" he asked tentatively. She shook her head. "You don't have to be worried about it. They are calling you a hero."

"Even after what happened in my kitchen?"

He nodded. "The sheriff, the DA, your captain—they're all standing behind you."

"Not everyone."

"Not the deputy's wife, of course. She's all over the TV, saying you drove her husband to suicide and that she's going to sue you and the department."

"I put a lot of pressure on him, it's true, and I purposely did it in front of his family."

"You couldn't have known that he'd kill himself."

"No, but if he hadn't blown his brains out in my kitchen last night, I would have confronted him at his house again this morning, or as he was dropping his kid off at school, to jack up the pressure to tell us everything or I'd take him down with the three rapists and killers that he was protecting. I wanted him to crack and he did. I'm just thankful that he didn't take his family or me with him."

Eve glanced at Daniel to see if she'd lost him with her lack of remorse, if his face registered disapproval or disgust. But instead she saw no judgment at all, just attentiveness and concern.

"I am, too." Daniel used his napkin to wipe some grease from her cheek. "How would you feel about chocolate ice cream and Oreo cookies for dessert?"

"Could we eat them out of their cartons here in bed?"

"Absolutely."

He got out of bed to get dessert. Eve watched his white butt go down the hall again and doubted that the LASD psychologist could possibly offer any therapy more helpful than this.

When Eve woke up on Thursday, her stomach felt like it was full of bubbling acid. She figured it was the combination of stress and junk food that was to blame.

"They say that breakfast is the most important meal of the day," Daniel said, buttering his bagel at the kitchen table and watching Eve as she sat down in the chair beside him with a handful of fruity-flavored Tums tablets that she'd found in his bathroom.

"I totally agree."

"Do you want milk and a bowl for your Tums or do you prefer eating them dry?"

"Dry." She was naked underneath his bathrobe. He wore a pair of boxers. She ate one Tum at a time.

He smiled at her. "You look like you're savoring each one."

"I'm pretending they're M&M's."

"Next time, maybe bring a salad instead of pizza."

"How about beets?"

"Sure, why not? I'm game for testing your theory about sex and its impact on postcoital appetite and taste. We can try a whole range of foods. Maybe I can write a paper on it."

"I can think of worse ways to get fat," she said.

He reached over and gave her hand a squeeze. "You're welcome to stay as long as you like."

"I'm not going to hide from the world." But it was certainly tempting.

"Is that what you're doing?"

"No, but I'm afraid that's what it would become. I feel so comfortable here with you."

"That sounds horrible," he said, teasing her. "I can see why you're worried."

Her phone vibrated. She glanced at it. It was 7:00 a.m. and the caller was Rebecca Burnside. Eve slipped her hand away from Daniel's, held a finger to her lips to signal him to be quiet, and answered the call.

"You're at work early, Counselor," Eve said.

"I've got a trial at eight. How are you doing?"

"I'm doing fine, thank you. But I'm guessing you didn't call to see how I am."

"Jimmy Frankel reached out from Soledad through his lawyer. He's willing to talk, but only to you. Alone."

The news excited her. She thought that this could be a decisive break in their murder case. It could also be a waste of time. But at least it would get her back to work, out of Los Angeles and away from the media for another day. The state correctional facility at Soledad was in the Salinas Valley, three hundred miles north, a five-hour drive up the 101 freeway.

"I'll leave in a few minutes. Frankel may be willing to cut a deal to testify against Towler and Harding in return for a reduced sentence," Eve said. "How much negotiating room do I have?"

"None. Only the DA can make deals. But you can tell him you've been told that reduced time is on the table or, if he killed Sabrina, the possibility of life in prison versus the death penalty. It all depends on the value and truthfulness of his information and the extent of his cooperation."

"I'll let you know how it goes." Eve disconnected and looked at Daniel. "I have to drive up to Soledad."

"You have such a glamorous job." He took another bite of his bagel.

Eve reached out and stroked Daniel's bedroom hair while he chewed. "We hardly know each other, but you were here for me, despite all of the baggage that I brought with me. That was very sweet of you."

She pulled Daniel close and gave him a kiss with a lot of tongue.

"I wish you'd warned me that a kiss was coming," he said. "I would have swallowed that mouthful of bagel first."

Eve laughed at his joke. "You may just be too good to be true."

The drive to Soledad followed the coastline, at times right beside the water, from Ventura to Gaviota, where the freeway turned inland, before heading due north again at Buellton, best known as the home of Pea Soup Andersen's, a truck stop–cum-hotel famous for a bowl of split pea soup that Eve thought looked and tasted like hot vomit. It was a pleasant scenic drive and Eve had the windows rolled down so she could enjoy the crisp fresh air and drown out the buzz of her phone, which was still vibrating with calls and texts, mostly from reporters or numbers she didn't recognize.

Eve was passing Pea Soup's distinctive shingled Danish windmill at about 9:45 a.m. when Duncan called. She answered that one.

"Are you sitting down?" he asked.

"It's hard to drive a car standing up."

"It's a figure of speech to prepare you for big news. Are you ready for it?"

"Yes."

"Celeste Crawford wasn't in school at Berkeley when her mother disappeared. According to her cell phone records, she was in Santa Monica."

"Nobody ever checked her story?"

"Why would they? As far as they knew, no crime had been committed—there was no reason to look at anybody for alibis."

"Maybe if somebody had, we might have discovered there was a crime a lot sooner."

"Celeste arrived in Santa Monica a day before her mom was killed. I've got the credit card charges for gas on her drive down the I-5 and for meals when she got here."

"Where was she staying?"

"My guess is with a guy. She made two calls on her way down to a number registered to Michael Morgan of Agoura. He was in her high school graduating class and was a student at Santa Monica College at the time."

"So are you going to talk with her?"

"I thought I'd wait until we got the DNA results on those garden tools. That'll give us a little more leverage. In the meantime, I'll start checking out the ladies who came to see Debbie Crawford that morning."

"You have a very suspicious mind."

"That's why I chose to be a cop and not a dentist."

"Well, that's one mystery solved."

"What mystery is that?"

"Why you chose not to go into dentistry. It's been driving me crazy since the day we met."

"Have fun in Soledad," he said and hung up.

She didn't think that was possible in a town best known for its two prisons.

CHAPTER
TWENTY-FOUR

"You could've brought me an In-N-Out burger or something," Jimmy Frankel said, sitting across from Eve at a metal table in a windowless interview room in Soledad State Prison. "It's lunchtime, after all."

Frankel was bald, with bulging eyeballs, a fat nose, and piss-yellow teeth in swollen gums. It made Eve wonder if he'd taken a vow not to brush or floss his teeth until he was released.

"I'm not Grubhub," Eve said.

"What is Grubhub?"

"Gee, you have been in here a long time, Jimmy. The world has changed a lot while you've been inside, not that it makes any difference to you. We could all be out there traveling by transporter beam, having sex with holograms, and living under the sea, but your life won't change. You'll still be here in solitary, exiled from the human race, waiting to die."

Frankel, as an ex-cop, was kept isolated from the rest of the prison population for his own safety. But now that Eve had met him, she thought perhaps he was actually kept in solitary so nobody could get killed by his breath.

"I'll get out of here in a few years," he said. "I didn't kill anybody."

"You're just a rapist, is that what you're saying?"

"I'm not saying anything until I know what's in it for me."

Eve shrugged. "Depends on what I hear. I'm just a detective. I'm not able to make deals. But the DA told me that lesser charges and reduced time are on the table, depending on whether I think that your information is good and that you're telling the truth."

He licked his lips, as if preparing to speak, but Eve held up a halting hand before he could start talking. "I'm going to inform you of your rights."

"I'm already in prison."

"Not for the rape and murder of Sabrina Morton," Eve said and recited his rights. "I want to underscore that anything you say will be used against you."

"Unless we have a deal."

"That depends entirely on what you tell me."

"So I'm taking a big risk talking to you without any guarantees."

"You're already in prison, Jimmy, and I can guarantee that if you say nothing, you'll probably be in here for the rest of your life. How much worse can it get? Unless, of course, you were the one who killed Sabrina. Then getting a promise of life in here, instead of the needle, for your truthful testimony against Towler and Harding would be a win for you."

He licked his lips again, not a good sign, and launched into his tale.

"There were two girls, not one, that we were partying with that night."

Eve tried her best to mask her surprise at Frankel's admission. A second victim wasn't disclosed in Lansing's press conference so, unless Frankel had some source in the sheriff's department who was feeding him information, this was an encouraging sign of honesty from the outset.

Frankel continued, "They saw us surf, we got talking, and we brought them back to Dave's van, he called it the *Love Boat*, that was parked right at the sand. He had a mattress and a cooler in there. So we smoked some weed, had a few shots, everybody was feeling good.

But then snap, the girls passed out and Chucky started laughing, said he was tired of them talking and giggling and that it was time to get the real party started."

Harding's van was something else that Eve didn't know about. If they were lucky, he still had it. "You're saying Towler put roofies in their drinks?"

"Chucky didn't come right out and announce it, but yeah, it was him. So he started banging one of 'em and I got busy with the other. Dave was sitting it out, looking kind of queasy, so Chucky, while he's still banging his girl, starts asking him if he was into men or women. What kind of man wouldn't want some of this action? So Dave says, 'Get out of my way,' and takes over with her. At first, he couldn't get it up, but he eventually got into it and did both girls."

"And afterwards?"

"We had some more drinks and went home."

"You just left two unconscious women behind on the beach."

"They were rode hard and put up wet, as Chucky liked to say. Sure, they were out cold, but this wasn't their first rodeo, I can tell you that. They got what they wanted."

"Then why did you have to knock them out?"

"We didn't. That was Chucky being impatient. Women fantasize about nights like that."

"Being gang-raped?"

"Having multiple men. I never did anything with a woman that she didn't want."

It was taking all of Eve's willpower not to punch Frankel's rotten teeth out. "If this was a fantasy come true for Sabrina, why was she killed?"

"She reported that she was raped, that's why."

"How did you find out about that?"

Frankel looked up at the ceiling, as if browsing back through the pages of time, but what Eve saw was him thinking about what lie to tell. "She came into the station and Dave saw her talking to a detective. It scared the crap out of him."

Eve thought it was interesting that he didn't say anything about Sabrina showing around drawings of the tattoos at the beach. "What made you think she knew you were deputies?"

"We didn't know if she did or not, but she came to Lost Hills, where we all worked. That was too damn close for comfort. She didn't see any of us that time, but what if she did later?" Frankel said, starting to fidget, another tell. "But the next day, Chucky told us that we didn't have to worry, he'd handled it."

"Meaning that Towler killed her."

"That was the implication. He didn't come right out and say it."

"How did he kill her?"

"I don't know and I didn't ask. She disappeared and that was the end of the rape investigation. We put it behind us and got on with our lives."

"Why didn't Towler kill the other woman, too?"

"Because she didn't file charges," Frankel said, showing a flash of anger. "We didn't know who the girl was and we never would have known who Sabrina Morton was if she hadn't cried rape. She got herself killed."

Eve had Frankel go through his story again and the basic details didn't change in the retelling. She believed what he said about the rape, but not the murder. He was too vague on the events surrounding the killing and displayed too many nonverbal signs of deception when he talked about it. She told him that she'd check out his story and the DA would get back to him if they were interested in cutting a deal for his testimony.

On her way out of town, she stopped at Carl's Jr. and ordered a charbroiled chicken salad, which arrived with wilted brown lettuce, even though Soledad was in the heart of the Salinas Valley, the so-called salad bowl of the world. The chicken had the consistency and color of Styrofoam.

She threw the salad in the trash and went across the street to McDonald's, ordered a dependable, if unhealthy, Big Mac, fries, and a Diet Coke and hit the road for Los Angeles, eating as she drove.

Burnside called as she ate her last french fry. "I've got Duncan on the line with us, too. I've got some good news for you."

"I have some for you, too, but you beat me to the call."

"The crime lab found Sabrina Morton's rape kit and they're processing the DNA now," Burnside said. "We all know it's going to match. Between the kit and Josie's clothing, we've established beyond any doubt that the rapes occurred."

"We have even more corroboration," Eve said. "In return for a reduced sentence on these new rape charges, Frankel is willing to testify that Towler drugged Sabrina and Josie and, once they were unconscious, the three men had sex with them. He'll also testify that Towler killed Sabrina because she filed a rape charge."

Eve repeated Frankel's story in detail. When she was done, Duncan was the first to speak.

"Well, that's it, case closed."

"Congratulations," Burnside added. "You two did remarkable work."

"Not so fast," Eve said. "I believe Frankel's story about how the rape went down, but I think he's lying about Towler killing Sabrina. He was vague on how Towler knew that Sabrina reported the rape and didn't say anything about Sabrina going around Malibu, showing people the tattoo drawing."

Duncan said, "Pruitt could have told Towler about it."

"But Pruitt is dead," Eve said. "He can't tell us who he told."

"I'm not worried," Burnside said. "I can convince a jury that it's likely that Pruitt told Towler."

"What if Frankel killed Sabrina and is trying to pin it on Towler?"

"No problem," Burnside said. "I can just as easily convince a jury that Pruitt told Frankel about Sabrina."

"So we're back where we started," Eve said. "Any of them could have killed her."

"Or they all did," Duncan said. "I'd like to track down Dave Harding's van. That would go a long way towards corroborating Frankel's story."

"Go for it," Burnside said. "I'll look at the evidence, listen to their stories, and decide who is the most credible and go from there. But I'm feeling very confident. Our case is strong. We'll get convictions on the rapes and the murder."

With that, Burnside said she had to go and hung up, but Duncan stayed on the line.

"You've missed some excitement around here," he said.

"That's okay, I've had enough excitement for one week."

"A weed abatement crew was clearing brush between the Backbone Trail and Piuma Road in Calabasas and discovered another skeleton." Eve was very familiar with the area. She often rode her bike up the steep winding road to the Malibu Canyon Overlook to see the spectacular view of the mountains. "Crockett and Tubbs caught the case. But they're getting off easy. The remains aren't in a burn zone and the bones aren't scattered all over the place."

"Are they bringing Daniel in?"

"I have no idea if Indiana Jones is out there, but it already looks good that the remains are Kendra Leigh, the old lady who went missing a month ago."

"They found her purse and ID?"

"No, but she liked to hike the Backbone Trail, her clothes match what she was last seen wearing, and she lived nearby, down in Monte

Nido." It was a heavily wooded, idyllic neighborhood below Piuma Road, a valley within the valley, that at one time so closely resembled a jungle that it was used as a location for the Tarzan movies and as Sherwood Forest in *The Adventures of Robin Hood*. "They've also got all her teeth and a hip implant. Those lucky bastards Crockett and Tubbs never have to work hard. They'll probably clear this case in a day without leaving their desks."

"That's the dream," Eve said.

"Do I detect a hint of sarcasm?"

"Not from me. You're talking to a woman who is going to end up spending ten hours on the road before this day is done."

"You don't have to do that. It's in our union rules. The department will pay for a night in a hotel."

"I've already got a hotel room waiting for me in Calabasas."

"Just don't fall asleep at the wheel."

"I'll stop in San Luis Obispo for coffee on the way down and invite Josie Wallace to join me."

"Good idea," Duncan said. "Give me a call when you get home tonight, just so I know you made it safely."

"Will do, Dad."

Eve was joking, but she was actually touched that he cared.

Josie met Eve at a Starbucks around the corner from her office and hugged her as she came in.

"What was that for?" Eve asked as they sat in side-by-side armchairs.

"I saw the news. You've been through hell for us. Now we're both scarred by those bastards."

Eve didn't think there was any comparison between the horrors that Josie had endured and her experience with Pruitt.

Confronting an unstable man with a gun and trying to talk him down was part of Eve's job. If she couldn't handle that, even when it went bad, she shouldn't wear a badge.

"I appreciate your concern, Josie, but I'm not scarred."

Josie reached out and squeezed Eve's hand. "Today it's just a wound. It takes a long time before you realize it's become a scar."

Eve got back on the road an hour or so later, wishing she'd just stopped for coffee and a donut in San Luis Obispo without meeting with Josie. All the talk of Pruitt's suicide, and Josie's well-intentioned interest in how Eve was feeling, made her dread returning the calls from her family, but she knew she had to do it eventually.

Just not tonight.

The stretch from Rincon Point, just south of Carpinteria, down through Ventura, was Eve's favorite part of the drive, because the southbound freeway ran right along the shore, and there were no beach houses or other buildings blocking the view of the crashing surf, just a simple guardrail, a sloped embankment of boulders, and, depending on the tide, a tiny sliver of sand. On stormy days, cars were splashed by waves crashing against the rocks. But the rest of the time, it meant the air was always full of sea mist, so she kept her windows rolled down to breathe it in.

It was dark, and she was about ten miles north of Ventura, feeling nice and relaxed, when she noticed two cars in front of her, weaving across the four empty lanes of traffic.

At first, she thought it was two highway patrol cars, running a traffic break, because they were both black-and-white Crown Vics with steel ram bars on their front grilles. But as she got closer, she realized that they were actually used patrol cars—the kind with two hundred thousand miles on the odometer that departments stripped of insignias, repainted, and sold to the public for a grand or two—and that they didn't have license plates.

No plates?

She glanced in her rearview mirror and recognized the grille of another Crown Vic closing in fast, its huge V-8 roaring, its ram bars like bared fangs, and she felt a jolt of pure terror.

They want to kill me.

She was certain that in the next instant, the car behind her was either going to ram her little Kia Forte . . . or clip her behind a rear wheel to send her spinning out of control. Escape was impossible—she was boxed between the two weaving cars in front of her, the concrete median to her left, the guard rail to her right, and the monster roaring up behind her.

There's no way out of this. I'm going to crash.

That horrifying fact left her with only one option.

Brace yourself.

Or was that a mistake? She knew drunk drivers often survived gruesome crashes relatively unscathed because they didn't tense up, grab the wheel tight, slam on the brakes, and brace themselves for impact.

Drunks survive because they are loose and relaxed.

So in the split second remaining before violent impact, she did something counterintuitive that forced her to fight all her instincts and reflexes.

Eve lifted her foot off the gas, let go of the steering wheel, and closed her eyes.

CHAPTER
TWENTY-FIVE

It was a perfect PIT maneuver, the pursuit intervention technique seen a thousand times by Los Angelenos watching the nightly police chase on the news: the Crown Vic clipped her behind the left rear wheel and her car went spinning.

Eve felt like she was on a Tilt-a-Whirl, her favorite ride at the Ventura County Fair when she was a kid. She'd laugh uncontrollably as she spun around and around. She wasn't laughing this time. Her seat belt grabbed her tight, pinning her to the seat.

While the Kia was still spinning, the Crown Vic rammed it, and suddenly the car wasn't spinning anymore.

It was rolling.

Airbags exploded, windows shattered, sheet metal crunched. She took a hard punch in her chest, felt something snap inside her body, and a rain of pebbled glass hit her as the car rolled once, seemed to take flight, then landed hard upside down, the sunroof shattering, the top caving in.

The car settled upside down, Eve held in place by her seat belt, seawater sweeping through the open windows and across the dented ceiling, then receding again with the surf, washing away the pebbled glass. Deflated airbags dangled from everywhere. It felt like she had a spike in her chest, pounded in with a heavy slab of iron that was still pressed against her. But there was no spike or slab, just the seat belt, and as far as she could tell, she had no major injuries.

That could change if the deputies who'd boxed her in on the freeway and rammed her car were coming down to finish what they'd started.

She had no doubt that her attackers were Los Angeles County sheriff's deputies. Who else would want her dead? Who else would know that she would be here, on this stretch of road? Who else would choose decommissioned cop cars and have the training to execute a PIT maneuver?

She raised one hand to break her fall, unbuckled her seat belt, and hit the wet roof. Every breath felt like she was being stabbed, her neck ached, and the saltwater stung the cuts on her face and arms. She figured the Kia had clipped the guardrail and tumbled down the seawall of boulders to the water below . . . and that the deputies could be up on the freeway, guns out, waiting for a good shot at her if she emerged.

Eve rolled with the tide out of the open passenger window, drew her gun, and rose to her feet slowly, peering around one of the wheels of her overturned car, ready to battle for her life with fellow deputies.

The traitor bitch is here. Come and get me, you cowards.

But she didn't see anybody on the freeway shoulder and no sign of the three Crown Vics.

It was an enormous relief.

She holstered her gun and squatted down, the surf crashing against her, and looked for her phone, which was still wedged in the cup holder, the screen glowing. She reached inside the car and grabbed the phone, the action causing another sharp pain in her chest.

Before she could call 911, she heard sirens approaching and could see their flashing lights. *That was incredibly fast,* she thought, as she staggered over to the boulders, intending to climb up to the shoulder to meet the first responders. But the pain and pressure in her chest, and a surge of dizziness when she raised her head, changed her mind. She'd let them carry her up on a stretcher.

Eve sat down on a boulder, facing the water and the rental car. The Kia was totaled. She definitely wouldn't be getting a Christmas card from her insurance agent this year.

This is what it has come to, she thought. *I'm so hated by my fellow cops that they want me dead.*

It was a painful realization, and not just physically. Eve was human, she wanted to be liked by the people that she worked with. She wanted them to be her friends. However, if being hated was the price of doing the right thing, then she could live with that.

If they'd let her.

A motorist on the northbound 101 had seen her Kia flip over the guard-rail into the ocean and called 911. Ventura County Fire Station 25 was only a mile south, on the east side of the freeway, which was why fire engines and paramedics were able to get to Eve less than five minutes after the crash.

She identified herself to the firefighters as a detective with the Los Angeles County Sheriff's Department and informed them that the car, and the stretch of freeway where the ramming occurred, were crime scenes and needed to be secured.

Officers from the California Highway Patrol responded to the scene, since the crash occurred on the freeway, and so did deputies from the Ventura County Sheriff's Department, since the car landed in an unincorporated area of the county. Eve gave her statement to a deputy and a CHP officer while she was being carried up to the freeway on a stretcher by firefighters and examined on the shoulder by paramedics. The deputy and officer assured her that the attack would be thoroughly investigated and that they'd start looking for the three decommissioned police patrol cars.

The paramedics secured her neck and head with braces, ran an IV of saline solution into her left arm, and insisted that she be rushed by ambulance to Community Memorial Hospital in Ventura. The deputies took her gun, gave her the pink property record receipt, and she was loaded into the ambulance.

Eve called Duncan on the way to the hospital.

"You made good time," he said.

"I'm in an ambulance on my way to Community Memorial in Ventura. I was boxed in and run off the freeway by drivers in three used patrol cars. It had to be three pissed-off deputies from LA."

"Are you okay?"

She was shaking and she knew it wasn't just from being wet and cold.

"I've taken a beating, but I think I'll be fine. I gave my weapon to a Ventura County deputy who is probably still arguing with CHP about who is going to handle the investigation."

"*I* will," Duncan said. "I'll be up there in forty minutes."

At the ER, her blood was drawn to determine if she was under the influence of drugs or alcohol and she authorized the hospital to share the results with law enforcement. The doctor, an earnest Scotsman who immediately reminded her of Scotty on *Star Trek*, sent her for X-rays and an MRI, which revealed that Eve had a broken sternum but no other internal injuries.

"There isn't really anything we can do about the broken sternum, except give you something for the pain and urge you to take it easy for a few weeks," Scotty said. "Your neck is strained, not sprained, which is good news. We'll give you some ice packs to reduce swelling and a neck brace to wear."

Otherwise, she had numerous cuts, none that required stitches, and a nasty bruise on her chest where she was hit by both the belt and the airbag. The real injury was emotional.

Her own people did this to her. People with badges.

Scotty insisted that Eve stay overnight for observation as a precaution and she didn't argue with him.

"There's a reporter outside from the *Ventura County Star*," Scotty said. "Do you want to talk with him?"

"I don't want to talk to any reporters," she said.

"I'll pass the word along."

"Thank you. How are the dilithium crystals holding up?"

He looked at her with a bewildered expression on his face. He'd obviously never seen an episode of the original *Star Trek*. "Excuse me?"

"Never mind."

He went off to treat another patient.

She was still on a gurney in the ER thirty minutes later, waiting to be taken to her room and lying with ice packs on her neck, when Duncan ambled in. He wasn't bruised and didn't have any broken bones, but she thought he looked worse than her. Worn out and feeling every one of his sixty years.

"I've only known you a few months," he said. "But in that time, I've visited you twice in the ER after car crashes. You keep this up, you're not going to make it to retirement in this job. You might not even make it to next year."

"I didn't cause this crash."

"Not directly. The three old Crown Vics that ambushed you were found abandoned in a vacant lot at the Sea Cliff exit—that's the first off-ramp from where you crashed, about a mile or so south, where the fire station is. They must've had a vehicle waiting for them there."

"I was set up. They knew I was coming."

Duncan nodded. "Looks like it. The three cars were stolen last night from a wholesaler in Oxnard that sells used state, county, and local government and law enforcement vehicles. The question is whether Jimmy Frankel was in on it or not."

"It would explain why he asked for me to come up alone."

"I don't know how else they could've known last night where you'd be today. I'm checking his calls from prison, but I doubt he was stupid enough to call a deputy directly," Duncan said. "How bad are you hurt?"

"Broken sternum, a sore neck, a few cuts, nothing serious."

"The CHP is handling the accident investigation, which was obviously no accident, and the Ventura County sheriff is investigating the attempted murder," Duncan said. "I've got to admit that now I'm afraid to answer your calls at night. It's never good news."

"In 108 days or so, you won't have to worry about that." And when that day came, Eve knew she'd truly be all alone at the sheriff's department with nobody she could trust, nobody she could call a friend. That realization hurt her more than her broken sternum or any of her bruises.

"You've still got plenty of time to total a few more cars or run into another wildfire before I go."

"That's true," she said. "I'll have to keep my eye open for opportunities."

"I've got your Glock, by the way. I picked it up from the Ventura deputy. You want to keep it under your pillow?"

"You can hold on to it. I think I'm safe here."

Duncan looked at the IV bag, then at her from head to toe. "It makes me sick to think that deputies did this to you."

"Don't be sick," she said. "Be angry."

That was what she was telling herself, too.

"The doctor says that if you do well tonight, and nothing comes up in your next exam, he will let you go at noon. I'll be back tomorrow to give you a ride home."

"You don't have to do that," Eve said. "I can get a rental car."

"Who is going to rent you a car after this?"

Injured cops often get preferential treatment in hospitals, and it was no different for Eve. She was given a private room and her bed had an iPad-like touch screen device mounted on an adjustable arm that she could use to watch television, order food, or access the internet.

The painkillers had kicked in, and her neck was immobilized in a foam brace, so she wasn't hurting so bad anymore. But she felt a strange crackling sensation, like her sternum was separating into sharp pieces, every time she took a breath. Even so, she was feeling comfortable enough now to notice that she was hungry.

Eve was sitting up in bed, scrolling through the cafeteria menu on the touch screen and trying to decide what to order for dinner, when her mom came in, carrying a grocery bag. It was an unexpected, and unwelcomed, surprise.

"Mom, what are you doing here?"

"You're in the ICU, fighting for your life. I'm your mother. Of course I'm going to be by your side."

"I'm not in the ICU and I'm fine."

"You don't look fine to me." Jen set the grocery bag on the night-stand and began unpacking items onto Eve's tray table, which was also on an adjustable arm beside the bed. "I brought you sushi from Bristol Farms. I don't trust the sushi at Ralphs. It's cheaper there, but the gal who makes it is white. They have a real Japanese guy at Bristol Farms."

"How did you know I was here?"

"A reporter from the *Ventura County Star* called me," Jen said. "I had no idea you were in Ventura. God forbid you should call your mother, even when you're lying naked and bleeding in a ditch a few miles from her house."

"I wasn't lying naked and bleeding in a ditch."

"It's a figure of speech."

"No it's not." Eve felt her shoulder muscles tightening up, which made her neck tighten up, which sent a stab of pain straight into her skull. "What did you tell the reporter?"

"The truth, that I haven't heard from you since your press conference. What kind of daughter doesn't call her mother after a lunatic blows his brains out in her living room?"

"You didn't say that to him, did you?"

"I also told him that you demonstrated the relentless dedication to justice that I've instilled in you since birth." Jen unwrapped the sushi and set it on the tray table. "I think the crab is krab with a *k*, the fake stuff, but it's still fish. Did you have a plastic surgeon look at your face?"

"No I didn't."

"You really should. You don't want to be disfigured for life."

"Disfigured? Is it that bad?" Eve realized she hadn't looked at herself since she'd brushed her teeth at Daniel's apartment that morning. "Give me a mirror."

Jen dug around in her purse for her compact mirror. "You never asked me for a mirror before. That's a good sign. You've turned a corner in your recovery already. You want to live."

"I'm not dying, Mom. Stop being so dramatic."

Jen handed her the mirror and Eve studied her reflection. There were tiny cuts on her face, most no worse than the nicks a man might get shaving with a lousy disposable razor, and she had a black eye. She'd also cut her lower lip, so it was slightly swollen. Overall, it wasn't so bad, considering the severity of her crash.

"I've looked worse." Eve gave the mirror back to her mom and had a piece of the California roll. It was tasty and she couldn't tell if it was crab or krab.

"Tell me about your accident."

"It wasn't an accident, but I can't talk about it. Police business." Eve gobbled down another piece of sushi.

Her mom took a piece of the rainbow roll and popped it in her mouth. "Okay, is it true what that crazy woman is saying on TV about you harassing her husband into killing himself? Because I know what you can be like."

"What is that supposed to mean?" Eve wished she had a morphine drip, because she would be urgently pressing the button for a dose right now. Her shoulders were like rebar and her neck was an iron spike being driven into her brain with each word her mother spoke. She had another piece of sushi instead.

"You can be intensely judgmental. Not everyone can take it. Not everyone is as strong and as understanding as I am. I know the real person that you're judging is yourself."

"No, it's you. It has always been you. You made me who I am."

Jen kissed Eve on the cheek. "That is so sweet. Why do you have to be on the edge of death before you'll say nice things to me?"

She was about to argue that she wasn't on the edge of death, but she realized she soon might be if her mother stayed any longer.

"With injuries this severe, Mom, the doctor says it's crucial that I get my rest. This has been nice, but I really need some sleep. You should leave the sushi and go."

"Okay, dear, but where are your valuables?"

"What valuables?" It seemed like everyone was interested in them lately. First the crime scene cleaner, now her mother.

"Your keys, wallet, phone, badge, and gun?"

"My partner has my gun, the nurse is charging my phone for me, and I don't have any jewelry. Everything else is in a bag in the nightstand drawer."

"All women have jewelry, honey. The badge is yours. You love wearing it. You probably wear it to bed," Jen said. "Maybe you should give everything to me until you leave."

She wasn't going to give her mom her badge or anything else. "Why would I ever do that?"

"Because I know from my experience working in the health care industry that there's an underground network of nurses and orderlies who steal valuables from patients, particularly those who are near death."

"First off, I am not near death and the only working you've done in health care was as a background extra on *General Hospital*."

"There was a head nurse while I was there who used stolen valuables to finance her sexual reassignment surgery so she could seduce and marry the straight woman she was in love with." Jen leaned close to Eve and whispered, "Have you taken a good look at the nurse out there? She looks more masculine than feminine to me."

"Goodbye, Mom," Eve said.

Jen kissed her on the cheek. "Sleep with one eye open."

CHAPTER
TWENTY-SIX

But Eve didn't sleep, with one eye open or otherwise. She didn't know whether it was the shock to her system from the accident, the pain, the discomfort, the side effects of her medications, the stressful conversation with her mom, or all of the above that were preventing her slumber.

Around 3:00 a.m., Eve got out of bed, grabbed hold of her rolling IV stand, and wheeled it with her into the bathroom to pee. It was not a pleasant experience and retying her hospital gown, which cinched behind her back, afterward turned out to be a difficult and painful ordeal.

She shuffled out of the bathroom, wheeling her IV stand beside her, and decided to take a little stroll through the hospital instead of getting back into bed. Perhaps stretching her legs, and getting the blood flowing, would loosen up all the tight muscles in her body and allow her to get some sleep.

Eve stepped into the corridor and was startled to see a man sitting in a chair outside of her door. She recognized him. He was a Lost Hills deputy named Tom Ross, an ex-marine. He was in jeans and a T-shirt, a badge and a holstered gun clipped to his belt. Her heart began to race.

"Come to finish what you started?" Eve said, looking around and seeing no one at the nurse's station. *Where the hell is everyone?* She was in no shape to defend herself. The most she could do was scream, and was considering it, when he spoke.

"You can stand down. I'm not going to hurt you."

"Are you a Great White?"

"Uh-huh." Ross leaned down, lifted up his pant leg, and showed her the tattoo.

"So you're here to deliver a message."

"I suppose you could say that. I'm proud of this tattoo and what it represents. This one, too."

Ross straightened up and pulled off his T-shirt. He had six-pack abs and stone-hard pecs. But what drew Eve's attention was the vivid tattoo on the cap of his right shoulder. It was a skull with three bullet holes in the forehead, set against crossbones comprised of a sniper rifle, a knife, and an oar.

"It's scary if you don't know what it means," he said. "It's a death head with three bullets through the skull. The bullet holes symbolize the three shots we take before the enemy even knows we're there. The bullet holes also represent the three words of our Marine Corps recon unit motto: swift, silent, deadly."

"It still doesn't look like Hello Kitty to me."

"It means you're willing to kill for your country and probably have. It means you have a code of honor, courage, and commitment you will live, kill, and die by. I wear the tattoo with pride. Same as the one on my leg, which represents my dedication to the badge, to my fellow deputies, and to our community."

"You're telling me that I betrayed that."

Ross stood and faced her. She was very aware of how much bigger and stronger he was than her.

"I'm here because Towler, Harding, and Frankel did. I'm here because the bastards who trashed your car at the hotel and ran you off the road tonight did. They don't represent who we are or what we stand for. So the message to you, and to them, is that you're one of us and we've got your back."

Eve wasn't sure that she'd heard him correctly. "You're here to *protect* me?"

"There will be an off-duty deputy by your side twenty-four seven until this bullshit stops."

It may have been the nicest thing anyone had said to Eve since she'd become a homicide detective. She wasn't alone. She wasn't hated by everybody. There were people she could trust, who cared about her even if they didn't actually know her.

Eve wanted to hug him but didn't because it would hurt too much. And because she was afraid if he squeezed her, even a little bit, it might break her sternum in half.

Instead, she held out her hand to him. "Thank you."

He shook her hand. "Just doing my duty."

She looked over his shoulder and saw a nurse coming down the hall. "Maybe you should put your shirt back on, Tom."

Ross picked up his T-shirt and pulled it over his head, but not before he got an appreciative smile from the nurse as she returned to her station.

"No need to put that back on for me, Deputy," she said. "No need at all."

Eve turned to Ross. "I'm going to take a walk."

"I'll come with you."

"That's not necessary. Stay here and guard my valuables. I'll be right back."

Eve moved slowly down the corridor by herself, wheeling her IV cart along. She didn't want him to see the tears that he'd brought to her eyes.

◆ ◆ ◆

The doors to most of the rooms on the ward were open, perhaps so the nurses could easily see how everybody was doing. Eve was surprised by how many patients were awake, too. Then again, it made sense, since many of them were in bandages or casts or had a bunch of tubes running in and out of their bodies. They had to be in a lot of pain and discomfort. She counted herself lucky. At least she was on her feet.

But she wasn't alone on that score, either. She saw a man in his thirties shuffling toward her, both of his arms in slings. Despite his two broken arms, he still managed to use one hand to wheel a rolling IV stand that also held a bag of urine from the catheter line that snaked under his hospital gown. She was glad she didn't have one of those.

He gave her a crooked smile as they came up side by side, like two cars in opposite lanes. "What are you in for?"

"Car accident. You?"

"Handicap ramp." He must have seen the confusion on her face. "I went to get my daughter a Happy Meal at McDonald's and tripped over the handicap ramp. Fell and broke both of my arms. One is a clean break, the other is a mess."

"Was the ramp over a cliff?"

The man laughed. "The curb wasn't even two inches high. Makes you wonder how Dwayne Johnson in those Fast & Furious movies can leap from the top floor of a skyscraper, fall thirty stories onto the roof of a BMW, and walk away."

"Because it's not real."

He slightly lifted his right sling. "Real is sixteen screws, three plates, and a titanium radial head from a trip-and-fall. I'm looking at months in a cast, followed by months of physical therapy, and I'll still never be able to play tennis or scratch between my shoulder blades again."

"That's one unhappy Happy Meal."

"At least you seem whole."

"Only on the outside. Broken sternum and a strained neck."

"Lucky you."

"I'm beginning to realize that," she said. "Have a good night."

"You too," he said and shuffled away. She watched him go and saw his bare butt, exposed by his loose gown. It made her wonder just how much she was showing.

Eve continued her slow stroll, her mind on the poor guy's unhappy meal—then her thoughts drifted back to the deputy who was guarding her valuables and she had a revelation, which came to her as an overwhelming cascade of facts, images, and bits of dialogue colliding in her head, creating a wave of dizziness and nausea that nearly brought her to her knees.

"I'd hate to see your career derailed by a bad decision made on your second murder case . . ."

"So we're back where we started. Any of them could have killed her . . ."

"All women have jewelry, honey. The badge is yours . . ."

"Sixteen screws, three plates, and a titanium radial head from a trip-and-fall . . ."

She closed her eyes and stood very still, clutching her IV stand for support, trying to settle her thoughts and willing herself not to vomit. After a couple of minutes, she began to understand how everything fit together and all the mistakes that she'd made. The dizziness passed, but the nausea remained, like a low hum. She must have been breathing hard, because now it felt like someone was pounding a stake into her heart.

Nakamura was right. She was a novice and a fool.

Eve opened her eyes and went back to her room as quickly as she could without making herself sick or creating too much pain.

Tom Ross was leaning on the counter of the nurse's station, talking to the smiling nurse, when he saw Eve approach and read the expression on her face. "Are you all right? Do you need a doctor?"

"Do you have a car, Tom?"

"Yes."

Eve turned to the nurse. "I need you to give me my next injection of painkillers and then get this IV out of my arm."

"I can't do that," she said.

"If you don't, then I'll yank it out myself. Either way, I'm leaving in five minutes."

"You've been in a serious accident. You need to stay the night for observation in case you've suffered internal injuries or complications that haven't become obvious yet."

"I need to go," Eve said. "Are you going to help me or not?"

The doctor on call was not pleased, but faced with Eve's obstinance and no authority to stop her, he gave in. He authorized her dose of painkillers and gave her a written prescription for more. The nurse removed Eve's IV line and helped her get out of her gown and into her underwear. Her clothes and shoes were still wet, so the nurse took pity on her, loaned her a set of surgical scrubs and slippers, and got her dressed.

"You're being irrational and making a big mistake," the nurse said.

"That's the story of my life," Eve said.

She thanked the nurse, grabbed her phone, personal items, and bagged clothes, and let Ross wheel her out of the hospital in a wheelchair to his Dodge Challenger, which was parked as close to the lobby door as he could get it.

"Where to, Eve?" he asked as he unlocked the passenger door.

"Lost Hills station," she said, trying not to cry out with pain as she got up from the wheelchair and into the car's bucket seat. It felt like every move she made drove a dagger into her chest. The painkillers must not have kicked in yet.

As they drove out of the parking lot, Eve called Daniel, waking him up.

"Sorry to wake you," she said. "I need to ask you an important question."

"Okay," he said, groggy.

"Were you called out to examine Kendra Leigh's skeleton in Calabasas today?"

"Yeah."

"How was she murdered?"

"How did you know she was murdered? I didn't know myself until I looked at the bones tonight under a microscope."

"Just tell me."

"Stabbed in the back. I could tell by the—"

"Thanks," she interrupted him. "Go to sleep. I'll explain this all later."

Eve ended the call.

"Shit," she said to herself.

The freeway was nearly deserted and Ross drove way over the speed limit, so they got to the Lost Hills station in only twenty minutes. When they arrived, Eve was in so much pain getting out of the car that Ross simply picked her up and carried her into the station. She didn't protest.

"Where to?" he asked, effortlessly holding her in his arms as if she were a very big baby.

"My desk."

He carried her to her cubicle and gently lowered her into her chair. "Anything else?"

"If you tell a soul about carrying me in, I'll shoot you."

"Understood."

"Can you please bring me the murder books on Sabrina Morton and Debbie Crawford? They are on Duncan's desk."

He brought her the two binders.

"Thanks." She gave him her hotel room key. "I'm in room 232 at the Hilton Garden Inn. Can you please bring me my duffel bag? I'm going to need to change out of these scrubs and slippers."

All the clothes and toiletries that she'd bought on Wednesday were in the trunk of her smashed Kia. *They're all trash now,* she thought. This case was going to cost her a fortune in insurance deductibles, hotel rooms, and lost clothing. She wondered how she was going to pay for it all.

"You're going to be on your own here until I get back," Ross said, breaking into her thoughts.

"I think I'm safe in a sheriff's station."

He didn't look too sure about that, but he left to run the errand anyway.

Once he was gone, Eve rolled her chair over to Biddle's desk, found the binder on the Kendra Leigh case, and quickly flipped through the pages. It didn't take her long to find what she was looking for: the details of the hip replacement that helped identify her. She took some quick notes on a legal pad, tore off the page, and rolled back to her desk. She opened the binder on Debbie Crawford, found the information on her knee replacement, and wrote it down on the same sheet of lined yellow paper.

Tom Ross returned with her duffel bag as she was opening the binder on Sabrina Morton.

"There was a note from the manager in your room," he said, setting the duffel bag beside her desk. "Your car has been cleaned and the keys are at the front desk. I'll be in the snack room if you need me. I've got to call Eddie Clayton, who is taking over for me at eight a.m."

"Thanks, Tom," she said, making a note from Sabrina's file on the sheet of paper with her notes on Debbie Crawford and Kendra Leigh. Next she went on the internet and searched for photos of Kendra Leigh. In every picture, Kendra wore a necklace with a tiny cross.

It was almost five thirty. The polite thing to do would be to wait another two or three hours before making any calls. But Eve was too restless and angry with herself to wait. She called the Mortons, awakening Claire, who answered the phone with a whispered "Hello."

"This is Eve Ronin. I am so sorry to wake you up, but I have an important question about your daughter's case that I need answered right now."

"It's okay, Detective," Claire whispered. Eve could hear Albert's heavy snoring in the background. "It won't be the first time I've lost sleep since she was killed. What do you need to know?"

"Did your daughter have any favorite pieces of jewelry?"

"Of course. Her Tiffany heart necklace. A ring she bought in New Zealand. Her grandmother's bracelet. So many things. Why?"

"Do you have them all?"

"Everything except her Tiffany necklace, which she wore all the time. She was probably wearing it when . . ." Claire's voice caught for a moment. ". . . when she was killed."

"You've been a big help, thank you."

Eve hung up and dialed Celeste Crawford's number, waking her up, too.

"This is Eve Ronin. I am so sorry to wake you up."

"I don't think you're sorry about anything. You knew my mother was murdered long before you told me. Is that because you think I killed her?"

"No I don't. But you can help me catch the person who did by answering some questions for me right now. Did your mom wear jewelry?"

"Of course she did. Tons of earrings, necklaces, most of them she made herself."

"Did she have a favorite piece?"

"She had a beautiful turquoise necklace she got at a Navajo trading post in New Mexico that she never took off."

"Where is it now?"

"You tell me. She was probably wearing it when she disappeared."

"Thank you, this is very helpful." Eve hung up. It was nearly 6:00 a.m. That gave her an hour or so to take a quick nap, shower, and change before making some more calls.

She got up, wincing with pain, and walked down the hall to the snack room, where Tom Ross was watching an old episode of *Hollywood & the Vine* on TV.

"You think I'd be a better cop if I was half-plant?"

"I don't see how," Eve said. "I'm going to the sleep room for a nap. Please wake me up before you go."

"Will do."

Eve went to the sleep room, eased herself carefully onto the cot, and fell asleep almost instantly.

CHAPTER
TWENTY-SEVEN

Deputy Ross dutifully woke Eve up an hour later, but it wasn't easy. She felt like she was struggling to awaken from a coma. It was a hard climb back to consciousness.

"You should go back to the hospital," he said.

"Don't worry, Tom. I always look like hell in the morning."

She picked up the duffel bag that Ross had brought her from the hotel and let him help her to the locker room.

Once inside, she removed her neck brace, splashed some cold water on her face, brushed her teeth, and stripped out of her scrubs. She was shocked by the huge black bruise on her chest. It hurt just to look at it.

She changed into a blazer, blouse, and slacks, which was a painful exercise. Her neck was sore, but she decided not to put the brace back on. She didn't want to look unfit for duty, though she probably was. But she had a job to do.

Eve staggered out of the locker room, grabbed a Red Bull from the snack room refrigerator, and returned to her desk, where she guzzled down the drink and began making calls. What she learned after the third call, this one to Sabrina Morton's surgeon, hit her like a gut punch and it made her sick.

There was no chance, in her condition, of racing to the bathroom in time, so she leaned over and puked into the garbage can that was beside her cubicle. The action of bending over and heaving seemed to tear at her broken sternum, making her whimper with pain, her head over the trash can.

That was the moment, shortly before 9:00 a.m., when Duncan walked into the squad room. He raced to Eve's side.

"What the hell are you doing here?" He gently held her by the shoulders and helped her sit up slowly in her seat.

"I'm beginning to ask myself the same question."

"Do you want to go back to the hospital or to your hotel?"

"I'm wondering if I'm qualified to be a homicide detective. I'm a total fuckup, Duncan."

"I wouldn't say that, but you are definitely crazy, perhaps even suicidal." Duncan held out his hand to her. "Come on, let's go."

She shook her head. "No, no, I'm staying. I need to see this through."

"See *what* through?"

She told him.

Duncan took a seat at his cubicle as he listened to her explain her failures as a detective and as a human being and everything that she'd learned from her calls that morning.

When she was done, he massaged his brow. "You're being way too hard on yourself. I was an equal partner in this."

"No, Pruitt was right about one thing. It's all on me."

"We can argue about that later. I'll call a judge, get the search warrants, and serve them. What are you going to do in the meantime?"

She massaged her wrist. It was sore. Her whole body was. She needed more than painkillers. She needed professional help. "I'll stay here, brush my teeth again, and see if I can beg my physical therapist to make a house call."

◆ ◆ ◆

Eve came out and met Mitch Sawyer in the lobby at 10:00 a.m. He was clearly shocked when he saw her. She wasn't wearing her neck brace, but there were cuts on her face and her eyes were bloodshot. The nasty bruise on her chest, which had turned black, had crept up to her collarbone and was hard to miss.

"Oh my God, Eve, what happened to you?"

"I had a little fender bender."

"Looks more like a train wreck to me." He dropped his gym bag and examined her wrist. "You're lucky you didn't break your wrist again."

"Yeah, but it hurts. Truth is, everything does."

"I'm sure, because you'd have to be in agony to give in and call me. Is there somewhere we can go?"

"Yeah, follow me." She held open the door. He picked up his bag and she led him down the hallway. "We can use a table in the snack room."

The only person in the snack room was her new bodyguard, Deputy Eddie Clayton, who was having some coffee and reading the latest issue of *Guns & Ammo*. At least, it appeared that he was. His eyes were hidden behind his ever-present pair of sunglasses.

Eve sat down across the table from Mitch, who said: "Let's start with the tabletop wrist flexion and extension exercise."

She set her phone on the table, then extended her right arm so that her wrist was hanging over the edge of the tabletop, her hand facing palm down. Without moving her arm, she lifted her wrist, closed her hand into a fist, and held the position for six seconds.

Mitch counted out the seconds, then Eve bent her wrist down, below the edge of the table, letting her hand hang, her fist unfurled. She held that position for six seconds.

"Very good. Let's do it slowly four times, but stop if you feel any pain." Mitch gestured to her chest. "Tell me about that bruise."

"It's a broken sternum," she said.

"Ouch. And you came into work anyway?"

"I've got three murder cases to deal with. That's why I couldn't come to you."

"I totally understand, though I appreciated your offer to bring an approved absence letter from the sheriff for your missed appointment."

"I thought you'd be impressed."

"Now, of course, I know why you couldn't make it. Congratulations on solving the Sabrina Morton case."

"Sorry I didn't return your call—it's been chaos since the news broke."

"No worries." Mitch glanced at Clayton, who was still absorbed in his magazine, and lowered his voice to a whisper. "I can't believe it was deputies who raped and killed her."

"It's been hard for all of us to accept."

"I was horrified to hear about what happened in your house."

"Yeah, I didn't see that coming."

"And yet after that horrible experience, and your car accident, you still came in to work?" He looked at her, incredulous.

"I'm not good at relaxing."

"That's the understatement of the century," Mitch said. Eve finished her last set of exercises. "How's your wrist?"

"It actually feels better."

"Good." Mitch took a rubber ball out of his bag and put it in her hand. "Let's try it with the ball."

Eve started doing the same exercises while gripping the ball. "This isn't going to be made public until later today, but we found Kendra Leigh yesterday. Her skeleton was in the brush near the Backbone Trail. She didn't have any ID, jewelry, or her phone on her."

"That's so sad. How do you know it's her?"

"From her hip replacement. We identified Sabrina Morton and Debbie Crawford, the two charred skeletons we found in Hueso Canyon, from their surgical implants, too. We traced the serial numbers on the devices back to their surgeons, who gave us their names."

"That makes things easy for you. It seems like just about everybody has implants of some kind these days."

"I don't."

"Not for lack of trying. Look at you."

"Good point." Eve's phone vibrated. She picked it up and glanced at the screen. It was a thumbs-up emoji and three photos from Duncan. She set the phone facedown on the table. Mitch gestured to her phone.

"Good news?"

"It's a big break. We found some of the jewelry belonging to the three dead women."

"Where?"

"I really shouldn't be talking about my cases, but I think you might be able to give me some professional insight into this."

"I'll be glad to help any way I can."

"I'm glad to hear that. The women all had different surgeons but they all shared one thing in common. The same physical therapist." Eve dropped the ball, let it bounce on the floor, and caught it again. "You, Mitch."

He smiled. "You're joking."

It had all come together for Eve after she met the patient with two broken arms in the Ventura hospital corridor and he told her that he was facing months of grueling physical therapy. In that moment, she remembered that all three of the dead women were in physical therapy before their disappearances because they'd all recently had orthopedic surgery. That was why the ME had been able to identify the women from the serial numbers on their implants. Then Eve thought about the deputy she'd left outside her hospital room to guard her "valuables" while she took her stroll down the corridor. That was when she recalled that no jewelry belonging to the dead women had been recovered with their remains, which were all found in canyons near the Backbone Trail in the Santa Monica Mountains. After realizing all that, it only took a few calls for Eve to discover the most important thing that the three murder victims had in common: a local physical therapist who was willing to visit his patients at their homes.

Mitch Sawyer.

Now Eve looked him in the eye. "I'm arresting you for the murders of Sabrina Morton, Debbie Crawford, and Kendra Leigh."

She read Mitch his rights. He leaned back in his chair as she spoke and glanced over at Clayton, who'd put down his magazine at some point and now had his hand resting on his holstered gun. Mitch was oddly cool, considering that he'd just been accused of being a serial killer. She knew an innocent person in his position would be furious or panicked.

When Eve was finished, she asked: "Do you understand your rights, Mitch?"

"Yes, but this is ridiculous. I have patients all over Calabasas, Malibu, Agoura, Westlake, and Thousand Oaks," Mitch said. "It's a coincidence that those three women were my patients, just like it's a coincidence that I'm treating you, the homicide detective who is investigating their murders."

"I thought so, too. There's just one problem, Mitch. We got a warrant to search your house. That's what my partner has been doing while you've been here. Look what he's found." Eve picked up her phone and showed Mitch the pictures of Sabrina's Tiffany necklace, Debbie's turquoise necklace, and Kendra's cross. "The missing jewelry."

"That's not what it looks like. Those were gifts."

"They gave you their favorite jewelry?"

"My patients love me. They always want to give me something, so I ask for anything that they think expresses their personalities and means as much to them as I do. Most of the time, it's pieces of jewelry."

Eve thought it was a good thing she'd already vomited that morning and hadn't eaten anything since, or Mitch's explanation might have made her lurch over a garbage can again.

"I think you made house calls on these women, providing them with physical therapy for their recent surgeries, and maybe you thought they wanted something more. But you were wrong. They rejected you and that pissed you off. These were rage killings."

"C'mon, Eve. That's not me. Ask Lisa. She'll tell you what a nice, sensitive guy I am."

"My sister doesn't know you like I do."

"She knows me better. She's slept with me. I'm not somebody who needs to hit on his patients to get laid."

"Maybe that's why you were enraged when they said no. You killed the women, kept a piece of their jewelry as a souvenir, and dumped their bodies in the nearest canyon."

"You must've sustained serious damage to your head in that accident, because you've forgotten that a few days ago, you stood in front of this building and told the world that three deputies raped and killed Sabrina Morton. You were certain of it. The sheriff even said the evidence was indisputable."

"The deputies raped her, there's no doubt about that, but they didn't kill her. You did."

"Make up your mind. Yesterday it was deputies, today it's me. Who is it going to be tomorrow? Or the day after that?"

"We know for certain it was you. When you took the bodies from the homes, you wisely left the women's phones behind. But you forgot about your own. A phone is basically a fancy tracking device, constantly following all of your movements. Here's a nasty little secret: your cellular provider keeps that data forever. We got a search warrant for yours. On the day each woman disappeared, we can track you from their homes to the spots where you dumped their bodies. Or is that just another coincidence?"

Eve bounced the ball and caught it again. Mitch crossed his arms over his chest and slumped in his seat. "I want a lawyer."

"We're not stopping our investigation here, Mitch. We're going to dig into your entire past. How many other women have you killed?" Eve saw a twitch in his cheek. A tell. "You can save yourself from the needle by cutting a deal now. The truth for your life."

"Maybe you didn't hear me. We're done," Mitch said. "I want a lawyer."

"Okay. Get facedown on the floor, put your hands out in front of you. Deputy Clayton is going to take you into custody."

Mitch did as he was told.

Clayton got up, went over to Mitch, dropped a knee on the center of his back to keep him down, and handcuffed him. The deputy pulled Mitch to his feet.

Mitch sneered at Eve. "Your sister was a mercy fuck."

"I'm sure you're right," Eve said. "She ordinarily goes for doctors, not orderlies. She must have taken pity on you."

Mitch lunged for Eve but Clayton yanked him back and dragged him out of the room. Eve bounced the ball, caught it again, and wondered how she was going to tell her sister about this.

Shortly after Mitch was booked, Eve went to her cubicle and called Scott Peck, the reporter at the *Acorn*.

"This is Eve Ronin," she said. "I have an exclusive for you."

"For me? Why?"

"Because I was wrong for giving you a hard time at the Hueso Canyon crime scene when you asked me if we were looking for a serial killer."

"Were you?"

"No, we weren't. But we should have been, because you were right, Scott. All three women were killed by the same man and we just arrested him."

"All *three*? There's a third victim?"

Eve could feel his excitement through the phone as she gave him the details and he asked her questions. He knew this could be the story that finally launched him into major league journalism. She hoped he was right.

Peck's last question was the big one, at least for her. "Are we on the record? Can I quote you by name on this?"

Eve knew that if she did, it would make Sheriff Lansing furious. But this time, she wanted to be the one to tell her story, without the hoopla and the spin. She didn't want to be portrayed as a supercop, but rather as the flawed, inexperienced rookie that she was.

That was when it occurred to her that she'd given the story a spin after all. She was such a hypocrite, as if she needed more proof of that.

"Yes, you can use my name, but give me an hour to call the sheriff before you call him for comment or post the news on the *Acorn* website."

"You called me before him?"

"That part is off the record," she said.

When she finished the call, she got up and went down the hall to Captain Moffett's office to tell him that she'd solved the murders of three women but that they'd have to drop the homicide charges against the three deputies.

Moffett didn't take it well. While he was glad to hear that three homicide cases were closed with one arrest, he was afraid that the good news would only slightly mitigate the major embarrassment of having to drop the homicide charges against Towler, Harding, and Frankel that they'd announced with such fanfare.

She left it to him to brief Lansing and Burnside on everything and walked out, using the excuse that she was about to collapse from pain and exhaustion. It wasn't hard to convince him of that because it was true.

Deputy Clayton drove her back to the Hilton Garden Inn and then remained in the lobby to keep watch over her.

Eve managed to time things perfectly. She was already in bed, knocked out cold by painkillers, with her room phone unplugged and her iPhone off, when Moffett and Lansing got calls from the *Acorn*.

CHAPTER TWENTY-EIGHT

Three days later, early in the morning, Eve sat in the lobby of the Hilton Garden Inn at a table with Linwood Taggert and signed a representation agreement with CAA. It wasn't something she wanted to do, but her bills were piling up fast and she was expecting to face huge legal fees to defend herself from the inevitable lawsuit from Pruitt's widow. Eve needed the money from a Hollywood deal.

Taggert shook her hand, took back his gold pen, and gathered up the contract. "This is very exciting and things should start coming together fast. I've already got a short list of showrunners and leading ladies to package you with. I'll get you DVDs, scripts, and credits to look at tonight."

"It's too soon to talk about actors. The most important thing to me is the script. If I don't like it, there's no show. I want creative control. That has to be clear from the outset with any writer we get into business with."

"Top showrunners will balk at that. It's going to be a hard sell."

"That's why I have a big shot agent."

"You're not going to make my job easy, are you? I like that. Make me earn my commission. I'll set up some get-to-know-you meetings with showrunners this week."

"That's not necessary. I'm having lunch with Simone Harper tomorrow. I've got a good feeling about her."

"She's a very talented writer and producer, but she's not one of our clients."

"Why should I care?"

"Because you're part of the CAA family now."

"I've already got a family."

That was when Duncan came in, spotted Eve, and ambled over. "Are they still serving the breakfast buffet?"

"Help yourself," Eve said. "Duncan, this is Linwood Taggert, my new agent."

Taggert stood up and shook Duncan's hand. "It's a pleasure to meet you."

"Brad Pitt would be great as me. See what you can do about that, Lin." Duncan patted him on the back and headed for the buffet.

Taggert smiled and turned back to Eve. "He's quite a character."

"So is everybody in my life now, including me. That's going to take some getting used to."

"Champagne problems," Taggert said and went outside to his Bentley, which he'd parked in the handicapped spot. Before Duncan came in, Eve saw her partner slip a parking ticket under Taggert's windshield wiper.

Duncan joined Eve with a mug of coffee and a plate piled high with microwaved scrambled eggs, microwaved bacon, microwaved waffles, and a defrosted blueberry muffin. "Aren't you eating?"

"I already had some fruit and yogurt."

"That's sickening." Duncan sat down.

She knew that he'd been busy over the last few days, going through Mitch Sawyer's patient files to see if there were any more murder victims in his past. So far, no more victims had emerged, but it was still early in the investigation and Burnside was putting together a task force of her own to look into it. Eve was sure they would find at least one more victim, perhaps a woman who hadn't been one of his patients.

"So you're finally going Hollywood," Duncan said.

"I'm not going anywhere. I'm coming back to work on Monday. I'm selling out for the money."

"Why not? You've already got the fame and the sex."

She certainly had the fame. Catching a serial killer and arresting three deputies in a cold rape case had made her a hero in the media again, despite her own efforts to cast herself as a flawed individual, the lingering questions about her role in Pruitt's suicide, and the murder charges that were dropped against Towler, Harding, and Frankel.

"What makes you think I have the sex?" she asked.

"I saw Daniel's car leaving when I drove in."

"He's off to Tarawa, some atoll out in the South Pacific, for two months."

"Why don't you go with him for a while? You must have a bunch of vacation time and sick leave left."

"It's not a tropical resort. It's a project to exhume and identify the remains of hundreds of American soldiers who were killed in a battle against thousands of Japanese soldiers and Korean slaves in 1943. When the anthropologists aren't working, they'll be living in tents, fighting off mosquitos, and digging latrines."

"You should still take a vacation."

"This week of sick leave that's been forced on me is plenty, thanks. I'd come back to work tomorrow if I could." The bruise on her chest was turning greenish yellow now, which she assumed was an improvement, but it still felt like she had shards of broken glass inside and just about every move she made caused her some pain. She was eager to get back to her job, even though she wasn't sure if she'd ever be able to entirely trust the deputies around her.

Duncan's efforts to find the deputies who tried to kill her in Ventura were going nowhere, mainly because it was a one-man investigation. Neither Lansing nor Moffett were eager to devote manpower and resources to an internal investigation that would inevitably create another embarrassing scandal for the department and put Eve on a pedestal yet again. Duncan had also heard that Lansing had applied pressure to his counterparts in Ventura County to make sure the case wasn't a priority for them, either.

"You can't keep going on this way," Duncan said. "You're too driven. You're all about the case to the exclusion of everything else. Well, I'm telling you that lifestyle will kill you. One way or another. You'll start making some big mistakes."

"I'm already making big mistakes."

"I'm not talking about your work. You solved a cold case rape from six years ago and three murders. Those weren't mistakes. That was skill."

Eve shook her head. "Nakamura was right about me. I made the evidence fit my theory of the case and I missed the pattern that was in front of my eyes. The real killer almost got away with it."

"But he didn't."

"But he could have."

"*But he didn't.* That's all that matters. You're always going to make mistakes in an investigation, especially when you're new. It's called 'learning from experience.' I'm not worried about your skills as a detective. You've got a gift. I'm worried about your skills as a person."

"You're saying I'm a terrible person?"

"You're not evil," Duncan said. "You're just self-destructive and not very likable."

"Gee, thanks."

"You can't be a loner on this job. You have to rely on others. It's not you against the world. That means making friends and establishing trust."

"But you're the only one I trust," she said, though that wasn't entirely true. Deputies Ross, Clayton, and a handful of others had taken turns during their off-duty time protecting her, right up until this morning, when she'd politely sent them away. She appreciated their concern for her and the visible show of support, but she didn't want a security detail anymore, volunteer or otherwise.

"That's going to be a problem for you because I'm retiring soon," Duncan said. "I'm not going to be around to watch your back."

"You could watch my fictional back."

"I don't understand."

"You could be a technical consultant on my show. I don't want to worry all the time about what they are doing. But if you're there, I won't have to. You can keep them honest, guarantee the realism, and stop them from making me into something I'm not."

"Likable, for instance."

"Anything but a big-boobed blonde who rides her Harley to work, flaunts her cleavage, wears her gun like a fashion accessory on her tight jeans, and never makes a mistake."

"Why not? That would be a definite improvement. You ought to try that in real life."

"I'm serious, Duncan."

"So am I."

"This is a way to retire and use your experience doing something besides security work."

"Yeah, but I'd have to spend all day around actors who are pretending to be cops. People like Nick Egan. That would drive me nuts. I'm not in love with the business like Garvey. Hey, why not go to him? He'd love this."

"Because he'd let the actors, writers, and producers do whatever they want. But you'll give them the same shit you give me. You'll be making really good money doing nothing but criticizing people and offering Pavone's pearls of wisdom."

"You can get paid for that?"

"Wait, there's more. They have caterers on the set every day. Breakfast and lunch are free."

Duncan's eyes lit up. "Free food?"

"It never ends. They have a table on the set that's always full of cake, cookies, chips, and candy."

"I'll think about it," he said. "There's no hurry for me to decide. I've got a few months left on the job and you don't have a TV show yet. Besides, the way things are going, you probably won't survive to see it."

Eve smiled. "I can always count on you to see the positive side of things."

"That's me," he said. "Mr. Sunny-Side Up."

Author's Note and Acknowledgments

The Lost Hills sheriff's station in Calabasas, California, is a real place, but the characters and events portrayed in this novel are entirely fictional. I've also taken substantial creative liberties regarding the way the sheriff's department allocates its manpower and resources. While many of the streets and other places mentioned in the book *do* exist, Hueso Canyon does not, though it is inspired by an actual location in the Santa Monica Mountains near Latigo Canyon Road and Kanan Dume Road.

There wouldn't be a second Eve Ronin novel if not for the enthusiasm, insight, and support of my editors Gracie Doyle, Megha Parekh, and Charlotte Herscher, the marketing and promotional efforts of Dennelle Catlett and Megan Beatie, and the negotiating prowess of Amy Tannenbaum.

To research this book, I attended several homicide investigators' training conferences for law enforcement professionals. I am grateful to the organizers, instructors, and attendees of these conferences for allowing me to participate and learn from their experiences. Special thanks to Jason Weber, public safety training coordinator, Northeast Wisconsin Technical College in Green Bay, and John Flannery, director of public safety, Madison Area Technical College in Madison, Wisconsin.

I am deeply indebted to Paul Bishop, Robin Burcell, Lee Lofland, David Putnam, Kathy Bennett, and Patricia Smiley for letting me draw on their law enforcement backgrounds to get the cop stuff right . . . though at times I've intentionally bent reality to suit my fictional needs. They were incredibly patient with me and answered my dumb questions in astonishing detail.

There is a lot of forensic stuff in this book, and to sort through it all, I relied upon the wise counsel of Dr. D. P. Lyle; Daniel Winterich, professor of criminal justice, Lakeland Community College; Pamela Sokolik-Putnam, supervising deputy coroner investigator, San Bernardino County Sheriff-Coroner Department; Katherine Ramsland, PhD, professor of forensic psychology, DeSales University; Danielle R. Galien, criminal justice professor, Des Moines Area Community College; and Katherine Ann Roberts, PhD, executive director, California Forensic Science Institute, School of Criminal Justice and Criminalistics, Los Angeles. Any errors in forensics, science, or procedure you encountered are entirely my fault and quite possibly premeditated.

I also appreciate the help of Lieutenant Colonel H. Ripley Rawlings IV, USMC, for showing me the wide range of military tattoos and explaining to me their symbolism and meaning.

There were several books that were especially useful to me, including *Practical Homicide Investigation*, fifth edition, by Vernon J. Geberth; *Introduction to Crime Scene Investigation*, third edition, by Aric W. Dutelle; *Advances in Forensic Taphonomy*, edited by William D. Haglund and Marcella H. Sorg; *Death Scene Investigation: Procedural Guide*, second edition, by Michael S. Maloney, MFS; and *The Analysis of Burned Human Remains*, second edition, edited by Christopher W. Schmidt and Steven A. Symes.

Finally, I want to thank the authors of these exceptional articles and papers:

"Forensic Anthropology: What Bones Can Tell Us" by John K. Lundy, PhD (*Laboratory Medicine*, volume 29, number 7, July 1998).

"The Forensic Evaluation of Burned Skeletal Remains: A Synthesis" by Douglas H. Ubelaker (*Forensic Science International*, volume 183, January 2009).

"Assessment of Skeletal Changes after Post-Mortem Exposure to Fire as an Indicator of Decomposition Stage" by N. Keough, E. N. L'Abbé, M. Steyn, and S. Pretorius (*Forensic Science International*, volume 246, January 2015).

"Exploding Skulls and Other Myths about How the Body Burns" by Elayne J. Pope, MD, O. C. Smith, MD, and Timothy G. Huff, MA (*Fire and Arson Investigator*, volume 54, April 2004).

"The Use of Orthopedic Surgical Devices for Forensic Identification" by Rebecca J. Wilson, MA, Jonathan D. Bethard, MA, and Elizabeth A. DiGangi, PhD (*Journal of Forensic Sciences*, March 2011).

About the Author

Photo © 2013 Roland Scarpa

Lee Goldberg is a two-time Edgar Award and two-time Shamus Award nominee and the #1 *New York Times* bestselling author of more than thirty novels. He has also written and/or produced many TV shows, including *Diagnosis Murder*, *SeaQuest*, and *Monk*, and is the cocreator of the Mystery 101 series of Hallmark movies. As an international television consultant, he has advised networks and studios in Canada, France, Germany, Spain, China, Sweden, and the Netherlands on the creation, writing, and production of episodic television series. You can find more information about Lee and his work at www.leegoldberg.com.